A Tale Etched In Fire

ANASIA EDWARDS

-A Tale Etched In Fire-

First published in Australia in 2024

ISBN: 978-0-646-70266-7

Printed and bound in Australia by IngramSpark LLC

a.tale.etched.in.fire@gmail.com

~ ~

-Anasia Edwards-

~~

To all the people who believed in me and helped me along the way, this achievment is one we all share.

~~

Capital
Village
Arcarlia
White Castle
Village
Capital
N
W
E
S

-Anasia Edwards-

~~

PROLOGUE

200 years ago

A woman was wandering in a rainforest. She had long dark brown hair bouncing up and down on her shoulders and big teal eyes. Freckles surrounded her pale cheeks, exposing a fraction of sincerity when her dimples paled as the breeze swept through her. Her emerald dress blended with the colours of the rainforest. The only thing disturbing about her was the runed sword in her scabbard. She glanced around at her surroundings. The rainforest was such a beautiful place. Adorned with life, some still, swaying in the breeze. Others loud and alive, happily scurrying around the forest floor. The woman gazed towards the sky, the leaves and branches of the trees peacefully swaying from side to side. The woman smiled.

"What a sight." She said quietly to herself. A home for all. Animals, humans and the supernatural alike. The woman wandered through the forest made path, a sign of nature. She gazed at the hill in the distance, full of bountiful meadows and colourful butterflies. She turned her gaze to her left, where a hidden pathway had been placed. The weeds were covering it strategically to hide any signs of adventure. No one would be able to accidentally stumble across it, a strong spell had been placed there. If you wanted to enter the path you had to know what to do, and where to go. Fortunately, this woman knew. The woman closed her eyes and imagined the weeds slowly shifting away from the path. Her palms glowed with a yellow, fluorescent colour; the mist-like aroma crawled its way from her fingertips all the way to her shoulders. The woman muttered something under her breath, her arms glowing brighter and brighter. She pressed her arms into a cross and placed them tight on her chest.

The woman snapped her fingers. Her eyes snapped open. A smile escaped her lips. The path opened for her.

The woman strode confidently through the path. Her answers to all her questions lay just a few hundred steps ahead of her. The strange aroma surrounding her arms faded away after each step she took, eventually the blinding light completely left her arms, dissolving into the air like sparks on a flame. Rustles echoed throughout the green shrubbery. The woman's eyes narrowed as a voice cut through the air.

"Wasn't expecting you to come so soon Celestial Tien. I suspect things are growing more and more restless in these lands, correct? Well, at least in your opinion. No one believes you, by the way. They all think you've gone crazy."

Celestial Tien paused. Then whirled to face the stranger with a glare. She sighed and shook her head. *They would never understand. No one would.* "I am already aware of that, Lord Tiergan." She hissed through her teeth. She detested this man, High Wizard or not. "Things will become more dire in the next few hundred years. I'm just here to ensure a select two are to rise. The prophecy is true, and this will prove it." She added, looking directly at Lord Tiergan. His face smirked right at her. "Uh huh.

Look, I personally think you've lost it. If Celestial Margerith hasn't detected anything disastrous in the future, why are you so worried? She's double-checked the future countless times." Tien shot him a dangerous look and shoved him away, leaving him stumbling towards the bushes.

"Now I can smirk you ignorant fool." She said under her breath as she continued down the path praying for no more interruptions. Such as Lord Tiergan muttering something unintelligible under his breath.

He was right She thought to herself. *It doesn't make sense, but I saw it. I saw it in that vision. I have to prove it's true.* A roar silenced her thoughts and turned her smirk into a frown. She twisted her head and her lips pressed into a thin line. A demon. A demon that had already taken Lord Tiergan's arm.

Her eyes narrowed as she pulled the sword from her scabbard, adjusting herself as she went into a defensive stance. High Wizards of his specialty are useless in physical combat. He can heal miraculously and do range spells, but he's long forgotten how to properly fight. She glared at Tiergan. *Pathetic.* The demon was an exaggerated size, with one eye in the centre of its head, its skin was a stone grey, with four arms dangling from its side, sharp claws scraping at its tough skin. The demon's vampire-like teeth gleamed in the sun as it took notice of Tien. The Celestial took a breath, then charged towards the demon. Swiftly leaping through the air, she succeeded with landing on the demon's back and pushing her sword through its spine. The demon screeched and went limp, collapsing on the path in a growing pool of transparent blood.

Tien scowled at the demon's broken body as it dissolved into ashes. She bent down to inspect Lord Tiergan, sliding her sword into her scabbard. He groaned, touching where his arm used to be, he closed his eyes and muttered something under his breath. A wand appeared next to him, in the lifeless hand of his detached arm. *He really just summoned it into his wrong arm. The Second Ranking High Wizard himself.* The Celestial rubbed her temples in pure disappointment.

"Why'd it have to be my good arm?" The High Wizard pouted.

"You can't do anything right, you buffoon. You can't even defend yourself against some pathetic Inconi."

"I am not a buffoon. Plus, that was ranked way higher than an Inconi. If that was an untrained demon, I could have easily killed it."

Tien looked unimpressed. "Just regenerate your arm and leave me alone." She glared at him. "By the way, summon your wand into a hand that's actually attached, Lord Tiergan."

Tien spat out his name. Then continued down the path at a quicker pace. Celestials didn't usually interfere with the problems of mortals, yet Tien needed answers, and so she trudged on.

Half an hour later Tien arrived at her destination. She stopped in her tracks as she took it all in. The shrubbery that had surrounded the path now led in a circular area surrounding a cozy wooden cottage with a few steps leading up to the painted oak door. There was a granite path which the Celestial carefully followed as she made her way through the path. Colourful birds soared and sang in the sky as Tien glanced up to gaze at them. She turned her attention to the left which had a small river that led downstream towards the entrance of the small cottage.

As the Celestial grew closer to the door, the more she heard someone scurrying around the cottage. Her smile grew. The one she was meeting with was home. Tien raised her delicate hand to knock on the door. A soft knock and the door opened all by itself. The Celestial ducked to enter through the door, the cottages' inhabitants must be dwarf-size, which is rather unusual, considering the species got wiped out long ago during the Human Revolution. Tien ignored her superstitions and set foot in the cottage.

The cottage was adorned with many paintings, all decorated with paintings of the hill near the forest-made path Tien had seen earlier, except they had castles on top of them. Tien tilted her head at them. She suspected that maybe the cottage's inhabitants were one of the few with the gift of sight. The Celestial smirked. If this was true, she was at the right place.

The next step she took gave her a larger view of the cottage. There was a small velvet couch that took up the entire left wall, with a small oak table directly in front. In the centre of the cottage was a strange circular shaped kitchen, behind it was a double bed with pillars of stripped wood strategically placed in each corner of the bed.

The door slammed shut behind her. The Celestial jumped, and she twisted her head round to see the cause. A short, plump dwarf stood to her side, watching her with its beady emerald eyes. The dwarf had short smooth black hair, with a small goatee dangling from its chin. Its skin tone was a warm brown, shining as the sunlight from the windows bounced onto the skin and back to the wall. Its fluffy eyebrows furrowed as it glanced down at her scabbard. The dwarf snorted as it squinted to see Tien's face better.

"Celestial scum." It muttered under its breath. Tien furrowed her eyebrows at the dwarf. "What do you want?" It barked huskily at the Celestial, the dwarf's face reddening in fury. "And how'd you find my cottage? You some sort a' spy?" The dwarf growled at Tien. The Celestial took a deep breath, then raised her hand to speak.

"I am Celestial Tien. I am the watcher of the land and waters. I have come for your assistance, but first

I would be grateful if you gave me your name, if you don't mind."

The dwarf snorted. Tien raised an eyebrow at it. *It doesn't seem at all bothered by my presence. Normally they bow and hurriedly apologise.* She smiled. *How interesting.*

"Pravadi Blazeringer, but that is Soothsayer to you, Celestial. Now what do you want to know?" The dwarf paused as a smirk lit up his face, his emerald eyes gleamed with mischief. "But the better question is, what do you have to trade?"

Tien froze. Of course, the dwarf wants something in return. "Give me a moment to think."

The Celestial turned her back onto Soothsayer, deep in thought. She didn't have much to trade, let alone something a dwarf could possibly have any interest in. She glanced down at her emerald dress, which was decorated with the rare gems. A smile formed from Tien's lips. She tore 3 emeralds off the dress and whirled around to face Soothsayer. She presented the emeralds to him, and to her delight, Soothsayer snatched them out of her hands in glee. Soothsayer admired the emeralds for what seemed like hours. Tien sighed. Dwarves are something else entirely. Soothsayer slowly glazed his stubby finger across one of the emeralds, taking in its unmistakable beauty. Tien coughed to get his attention. His head snapped up as he slowly came back to reality. Soothsayer snorted at the Celestial as he placed the emeralds down onto a sleek bench. "Fine. You win then, Celestial."

He waved his hands at her in a way of saying, 'follow me'. Soothsayer led her to a small four-person table. Tien sat in the seat closest to the door, just in case. Soothsayer sat directly opposite her. He placed his hands in front of him and sighed, his gravelly voice somewhat comforting. "So, Celestial, what do you want to know?"

Tien gazed at him, then rolled her eyes to the left and the right to ensure no one was watching. She took a deep breath, then lowered her voice to a whisper. "I'm sure you have heard of the Barren Prophecy, correct?" Soothsayer nodded, his eyes growing more and more curious after each word. Probably the most entertaining thing he's had in a while.

"Well, I am here to ask you a question. Will the select few of the Barren Prophecy rise? I know I will be weakened during those times, so will Mistlon, so you understand." She tensed slightly. "No one believes me, but I know He will turn the tide of battle when the time arrives."

Soothsayer nodded approvingly, then let out a deep breath. He closed his eyes with a bright light flowing out of his fingertips. Miraculously, the world faded away, into a pit of nothingness.

Tien gasped. It was like she was in the water, swimming gracefully. But she knew better. The Void.

I didn't know he was capable of opening this dimension up. Not even the Celestial of Time herself can. At least, not for a long period of time. How remarkable. She held her hands out, colour was slowly fading from her arms, leaving it the same shade as everything around her, pure white.

Slowly but surely, colours emerged from the nothingness. Shades of green appeared to her left; Tien tilted her head at it. Eventually an image appeared, it contained a young girl with rich brown skin and straight black hair. Her eyes were a unique shade of grey, one the Celestial was familiar with.

One of the Ignei family line. The Celestial watched her grow, the years filtering by as if it were nothing. *It makes sense on why one of the Ignei's would be a part of this prophecy.*

Soon a new image appeared. This one resembled a young pale girl with dark brown hair. She too began to age rapidly, but Tien couldn't recognise who she

was. Her eyes were also what stuck out to her, a piercing green. Whatever that meant, the Celestial hadn't the faintest idea. *Just a normal human, with a small amount of potential. How disappointing.*
Roots pulled the image away, deep into the endless world of white. Tien caught her throat when another figure majestically appeared in front of her. She gazed at it, only to find it was blurred. She swam closer to it. Her body slowly moved through the eternal pit of white. Tien reached out her hands to touch the blurred figure. As her fingers braced it, the figure disappeared into a pit of blinding light.
"Strange." She told herself. *Soothsayer must have run out of energy. Shouldn't be a problem.* She held her hand out in front of her, watching as the yellow aura sparked up again, flickering around her fingertips.
I'll give him a blessing of my own, recharge him. I need these images. As these intentions flooded through her mind, a voice came from behind her.
"Hello Miss Tien."
Startled, the Celestial whipped her head around to meet a friendly faced woman, she had long brown hair that led down to her waist, she also had piercing blue eyes that stood out in the colourless world. Tien stared at her. *Did the dwarf allow someone else to enter? Why?* She narrowed her eyes on the woman. *And without warning me? I'd have his head for this if I didn't need his abilities.* The woman sighed.
"I'm sure you have questions on how I am here, but I need to explain something important to you."
Tien tilted her head at the mystery woman, eventually she decided to slowly approach her.
"What exactly would that be?" The Celestial pressed.
The mystery woman paused, then laughed. "I figured you'd say that, but first I need your help urgently."
The woman's smile faded. "He has killed a mortal."

CHAPTER 1: LEXI

One Month and One Week Earlier from Present Day

I stood in the room with no fear in my mind. I could imagine Grady on the other side of the arena advancing slowly, a grin on his face. Today was the day of the trials, the final trials before we were sent out into the real world to help Sorvia win the war. So yeah, I suppose it is a fairly big thing for us initiates. That and finally being aboveground for the first time in years. I felt my fingers slowly grip the dagger tucked inside of my belt, I would need it in a few minutes. The trial was set to find the victor crowned by first blood, otherwise known as Trial Of Unknown Combat or known more amongst us contestants as "TOUC". The boys and girls were separated to train in groups of their own gender, as they'd be versing their opposite during the trial. They were assigned their opponent through skill and careful assessment. I was ranked first amongst the girls, so therefore I have to verse Grady, first of the boys.

We were fighting in front of all of Sorvia, which was enough to make some initiates regret applying for "TOUC". *Well, more like the CrysTalk versions of all of Sorvia. It would be stupid to move over fifty thousand people from our original base to the arena each year.* Regardless, no pressure, right?

Of course there's pressure. The one fear I have, they decided to put in front of me. *Crowds* I thought to myself, after glancing out into the stadium to see swarms of people appear almost magically in their seats.

A gust of wind blasted my thick, braided hair right into my face as the rusty old door behind me swung open. I was met by both of my instructors, scowling Sire Lewis and bubbly yet deadly Sire Cleo. Sire Lewis had a shiny, pale bald head with jet black eyes and his usual expressionless pointy face and thick grey eyebrows. Compared to stunning Cleo, he looked like he just came out of a Ranger's nest. While Cleo's dark skin matched with pale blond hair was unusual, it was a side effect to being an Aerial, or an air elemental. Her brown eyes lit up like stars as she gazed at me, her expression proud.

"I knew you could do it Lexi! You were always a talented Ignei!" She squealed excitedly, her enthusiasm building as her eyes were drawn to my dagger. "There isn't a world where you lose this Lexi."

"And if there is, I'll be extremely disappointed, Ignei." Huffed Sire Lewis, his eyes narrowing. "Not a single initiate that I have trained has lost a single trial. Try not to be first, it will look worse on me than it will on you girl."

"Lewis-" Cleo started, but stopped and sighed when she noticed Sire Lewis's death look. "Sorry, Sire Lewis. She got to the finals, top of her class! Can't you not be annoyed at the world and just congratulate her?"

"I'll congratulate her if she wins."
"When, you mean Sire. When I win this." I told him, my face set in a determined look. He was right about it looking bad on him if I lose. He has had the greatest reputation of training initiates in the entire 30-year long war, not a single one being eliminated from the trials. Many desperate parents pleaded and bribed for his teachings for their children, but instead he took on the world's most infuriating job. Mentoring an Ignei. Otherwise known as the strongest, most uncontrollable Flammous family line in history. Sire Lewis gave me an appreciative nod, his way of saying I did well. A little spark of pride opened up in my chest, sending butterflies all over my skin.
"You're right Lexi. You are completely right. When you win. That is the confidence you need! Remember that wisely." Cleo spoke, her voice serious. "You will win this, then you will be given your war profession. Hopefully you'll get a Tank, that would suit you well I reckon."
I nodded obediently in return. A Tank was one of the seven professions you could get. It meant being part of the first charge into battle or an ambush, possibly the deadliest. Only the strongest are given that role. The others are Scout, Archer, General, Knight, Tactician, and finally the rarest and most difficult to obtain out of them all, Assassin. There haven't been many Assassins in the last three decades. It was a difficult job, and only the Sorvian Council and Royals can pick them out. To be an Assassin is possibly the greatest honour in all of Sorvia. It means going into the enemy's own grounds, getting in close enough to them, and then finally completing their deed to Sorvia's future. Out of all the professions, I've concluded that it will be most likely for me to get Archer, Tank, or maybe Scout. My ability makes it easier to rain fire down on enemies as an Archer, my strength would make me a good Tank, and I suppose

I have good scouting and observation abilities. It's important to know what you can and can't do in this world. One misstep can cost you everything.

A large and ear shattering bell sang loudly then, signalling the end of the initiates' time with their Sires. "Remember Lexi, the Judges and Council will be looking for your reaction time, your agility, your strengths, and your weaknesses. Okay? Show them everything you've got." Cleo reminded me, resting her hand on my shoulder before abruptly letting go to follow Sire Lewis out of the room. Another announcement came by, stating that there were only two full minutes before it all began. Yesterday if I heard that announcement I would've nodded quietly, knowing my chances of victory were only at fifty percent. Yet for some reason, today I feel completely different. My fingers grazed over my dagger as I slowly lifted it out of its hilt. Today the feel of cool metal against my skin was comforting. Maybe it was because of the anticipation of the trial, I'm not sure.

Don't go into battle too cocky Lexi. That's how you fail. The crowd outside grew louder, so much louder the sound was deafening. *The two minutes must already be up* I thought to myself silently.

I walked over to where the beige curtains were, which was going to open in a few moments and present me to the kingdom of Sorvia. *No pressure.* I then heard the announcer's voice ring out once again.

"Ladies and gentlemen! Boys and girls! Welcome to the final round of our 30th Trial Of Unknown Combat! In our final round, we now have the best of the best of both groups competing for a place in our Elites. Place your bets and let us introduce our final two initiates!" Proclaimed the announcer, causing a massive uproar of the ginormous unknown crowd outside.

-A Tale Etched In Fire-

"Presenting from the left, we have Grady Cross!" The crowd roared its approval loudly as Grady's curtains must have opened. The announcer stayed quiet for a moment, clearly letting Grady soak up the applause a little while longer before he spoke again.
'Now for our final initiative of the "TOUC", presenting from the left, we have Lexi Ignei!'
The curtains immediately swung open, revealing myself to the massive crowd surrounding me. The arena was massive and made completely out of stone bricks, with the centre of the arena covered in a perfect circle of completely dead grass. There were thousands of people in the stands, each on their feet screaming and cheering with the biggest smiles on their faces as I walked into the arena. My surname was well-known across Sorvia. Ignei's are expected to be the best. Nothing less. On the other side of the arena stood Grady with his blonde hair and hazel eyes holding his own dagger firmly while watching me with his eyes narrowed. Normally he would grin at me and laugh, but not now. We were declared competition not very long ago, to act like my friend now would be a severe sign of weakness and an immediate minus in how the Council graded him.
I found myself already predicting his next few moves while the announcer began to go over the rules we had heard what felt like a million times before. Grady was the kind of person to rely on his strength and elements first to weaken his opponent so he could then deliver the final blow. How did I know this? By watching him verse others who were on a similar level to him. He does it every time, and to give him points it does work every time. It's smart, but predictable. All I have to do to beat someone as sure headed as him is simple. Let him believe he's in charge of this match and play with him. By the time he's figured my plan out, his defences will be down slightly. That will give me all the opening I need to do one swish of my dagger to let a drop of blood touch

the ground, and I'm crowned victorious. It sounds easy and simple enough, but the hard part? Grady isn't very well known for missing. The other hard part is that I am a Flammous, and he's a Liquarn, so I already have a disadvantage. Water and fire don't mix.

"Ladies and gentlemen! This concludes our time for betting, so please quiet down! Then we will start the countdown for our final round!"

I took a few more steps forward to meet Grady in the middle, our eyes fully locked with a tingle of tension between us as we drew ever closer. My hand tightened on the handle of the dagger, and I could see Grady doing the same.

"Five!' The crowd began to count down.

"Four!" I started to notice my heart rate quickening, which I steadied almost immediately.

"Three!' I readied myself into a good enough position to propel myself backwards away from Grady.

"Two!" The crowd is freaking out now, clearly eager to see the best of the best, fight each other.

"One!" My hand closed tighter around my dagger.

"Begin!"

Grady leaped forward for the swipe of his dagger while I shot backwards, dodging his attack by a mere second. I landed neatly on my two feet, bracing myself for Grady's next attack. It should come sometime soon...

Now.

An icy cold stream of water shot by my head like a torpedo so fast it almost hit me. Almost. My head swerved out of the way just in time. I threw a fireball at him, in hopes to distract him while I think. He dodged pretty easily. I glanced up and saw his face, determination filling every pore. My plan didn't seem as simple now, and the hard parts felt far more difficult. I paused for a split second, calculating my next move. I didn't have the greatest chance dodging his every move, but then again it was one of my only options that I even had. My only advantage over him at the moment was the fact that I was faster than him in almost every way.

I heard a sloshing sound then coming from Grady, to which I quickly realised that he was conjuring a massive bubble of water, letting it rise higher and higher to the point where its height was taller than I was. He then began to shape the bubble into a pointy shape, his hands moving in the current of the water he himself had created until it was in the shape of a massive, very pointy spear. He saw me watching and his face twisted into a self-righteous smirk.

"Grady…" I called out wearily, my eyes following the water spear as it slowly turned to face me. "I would recommend putting the water spear down and just go with the nice hand-to-hand combat we all know and love." *Come on, let me lure you into this trap.* "There is no need for you to launch that-"

The spear shot forward so fast I almost didn't get out of the way in time. *He's even faster.* I turned my head around to see the water spear rebound off the arena walls, before propelling back to me. *Well, this is unexpected.* I felt the icy cold-water pierce through my chest, swirling around me, until before I knew it, I was encased in a massive bubble of water with the crowds' cheers muffled from the liquid. I don't particularly like water. At all. I turned and thrashed to escape the bubble, but Grady had surrounded the bubble with a thin but strong coat of ice to prevent me from leaving. Smart of him.

Damn it, I was hoping I wouldn't need to do anything too disastrous I thought slightly frustrated, focusing all of my willpower into my left hand. It would need to take a massive spark to start a flame big enough to dissolve the water into steam. The fact that I couldn't hold my breath for much longer added on to the list. The moment I slipped unconscious would also mean a solid win for Grady, and all my hard work would've been for nothing.

I reached my left hand out to touch the encirclement of ice. It was freezing to the touch, so cold that even though my hand was slowly heating up, it still felt like enough to give me frostbite. I could see my hand start to glow a faint red, my skin disappearing under the heavy glow as the water around heated up in temperature. I could see faint steam coming from the ice and fading into the water. A faint hole began to open up where my hand was placed, cold now boiling water seeping through the cracks and gushing out the other end. I threw my head upwards and inhaled a massive gulp of air that had now been created at the top of the inside of the sphere. Relief flooded through me but was short-lived as Grady let go of his magic, letting the once water filled ice ball completely evaporate, forcing me to drop to the ground unexpectedly. *He shouldn't have dropped me. He knows what I specialise in, if he kept adding layers to that bubble I was never going to get out.* I grinned at him. Surely he knows when he's beat. I immediately leapt up, ready for the attack, hands sweeping soaking wet hair out of my eyes as I scanned the arena for Grady. He was standing shakily, legs swaying slightly as he stared at me with a baffled look on his face.

He clearly didn't expect that.

The crowd roared its approval, each talking amongst themselves loudly and excitedly as if they had just witnessed a life-changing moment in history. Like animals eager to have a fulfilling meal. Grady on the other hand looked the opposite, his eyes piercing me with a dirty glare, as if I had just made a complete fool of him. I could also see him gaining his balance back quickly. I tensed slightly. Me burning through his ice-sphere had only stalled him temporarily, and for some odd reason I hadn't thought about the fact that he could easily regain his energy afterward. I should've immediately gone in for the attack, not just stood there watching him and dragging the fight out even longer.

Why didn't you think of that? A small part of my consciousness whispered in my ear. This fight should have been over long ago.

And I couldn't help but agree with my consciousness as I noticed Grady edging closer, now very balanced at this point. I cursed under my breath. He then stopped in his tracks, his eyes narrowed, and his hands hidden behind his back. I readied myself for an attack, genuinely curious on what he was going to do. The crowd had gone quiet at this point, they were probably as baffled as I was at what he was going to do. A strange gurgling sound then echoed out around the arena's silence. Confusion washed over everyone else, but I knew what he was going to do just a few seconds before it really happened.

"You have got to be kidding me-"

I spat out as I dived a little too late to the side, still managing to get kicked in the gut as Grady's foot came flying forward from his water jet that he had used to propel himself forward over a hundred metre distance at a shocking speed. I was flung to the ground with a large thump as sand went flying. I gasped, inhaling air roughly as I looked upwards to see Grady towering over me already, having walked over here already with his long legs. He isn't giving me time to react. He grinned slightly, raising his dagger up to the light, then slamming it down aiming for my arm. I spun to the side, dodging his attack as he tried again and again until finally he pinned me down with his knee on my chest to make sure I didn't move. He then raised his dagger one final time, taking his time to get it into position. Panic flooded throughout me. Grady outmatched in pretty much everything. Strength, Decisiveness, and what feels like almost everything else. My eyes widened in realisation.

Almost everything.
I still have my speed.
My hands shot up just a few seconds before Grady's landed, pushing all of my energy as I blasted out a massive stream of pure fire out of my hands. Grady launched backwards in surprise, giving me enough time to grab a fistful of sand to throw into his eyes, blinding him temporarily. He let out a guttural screech at that, his eyes squinted shut in agony. While all of this happened, I calmly grabbed my knife from next to me, before swiping a clean strike onto Grady's cheek. I felt a sense of pride as drops of blood trickled down his cheek and onto the sand, staining it a deep red.
The crowd roared in response, knowing I had won the match. People threw their digitalised silver out into the arena, only for it to fizzle out of reality before touching the sands. Grady slumped down to his knees, defeated. I could hear him curse under his breath. I frowned. *Being a sore loser won't do him any good, and I can't exactly have him attacking me because of that.* Shrugging, I did the thing that he would've done in that situation. I gave him a hard kick, the heel of my boot connecting with his head with a loud thump. The crowd went silent at my move. I ignored them. Confirming victory, that's all.
And with that, I waltzed out of the arena.

CHAPTER 2: LILA

Present

"Once upon a time, the world of Mistlon was whole. Elves, dwarves, humans, wizards, Celestials, elementals, even demons lived in harmony. All the species were close, there were no recorded wars. The four human kingdoms lived cooperatively with each other; Arcarlia, Krinia, Sorvia, and White Castle. The dwarf and elf kingdoms Rumah and Siniru were thought of as the closest species, distance wise and friendship wise. The wizards and elementals usually had homes scattered all throughout Mistlon, always having a tendency to explore. The Celestials rarely came down to Mistlon, only ever on specific days of the year when they were celebrated. The demons, however, took care of the dead in the underworld which was sometimes referred to as 'hell' for some people."

"Hundreds of years later was when the dwarves were identified as traitors to the peace we had once had. Furious with humanity's decision for war, the elves joined forces with the dwarves to fight back against humanity. T'was the age of The Human Revolution. After over three hundred years of battle, humanity reigned victory, annihilating the dwarves and elves. The supernaturals felt intimidated by humanity's power and retreated to an unmapped location, which is still unknown today."

"All was going well for the humans, that is until an endless drought swamped Krinia and Sorvia, turning their lands into a barren-"

"Oh! I know this bit!" Mother exclaimed, sitting elegantly as always.

"Mother! I was in the middle of telling the story! And of course, you know this bit, it's happening right now!" Jackiel snapped at her.

"Guys, come on. No fighting! Not when we are so close to finally getting home!" I said, a massive grin adorning my face.

Jackiel rolled his eyes at Mother, before clearing his throat to continue. "- a horrific wasteland where all the surviving inhabitants fight for food and water sources. Unlike the other two kingdoms however, White Castle and Arcarlia have always been able to grow food and produce water. Krinians and Sorvians were jealous of the wealthy lands, so their Leaders bound together an alliance between their kingdoms. This is the exact reason why a war started between the humans, a fight for the wealthy lands. White Castle's ally in this war has always been Arcarlia, as they would ship each other supplies once a month to symbolise their healthy alliance."

I tilted my head at Jackiel. "I always thought Arcarlia simply did it because we usually sent them gold in return," Mother gave me a death glare. "But now that I think about it that is how these things work huh?" I quickly added with a fake smile.

"I think that's enough reading for today." Lexi told him, pointing at his book. I was surprised to hear her voice. She hadn't talked much for the whole trip, but

I suppose even she was getting sick of the conversation. Her full name was Lexi Wellfire. The name most people called her? Lady Lexi Wellfire of Moralvelle. Mother had suggested picking her up on our way back to the castle instead of her having to organise a whole bunch of security guards for herself. She probably doesn't trust her, or maybe she wants to learn more about her beforehand. She came from an island called Moralvelle, to which she is the ruler of. She'd sent us a letter around a month ago, listing that they wished to join our alliance and aid us in our war against Sorvia and Krinia. I took a liking to her immediately. She had rich brown skin and straight black hair with braids running through it, and beautiful grey eyes to go along with it. It was hard not to agree with everything she said.

We all nodded in agreement. Mother sighed and turned around to lean against the side of the carriage, gazing out the window with her dark brown hair flicking onto her face. Lexi leaned back lazily into her seat, sitting with a comfortable expression adorning her face. Jackiel held his hands up to his face and fiddled with a watch that seemed to be perfectly fitted onto his hand. We were all coming back from one of the Royal families' country homes far enough from the main castle. We had gone to the country home to escape a potential threat from one of the enemy kingdoms, Sorvia. We had received intel from one of our scouts that one of the enemy kingdom's were planning an attack on the castle, so we were told to flee to the country home for safety while our Father stayed behind to manage the capital. After two weeks, We finally had permission from our Father that we could come back home to reunite with him once again, claiming the area was safe. The warning had been false after all.

I gazed out the window at the trees rushing past us and the carriage gradually built up more and more speed as we tumbled across rocks, sending the carriage flying into the air before landing onto the ground. Which earned me a decent amount of stomach flips that made me feel like I was about to puke. At this point, we have now almost arrived at the entry point to the capital, the drawbridge. It usually looks beautiful, like a doorway opening into the light. As the drawbridge lowers, the capital would usually appear in its majestic form.

"So how does the capital look?" Lexi asked, looking out the window. I was surprised to hear her speak again. *She doesn't seem like the person to start a conversation.* "Anything that makes it overly unique?" *Lexi seemed the type of girl who observed rather than talked. I could get her to talk way more, of course. After all, it might be best if she wants to become allies with us.* I giggled. *We're pretty talkative.* Finally, I answered her question.

"The capital is mainly full of lots of houses, markets, and sacred sites. One of the more important sites being that one closer inward of the city, that's dedicated to Celestial Tien. The castle is really pretty though! At least on the inside, in my opinion we could probably do with a nicer looking exterior." I gave Mother a side glance. "But something that makes it unique? Probably the people. They're the most joyous civilians in all of Mistlon!" I said, proud. "But!" I grinned, thinking of all the fun things we could do together. *I've never had someone who could relate to my position in the royalty system, the only other Princess is Princess Jassai, and she's way out of my league.* "It would be pretty fun to go swimming in that river like Jackiel and I used to when we were younger," I playfully nudged my older brother and he grunted, shuffling away from me in annoyance. I simply laughed at his reaction. "Though it would still be just as fun as it was to do it together."

Lexi nodded slowly, as if not feeling my excitement. *It's almost like she doesn't want to be here at all, so weird.* "Maybe another time. I think I'll be pretty focused on working out the logistics of what it even means to be…" She fumbled with her words. *It kind of reminds me of when I fumbled my lines during one of the speeches I did.* "Partners with you all." She blinked, then realised what she said. "Not that we can't! We can definitely do it… some other time." She said, panicked.

She's really weird.

I smiled.

I like her.

For the next hour or so, all I did was try to get her to talk more. While the river came up multiple times, so did pranking the guards, playing hide and seek, and all sorts of entertaining things I could think of. *The hardest part about pranking the guards would be us getting in trouble with Father. Getting ourselves out of trouble would soon turn into a worthier test than the rest.* I thought to myself. I could hear Jackiel and my Mother groaning as they listened to my schemes. Jackiel rolled his eyes at my words, but the hint of a smile poked out from underneath. *He finds me entertaining. Rude.* Right when I was getting into the good bit of cooking up a way out of my Father's reach, the carriage went over a massive bump again, sending us all flying into the air before landing back down in uncomfortable positions on our seats. It was quiet for a moment, that is until my Mother's scoff filled the air as her hand had flung itself right into her face, smudging the heavy make-up that she was wearing. Jackiel tried his best to not smirk, as did I. My smile faded as I turned to face Lexi. *Wait, did she get injured? No, this will look horrible on us!* Lexi on the other hand had managed to land perfectly in her

seat, her face blank as she watched us adjust ourselves. *Woah.*
Mother's face went bright red, before shouting out to the driver. "For the love of Tien, be more careful!" Jackiel finally gave in, a smug grin on his face at Mother's rage. "Well, you're one quick to smirk Jackiel, look at you over there!" Mother had a point; everyone then turned their attention to Jackiel who was undoubtedly shaking, and his shirt was caught in the edge of the seat. I straightened my back and looked around awkwardly. *Mother, you're in the presence of another Royal! Maintain your Queen-like posture!*
This wouldn't have been so bad for any other person, but Jackiel always prided himself on that shirt. As he seemed to argue with the cleaners back at the castle all the time on how terribly they cleaned it, and that he could do, and they should do a far better job. He had quickly ended up with the title, 'Mr Perfect' from most of the servants at the castle. It was also a nickname I tended to call him whenever he decided to tease me, he would usually walk off grumbling something like, 'girls'. He never said it out too loud though, just quiet enough that I could hear it. Always made me smile every time at his back after he would slam the door behind him. *He was quite the Prince.*
"Oh my goodness! Your shirt, Jackiel!" I said, smirking at him. "Whatever will you do without it?" Jackiel shrugged at me, delaying the angry response I'd expected.
Lexi ignored the conversation, returning to staring out the window. *She seems really interested in what's out there. Or maybe she just doesn't really want to talk with us. Eh, I don't mind whichever turns out to be true.* I looked down on myself then, observing what I was wearing. *There doesn't seem to be any tears in my dress,*

thank goodness. But I feel like if I went with that green one instead it would've been more appropriate for the occasion. As I rattled off in my head about fashion, I didn't even notice that we had apparently arrived at the drawbridge leading inside White Castle's walls. The only reason I noticed was because Jackiel was tapping me on the shoulder quite vigorously with an annoyed look on his face. I turned around to see what he was looking at. *Ah,* the drawbridge. *It's slightly more used than I remember, with noticeable cracks running along the wooden contraption, metal beams holding it together had also gathered some very noticeable rust and damage, appearance-wise I'm surprised the structure is still standing if I'm being completely honest.* The drawbridge turns seemingly haunted as it creeps downwards to let us through, almost goth-like as it creates an ear-piercing noise. We all clasp our hands over our ears, desperate to block out the noise. It sounded dreadful, like nails on a chalkboard level, except the volume and pain-in-ears was ten times worse. Lexi grunted, and turned her head towards me so I could see her pained expression. *I have a feeling I looked the same.* A massive clunk shook the carriage as the drawbridge had finally reached the ground. Lexi and I both made a big effort to fully turn around to see the kingdom of White Castle emerge in front of us. Massive buildings stuck out of every corner of the space inside the walls, civilians running around as the carriage emerged into the kingdom. You could hear all sorts of sounds; children laughing, adults joking, blacksmiths clanking away at swords and weaponry, bakers coughing as the smoke from the oven became too much, it felt so much like home. Lexi looked back at me, curious.
"You weren't kidding. It really is just houses and shops." She seemed unimpressed. Lexi jabbed her finger in the direction of two knights laughing and

walking through one of the busier streets, happily munching on breadsticks as their swords bounced up and down with each step. *It felt so much like home.* "Do your soldiers normally slack off like that?" *Wait, what did she just say?*

Mother went bright pink and guided her attention over to somewhere else.

The buildings in the kingdom were similar to the ones of the past. Concrete walls and visible wooden beams to hold it in place, the roof's tiles were usually carefully fitted wooden tiles. The castle on the other hand was different. It was carefully created with all sorts of spirals and towers located in the middle of it. The castle was close to a kilometre in length, stretching out and covering a majority of the capital.

I frowned as I recognised my least favourite part. *The colour is hideous.* All of a sudden, the carriage stopped in its tracks right in front of the food market stalls. Mother smiled, then nodded at all of us.

"I had assumed it would be a good idea if we stopped at the food market, don't you think?" I nodded at her. "Fantastic! Coach!" She called out. "Fetch us something to share, will you?"

"Of course, Your Majesty." They responded, and the feeling of the carriage shaking as they hopped off was imminent. Lexi stared out the window again, watching the Coach get our food. She had a judgemental expression on her face.

Is she judging the Coach? Or us?

I couldn't tell.

CHAPTER 3: LILA

The four of us looked up to the large castle. It had perfectly polished grey bricks running down its sides and tall pillars for support. Mother gripped my hand tightly, I turned to her to look at her face. It was full of relief. I then turned to Jackiel, who was scanning the walls with utmost curiosity. Lexi was looking quite tense as she gazed at the castle, I was probably copying her expression now that I think about it. I sighed. It probably isn't even close to how her castle looks, is it? Hers is probably bigger and grander with lots of pretty colours on its walls. I crossed my arms.

Well, wait till she sees how it looks inside.

"Is that how it is meant to look?" Lexi said matter-of-factly. I don't think she meant for it to come out offensive, just saying what was on her mind at that moment.

Mother's hand tightened on my wrist, some kind of death grip. I could see her purse her lips together tightly, smudging her make-up again slightly. She isn't used to people judging our castle. Especially not like how Lexi is now. I turned to look at her, with her eyes still roaming the castle walls.

"It's home, as it always is." Mother sighed, before giving Lexi a bright smile. "Yes, that is how it's meant to look. We focused on defences other than wasting materials on any eye-appealing properties. Surely you understand." She crossed her arms behind her. "I can assure you that the inside is much more magnificent."

"Mother!"

Mother turned around to see Jackiel looking at her with a sincere expression. Everything about him seemed so relaxed at that moment. *He's been acting like that for a while now, I wonder what happened?* "Do you think I could head in now? I have a number of things I need to attend to." He asked politely. I almost snorted at his words. He's rarely this sophisticated behind closed doors. At least not to Mother. Mother nodded at him. "Greatly appreciated, Mother." He bowed, before standing back up and hurrying over to the big double doors. He swung one open before slamming it shut behind him, clearly in a hurry. The guards didn't even get a chance to open it for him.

Mother beamed at us, gesturing to where two guards were stationed at the entrance. "How about we head inside now?" She said, before shooting the guards a look. "Just the three of us." Lexi squirmed uncomfortably, before replacing it with a small smile, nodding along.

No one spoke as we slowly made our way to the oak entrance's double doors, which created a creaking sound as the guards slowly opened them for us.

Inside the main entrance room, we swerved through the statues of great kings and queens, some holding sceptres, others swords, and the one wizard in the room, King Triarch, was the only one holding a staff. Many people believed that he was the ancestor of the

Camhok family line. *Not that he ever existed in the first place.* My ancestors created him ages ago, to keep faith in the royal family of White Castle. The people believe that his gifts were passed down, which makes for awkward conversation. For the best or the worst, no one was entirely sure whether it was a good idea or not. Lexi stopped walking to take a better look at King Triarch, she then turned to face me for what felt like the first time today. "You had a wizard in your family?" She mused at me. *Oh.* I felt my face heat up. She doesn't believe it at all, I can hear it in her tone. *She's really quick to catch onto things, we hadn't even mentioned him yet. Let alone gave the statue more than a glance.*

Mother turned to look at Lexi with a thoughtful expression emblazoned on her face. She nodded, her face slowly brightening up as she excitedly told Lexi all about the non-existent King Triarch. Although I knew most of the tale, Mother seemed to add additional false details to the already fake story. My Mother had explained how he had led White Castle a thousand years ago to victory in the war against Rumah, an ancient dwarf city that was eliminated by White Castle in the war that was called, 'The Human Revolution'. She told her he had been extremely powerful at the time, so powerful he could take on small armies all on his lonesome. *That's pretty exaggerated* I thought to myself, amused by the thought. Apparently because of King Triarch's reign, White Castle became a significant and very large kingdom that people respected for our power.

I sighed, then rolled my eyes at Mother. We continued throughout the path. There were thousands of generations carved into this hall, and every single one of them did something inspiring to make them be placed here. *I always wondered what my great deed would be, perhaps ending the war?* It seemed impossible, after all the first and last one to try settle with Sorvia and Krinia had their head chopped off.

For what felt like no apparent reason. I suppose it is a dream though isn't it? Dreams don't always come true; they simply live in our deepest fantasies. Maybe mine will come true one day. I can only hope. I cleared my throat, positioning my dress a bit better as I led the charge. *I'll do something to be worthy of being in this place someday, I know it.* A loud and exaggerated cough came from somewhere behind me, l swivelled my head round to see Lexi examining another statue.

I took a few steps toward her, leaning in to get a better look at the statue Lexi was looking at. The statue showed a young woman holding a harp. It seemed normal at first, a mere statue in a specific pose. Then I tilted my head at it more, inspecting it more closely to see that the young woman's nose was extremely pointy. *Ah. Princess Crelle.* I snorted in amusement as I raised my hands to my nose and used my pointer finger as an extension to mimic the statue.

Maybe just talking to her isn't the way to go, maybe I should use humour. Lexi stared at my attempt, before shrugging it off. I stared forward, defeated.

This girl is impossible.

We kept moving through the hall, catching back up to Mother. She rolled her eyes at me when she saw me, but her expression changed to something more positive the moment her eyes locked with Lexi's.

Great, favouritism I thought to myself bitterly, not taking my eyes of Mother. Lexi gave me a funny look; she clearly saw the difference in expression. I shrugged it off. Mother then cleared her throat, and we continued through the hall, this time in uncomfortable silence. Eventually after a few more metres we made it to the next set of double doors, the doors that would lead to the main room of the castle. I extended my arms out and pushed open the heavy doors, revealing a massive circular room the size of a ballroom. I turned back to Lexi to see her surprised, maybe even mildly impressed by the design. I couldn't quite blame her; the walls were studded with precious jewels such as rubies and emeralds. There were even some diamonds hung upon the chandelier in the middle of the room. I grinned. *Finally, she's impressed by something.* Maybe I can use this to my advantage.

At the farthest wall there were two grand staircases leading up to the second floor with a fancy dark blue carpet trailing each step. In the very centre of the room there was a massive statue of a smooth white marble tower with golden harps crossing through it, the symbol of White Castle. The floor was smooth, dark oak planks positioned neatly in rows of seven, and they were heavily polished. There were also four exits to the room, one on each wall in the square shaped room. Waiters, servants, and knights were making themselves busy by talking and cleaning areas in the room. The waiters were all gathered near the east exit, discussing excitedly as some of them locked eyes with us. While the servants and knights seemed to be having a heated conversation in the centre of the room, both sides snapped colourful words at each other as they argued on whatever was the main topic of the day.

Mother grimaced at them before striding up towards them saying something to them I couldn't quite make out, but in the end they saluted her with guilty faces and both servants and knights both dramatically walked out of the opposite exits, but not without shooting me a nasty glare on their way out. I could practically sense Mother's annoyance from a few metres away even with her back turned. Lexi looked almost amused. I just shrugged it off, as I usually do. The servants and knights always had a lot of beef with the Royals lately. As if we have done nothing for them. *Ungrateful servants.* Mother then turned back to us with a massive grin plastered over her face as she clasped her hands together loudly before exclaiming. "Ah Lexi! Are you ready to see your room? I sent some of the servants to get some snacks for you, for later." Lexi nodded politely while Mother ranted about how she'll love her new room way more than the one at her old castle. *Mother's trying to be a suck up even more than me.* "One of the servants will come by in a few moments to guide you to your room, feel free to follow too Lila, they spent a lot of time decorating it, so I figured you'd both spend a decent amount of time in there!"

Or establish a friendship that could aid in our Alliance. Right on cue, a young man, who looked to be in his twenties, strided up towards us, grinning like a madman. He had messy blonde hair that looked like a human version of a bird's nest, his hair also had some strands that were longer than the others that he had to keep batting out of his eyes. His eyes were a soft hazel, with freckles dotted everywhere around his face which gave him a friendly, cheerful appearance. He wore the standard servant uniform, a one-piece grey suit with the emblem of White Castle embedded into the middle of his chest. His sleeves were rolled up as well as his pants, which I was surprised he didn't change before coming up to us, especially considering Mother was looking him up and down with annoyance. It was a major breach of normal protocol, yet it seemed to make me like him more.

"Your Highness, Princess," he bowed to each of us before hesitating on Lexi. "And who exactly might you be?" He raised an eyebrow at Lexi, making her flush slightly.

"Ah, right. I'd thought that everyone would have already been informed." Lexi said through gritted

teeth, all while a smile was planted on her face.
"Lady Lexi Wellfire of Moralvelle, thank you."
The blonde servant went hot pink with realisation.
"Craig Burrowhill at your service, My Lady. I
apologise for not recognising you before!" His eyes
flashed with uncertainty. "I'm here to escort My Lady
to her room."
Craig then gestured his arms to the right staircase,
still embarrassed. Lexi nodded and left for the
staircase immediately. I stood still for a few
moments, deciding on whether or not to accompany
Lila. It's not like she seems to have any intention of
being friends with me. Mother then harshly slapped
my back then pointed in where Lexi had already
gone. "Follow her, Lila." She hissed into my ear. I
jumped at her sudden harsh tone. *Right.* I rushed
after her, surprised by how agile and quick she was.
Geez, she's fit.
I followed her up to the second floor, to where I
quickly realised how much the castle had changed.
The second floor used to be a long hallway with spots
every now and then for lounges so the waiters and
servants could rest from tending to people all day, yet
they were gone. Instead, those spaces in between the
rooms were being used as weapon racks and
gatherings for knights. Maybe that was why the
servants and knights are being so bitter towards us.
Still, there's no excuse. Changing more areas to
weaponries should make them feel more at ease, not
despise us. Lexi turned her head to see me right
behind her. Her face stayed the same. No sign of joy
to see me?
"Was that not there before?" She asked, genuinely
curious.
"Nope. In fact, it used to be a lounging area for
servants and waiters from tending to Royals, ladies,
dukes, and visitors. They often needed it for walking
around for such a long time." The blonde servant

appeared behind us, as if summoned by an otherworldly force. I jumped, surprised to see him. "What are you doing, sneaking up behind us like that?" I snapped at him. "Plus, I was going to answer that." I muttered under my breath, even though the area was new to me too. *Nevermind, he's just another ignorant servant.* I cleared my throat, deciding to ignore the servant. "So, what was Moralvelle like?" I asked Lexi in a more respectful tone, tilting my head at her curiously.

She paused, thinking. "Well, what do you want to know about it?"

"Oh! Uh." I was surprised to even see her answer my question. "What's your castle like?"

"My castle?" She looked slightly panicked for a moment.

"You- you do have a castle back at Moralvelle, don't you?"

"Yes! Yes, I do. Sorry, just not that many pleasant memories there." She shrugged. "But to describe it? It isn't as big as the one here, actually probably half the size." She kept having spaces in between her words, which I found weird. *Must just be her way of talking. I, for one, talk too much.* "But for what we lack in size, we excel in beauty. Since we haven't had the need to fortify it like you have, it's been decorated in many different ways over the decades. The outside of it looks somewhat like yours, grey walls and the occasional tower. But we have banners everywhere, symbols of Moralvelle."

"Oh, well that's nice." It was quiet for a few moments, walking side by side. Eventually Craig started talking again, explaining some of the history behind White Castle. Who founded it, what our currency is like, the basic stuff. "We are also very culturally appropriated with our food, you see. One of our most delicious meals would definitely be Pork-" Before he could finish his sentence, the servant walked into one of the waiters hurrying past with a platter full of expensive wine. Once they collided, the glasses went up in the air, with wine splattering everywhere on the walls. The passersby let out a horrified gasp as they were drenched in wine. I felt Lexi pull on the back of my dress with a sudden jerk that pulled me backwards, narrowly avoiding the wine that splattered right in front of me.

Lexi's reflexes are on another level! I thought, trying to comprehend what just happened.

I looked back to where Craig and that waiter was, and found shattered glass decorated all around them. The waiter was lying on her stomach, looking up and around to see the mess she had accidentally created. Craig merely stood there, arms out with red wine patches all over his shirt. The waiter looked horrified when she realised what she had done. "I- I am so sorry Craig!" She frantically sat upright, careful not to touch any wine or glass. She was also drenched. "It was an accident! I- I didn't see you there!"

Now as she straightened herself, I got a better view on the waiter. She had tanned skin with black hair carefully styled into one big braid, and silver earrings hanging out of her ears. Her bright blue eyes were wide open. My face fell as I slowly recognised her. I couldn't tell who she was at first, considering she had a whole new hairstyle and fashion sense, but there was no mistaking it. It was Evalune. The same Evalune who used to be my own personal nanny growing up. I narrowed my eyes on her. Just my luck I ran into her again. *At least she got a demotion, which she deserves.*

"Is that Evalune Woodbryne?" Called out a guard from the growing circle of bystanders. "Hah! I always knew she would find trouble somewhere." Chuckled another. The crowd began to grow with comments about Evalune. *Well, it's not like she's a very popular person after everything.* I mused to myself.

Craig turned back to us, visibly embarrassed. "I am so sorry about that, Your Highness." He bowed to me, while attempting to wipe off the wine. He was drenched in alcohol now; any normal person would assume he was drinking on the job. He gestured to the end of the corridor. "Your room is just down there, My Lady. I'm sorry, but I doubt you want this smell anywhere near your quarters. So, I'll leave you two to it." Lexi nodded, watching him hurry off in search of a change of clothes.

I started to grab Lexi's arm, trying to take her with me when she didn't follow. I blinked, staring at her. "Aren't we going to go now?" I said, confused as to why she wanted to stay. Lexi frowned at me, almost looking at me with an expression of disgust.

"Aren't you going to help her up?" She said, standing her ground.

"Help who?" I whirled my head around, before realising she was talking about Evalune. "Her? No, I'm not helping her!"

Lexi stared at me, not blinking. "Why not? She's one of your citizens. Isn't she?"

"Well-" I stuttered, lost for words. *Someone else will help her. Surely she realises that? It's not my problem.*

"What kind of example are you trying to set here?" Lexi questioned, raising her eyebrows. "Don't think I didn't notice how those guards had looked at you. They don't like you. Surely you realise that? You're just going to fuel their hatred?"

I was lost for words. I quickly rounded up an explanation. *Wait, why am I explaining myself? I've never had to do that to someone. Who is this girl?* "No, no it wasn't like that Lexi. It's just, everyone isn't used to people other than other knights and other waiters and servants to help them with this kind of stuff." I felt like slapping myself after I said that. *What am I doing?* "Okay, sure. It would make sense to make them like me more." Lexi nodded in agreement. "But just because we don't help people off the ground doesn't mean we don't do other good things?" I said hopefully with a wry smile, my dark brown hair slapping into my face as I continued to speak. "We also give out food for the poor, provide shelter, and we have a currency system for everyone."

"But isn't that what Leaders are expected to do? You don't do anything out of the ordinary, clearly." Lexi snorted.

"You're twisting this right now!" I exclaimed defensively, getting a little annoyed. "Just because we don't attend to their every need and call doesn't mean we don't make their lives easier!"

Lexi simply shrugged in response, clearly not changing her mind on the matter. "Okay then. I was just asking." She replied calmly.

Lexi then started to walk forward, and I followed. The commotion was still ongoing, with no one stepping in to stop it like I had hoped. I shook my head and kept going. *How can she make me question things I had originally thought were second nature? Especially over such a small problem?* I rubbed my temples and quickened my pace. *She really will make a good friend, she's stubborn.* I smiled. It'll be an adventure every day. Eventually, we reached the end of the corridor. I turned to face the door on my right and gripped the handles, slowly but dramatically pushing the door wide open as I gestured for Lexi to enter, once again silent. *This should be it* I thought to myself as I took in the room. I was surprised to see how stylish the interior of the room looked. The room was clean and sleek, and looked amazingly flawless. Once you entered the room, a massive double postered bed awaited you two metres in, with dark blue silk covers and pillows and a massive wooden mandala decorative piece located at the front of the bed. Then if you stepped further into the room you could see the rest of its contents. On the far wall sat a massive window made up of three smaller arched windows and a cushioned ledge going from one side to another just wide enough for someone to get comfortable sitting on. Then if you looked at the wall farthest to the left, you would see a dazzling looking fireplace with its structure carved out in swirls and specific patterns, as well as a massive painting illustrating a lone tower looking out into the never-ending sea. Candles were decorated all around the fireplace. There were also two cushioned chairs sitting out in front of the fireplace, creating an inviting and warm place to curl up and read a book. There was a fancy-looking analogue clock on the wall just above the massive bed, as well as a big, antique wardrobe cushioned into one of the far-left corners. As you looked up to the roof you would see a small chandelier about as big as a young toddler. The chandelier was moulded into multiple curves created to hold several candles to light up the room as much as possible. There were also two support beams built in place along the roof, with thick, green vines curling and dangling all over each of them for decoration.

"This really is something." Lexi breathed, her eyes widening at the sight.

My face lit up at Lexi's compliment, a smile beginning to form. *This is good progress.* I then turned to her. "I'll be sure to send some servants to send up your belongings. Later." I said, watching her reaction.

Lexi nodded at me, still taking in each corner of the room. She then sprinted towards the bed and grabbed one of the pillows. "Huh. These things are really fluffy." She observed, squeezing each pillow as if she was checking for something. She can be really weird.

"Do you like the room?" I asked, watching her with content as she began to search the place from top to bottom. She tilted her head to look under the bed, then, once satisfied, she took the liberty of scanning the room again. *I have no idea what she's looking for.* "Why wouldn't I?" She said with a small laugh, finally smiling when she turned to face me. "This room is amazing, actually. Definitely exceeded my expectations. It's hard to believe this was made in such a small amount of time." She sighed, then walked up to me. "Do you think it would be okay if I explored a little on my own? I'd like to get my own feel for the place, on my own if that's fine with your policies."

She already wants to leave? *That was quick. We just got here* I thought downheartedly.

"No, don't worry, it's fine!" I said, trying to shrug and keep a smile that was actually believable. "Just don't wander off too far though, this place is massive. Meet me back here in twenty minutes?"

Lexi's face flickered with uncertainty, as if she wasn't expecting that answer, then was quickly replaced with a sly smile, "Yeah, that should be okay. I'll try and get back before then."

And just like that, Lexi bolted past me and out the door with astonishing speed. I slapped myself in the face, I forgot to tell her about not running in the corridors, and certainly not when there's wine all over the floor.

Waiters and servants hurried past me, clearly on errands directed by some of the knights and higher positions in the castle. "Can't be late," some would say as they hurried past, while others muttered annoyedly, "I swear the people here have no patience." I missed the bustle of people in the afternoon before we left the castle, how they would gather in halls and gossip about the latest gossip about someone doing some other thing, or just about the daily dose of jealousy against the knights in their shining armour. It was all quiet here now, far too quiet for me. I was in the hallway, standing in the exact spot where Evalune ran into Craig. Even with her best attempts at clearing the floor of all the wine and glass, some remnants remained. No one seemed to care though, not yet anyway. Just wait until Mother comes by, she'll freak out as if her entire bed was full of cockroaches.

I knew Evalune since I was five, she had ended up becoming my personal nanny after Mother and Father kept attending meetings with King Stafran, discussing things that Mother had assured me were important enough for her to leave me for an entire week away with Father. Evalune - or Eva as I used to call her - was always there every second of every moment. A little like an older sibling who you did everything with, that was Evalune. While my parents were away, she taught me how to bake, cook, draw, and even showed me new games that I could play in the lake with Jackiel. Then Evalune suddenly stopped showing up. My parents assured me that it was for good reason, even though they couldn't even give me one. My faith in Evalune slowly died out after six months of her not being there, until eventually when she came back she pretended I was just a person she had to care for. I never knew what had changed, but it taught me a lesson. No one ever stays the same. *Maybe that's why I won't give up on Lexi.*

I continued to walk through the hallway, dodging waiters carrying meals, and servants scurrying through the halls trying to reach one of the rooms down the hall. I didn't have that problem of course, the benefits of being who I was meant I could walk through a massive crowd and there'd always be a gap surrounding me so I could never break my strut. I had only had two goals while Lexi was out exploring; try to avoid talking to anyone and find Jackiel. He was always terrible with change, even though we're now back to how it has always been, I still want to check on him just in case. Jackiel's room was at the very end of the hall, he spent most of his time there, usually having a nose in a book trying to hide from everyone. I liked the fact that we were complete opposites, I would do anything to live his life. He isn't the heir to the throne after all.

CHAPTER 4:
LEXI

One Month Earlier

"Lexi Ignei, do you pledge your full loyalty to the Council and this mission?"

"Yes, yes I do sire." I answered confidently, staring Sire Lewis directly in the eye. I wasn't letting anyone down on this mission. "Never for a second would I think twice about where my loyalties lie."
"And do you pledge to draw the blood of anyone who prevents your success?" Inquired the Sire, his tone without emotion. "Woman, man, or even a child such as yourself?"
I tensed slightly, I still had mixed feelings about the last one. Yet one of the targets is my age, so I'll just have to suck it up. "Yes, I pledge to draw the blood of anyone who prevents my success. Woman, man, or," I took a sharp intake of breath as I forced out the final word, "child."
Sire Lewis paused, examining me for a moment. His features stood out to me even more in that moment.

His shiny, pale bald head with a pointy face and sharp features. His jet-black eyes were heavily intimidating, which was funny for a person such as me to find intimidating. He wore a dark red suit that most suspected was meant to show off his scars as a sign of defiance and fierceness. I had gotten used to his harsh teachings and personality over the years, sure it was hard to adjust to but after almost a decade of his daily classes you end up finding it as a small sign of affection. Fairly different from what most children are used to, but it's the best I've ever got.

I was placed into an elite training program from a young age, making me one of the most intimidating seven-year-olds you would ever meet. Most children were put to a test before entering into the advanced program. I, on the other hand, was given free entry because I was... different from the other children. I was born into the Ignei bloodline. Our current world's version of Celestials, Gods. However, I am what people call a Flammous. Fire elementals, Army destroyers, all the same. It also made for a fairly chaotic training session, but we don't talk about that anymore.

My Sire sighed. He was the closest thing I had to a Father; I was taught to be grateful for that. "Don't think I didn't catch your hesitation there Ignei." His eyes narrowed into slits. "Tell me again, do you pledge to draw the blood of anyone who stands in your way, woman, man, or child?"

I snorted in response, a sly smirk lighting up my face. "Of course, Sire." I responded, my worries from before slipping away. "Why wouldn't I be?"

Then I balled my fists into bright, fiery flames.

Present

Lila was clearly a little upset about me wanting to explore without her so quickly. I could see her expression change then quickly form back into the smile she usually had plastered on her face. But I had bigger things to work on, one of them being responsible for her and her entire family's assassination. Possibly one of my gorier thoughts, but I'm used to it by now. My goal with my limited time away from Her Highness is simple. Be able to map out this castle for good escape points and note down people who aren't as oblivious as their Royals are to assassins. This friendship between the Princess and I will certainly be short-lived, that is if everything goes to plan. *Not that my lack of social skills is helping with that regardless.*

Yet I'm also starting to think leaving without Lila might have been the wrong decision. I had noticed how all the people who work here cleared a path for her as she walked the halls, but they clearly haven't done that for me. Frustrating, especially since this hallway is filled with servants just wandering past without a care in the world about the other person actually trying to get through. I take back what I said earlier, this is infuriating. Unfortunately, this next mob to wander past was a group of knights, squabbling with each other on who performed the best in one of their duels. Their shining armour had sharp ends, with their scabbards swinging around as they swayed closer and closer toward me. There was only a little bit of room on the left for me to squeeze through to not get squashed by obnoxious knights.

How many people are in this castle?!

I quickly made a quick dash to the left, pushing myself against the wall as hard as I could to avoid the guards. It would be stupid to get on their bad side this early in the plan. I bit back a sarcastic response as one of them turned around to snort in my face. *Definitely regretting going on my own that's for sure. Plus, they don't seem to have a single idea on what my new persona is.* I took a sharp turn left and found

myself standing in front of a massive, grand staircase. Surprisingly it was the one place where there were less people, something I took as an advantage. I made my way quickly down the steps, I was going to make the most of my limited time. Once I had reached the bottom, it didn't appear that much had changed. Only now there were more servants and the waiters who were standing by one of the exits had disappeared. Other than that, there was almost no one in the area. *Everyone seems to have gotten the memo that I had decided to try and walk through the hallway upstairs and clearly left the downstairs area alone.* I snorted at the thought. *No, Lexi. You need to be more mature, otherwise you'll get picked out quicker.*
I paused at the bottom of the stairs, wondering which exit to follow. I already knew where one of them went, the massive hall of old dead people then the exit out of the castle, but I didn't know about the other three entryways, however. There was one just in the middle of the two staircases. Then two others to the far right and left of the room. Where one of them went, I'll find out soon enough, that is if I haven't wasted enough of my precious time already. In the end I chose the one to the far left, which as I drew closer seemed to be an extremely, unnecessarily long hallway. A hallway with an opening at the end that seemed to lead out into some sort of path with dots of greenery at the end. I grinned. A garden. There won't be as many people down this path, gardens these days aren't that popular.
I made my way down the hall to notice a door on either side of the wall. Loud voices came from the door on the right, as well as multiple sounds of banging silverware. I whipped around in a defensive position as an ear-piercing bang rang from the door, followed by multiple screams and angry rants. Another reason why this kingdom is being targeted. *They hire psychos as chefs.* I conclude quickly in my

head. Opposed to the right door, the left was rather quiet with voices speaking in such low tones I could barely even hear them. What they were talking about was unbeknownst to me, making it more enticing to find out what. Ignoring any second thoughts I had on the matter; I leaned my ear right against the door and slowed my heart rate to a steady beat so I could just make out the muffled words.

"-fancy dinner tonight. Did you not hear about that?" Inquired the first voice.

"No, probably because someone could just as easily poison the food as they could simply breathe? Did that thought not occur to you?" Hissed the second voice.

"And why exactly would someone want to poison my wife's birthday dinner? You're overreacting."

"Oh, I don't know, maybe a spy from an enemy kingdom? A Sorvian? Maybe even a Krinian?"

"Sarn, where are you getting all this hogswallop from? Just because something happened to your family doesn't mean it will happen to mine." He groaned. "A spy? How much did you drink last night at Darrell's anniversary?" Groaned the first voice.

"Nothing! Again, I don't drink! Plus, it's not exactly like it isn't possible Felix! The spy I mean you buffoon!" Replied an agitated Sarn.

I went stiff against the door. How could there be suspicion of people already? All these years of training just to get caught on day one on the job? What kind of assassin am I? I haven't even met this oblivious Felix and his far less oblivious friend Sarn. I held back from stamping my foot in agitation as they continued arguing in far less quiet tones about this guy Sarn's drunk matters. After quickly deciding that getting caught eavesdropping on two people talking about a potential spy doesn't make me look like an innocent Lady, I forced myself to back away from the door. Not that there was really anything important they were talking about anyway. *I need to calm down, I'm rushing things and getting suspicious of everything I hear.* A fake smile is then plastered onto my face. One I hope looks pleasant and curious enough for any passersby.

I looked back down the hall, questioning if going to a garden was really worth the time I would waste in doing so. I shook my head. I haven't learnt anything so far; I need to continue looking around for more information. I took a deep breath then spun on my heel and waltzed back to the central room.

I just wasted so much time and learnt nothing. I groaned. I was back in the central room with zero idea on how much time had passed. Whether it was ten minutes, or more, I didn't really care. *Actually, I probably do, after all this has been a waste of my time.* I gritted my teeth and forced a calm expression onto my face. The Princess was just being protective with her damn time limit. I doubt she'll care if I'm a few minutes late. I made my way up the staircase, taking a longing look at the other entrances. I'll find a way to convince Lila to let me map out the place a bit more, it shouldn't be too hard. *She's nice, but she's not a genius* I thought calmly, my hand gliding along the railing of the staircase as I made my way up. I've become an expert at lying over the years. It's not exactly a new thing to ask for permission to go elsewhere for a false reason.

The hallway upstairs wasn't as crowded as it was before, with noticeably less people jamming themselves in the middle of the hallway. I took advantage of it, speeding through the hall without properly looking, and ended up running into something at full speed. Just like that good for nothing servant from before. *How can I possibly make the same mistakes they do?*

-Anasia Edwards-

"Hey! Watch it!" Snapped a frustrated voice, clearly the person I'd run into.
I looked up, a little dazed and a little frustrated to see a boy about my age with dark brown messy curls and bright blue eyes. Unlike me, his face was completely clear of freckles, leaving only olive toned skin. He was wearing some sort of chain mail chest piece bearing the emblem of White Castle, with a leather top underneath. He wore lightweight pants that were pitch black, probably a knight in training by the looks of it. His expression was hard and stern, which anyone would've expected considering I'd just ran right into him. While it would've been fun to play with his clear anger-management issues, it would've brought far too much unneeded attention. So instead, I went with the safe path.
"Oh! Sorry, didn't see you there. I'm new around here and I'm late to meet up with my friend, sorry again!" I replied cheerfully, shooting him my most sincere smile yet before getting ready to hurry past him. Long story short my face of pure innocence seemed to piss the boy off even more. *Lovely.*
"I don't care if you were meeting your friend!" He snapped back, rolling his stubborn eyes at the word. "Thanks to you, I'm now late to my Combat 101 class, or the class that I've been late to for the past three weeks! My General is going to kill me!" He shouted even louder. How could I make him late? Our encounter hasn't even reached the minute mark yet. The few people in the hall had stopped walking at this point and simply stared in astonishment, but by the looks on their faces I could tell this was a normal thing to see. However, his shouting is already drawing far too much attention onto me right now. My lips pursed into a thin line. He needs to get out of my way, now.
I gritted my teeth and tried to maintain my smile of innocence. "Ah well, in that case I'll just get out of

your way now so we can both get to where we want to go quicker."
The boy laughed darkly at that. "Don't bother hiding it, I can see your sarcasm as clearly as a torch in a pitch-black room. You might want to get that checked out before meeting your so-called friend, you know?" He said menacingly, his voice sending shivers down my spine.
I flinched. Who was this boy again?
He smirked at me, looking so amused and righteous as if he were royalty himself. That was, until someone cleared their throat and stopped the boy's next jab. It was one of the knights, except this one seemed older, with a long grey beard and grey hairs sticking out of his almost bald head. Yet there was something about him that simply screamed 'get out of my way' and everyone around us seemed to know it judging by the looks on their faces. His expression turned hard as he focused on the boy.
"Jesse Marks! What time do you call this? You were supposed to be at class ten minutes ago! Yet here I see you," the knight then noticed me while throwing daggers at the so-called Jesse. "Annoying one of our castle's guests instead?" He shook his head, disappointment spread all over his face as he scolded him. The old knight then pointed to me. "This is Lady Lexi Wellfire of Moralvelle. Someone of a far higher position than you ever will be." He spat. "I expected better from a Marks."
Jesse's frustration quickly drained from his face, replaced by a flushed expression. He mumbled what I assumed was an apology under his breath. He then quickly shot a quick death look in my direction before following the knight down the stairs, head bowed low. Whispers came from the witnesses as they quickly dispersed back into their schedule. I groaned. They almost definitely wouldn't forget this. Lila would find out within the hour, and the Queen.
However, I do need to find out more about this Jesse.

Why is it that all the angry people here seem to be more perceptive?
He's not afraid to speak his mind and he's intelligent.
That makes him dangerous.
I was about to continue down the hall and play it out normally when I saw a familiar face looking right back at me. Jackiel. He had his arms crossed as he watched me, a hint of a smile on his face. Jackiel then walked up to me. "Ah, your first Marks encounter. Always memorable, though not in a good way as I'm pretty sure you've gathered." He added as-a-matter-of-factly. "But don't worry, you should adjust to it."
I paused for a moment, taking in his words. We hadn't really spoken much since I'd known him, which wasn't very long anyway. It was mainly just me and Lila, though that was the plan anyway. Out of the two royal siblings Lila was supposedly the people's favourite and one of the most gullible. Plus, from what I hear she's the heir to the throne. It was a funny feeling talking to him, he surprisingly had humour that I didn't expect from someone such as him. Now that I think about it, it wouldn't exactly hurt to see if I could get on his good side. The more important roles on my side the better I can carry out the operation unsuspectedly. Considering these options, I decided to keep the conversation running smoothly.
"What, does he have some sort of reputation? You know the boy Jesse?" I asked, general curiousity filled behind each word. *Wait a minute.*
"You're way easier to talk to than before." I noted, immediately regretting my words as I said them.
Crap, I messed up already.
The Prince's face turned bright red, slightly embarrassed but more agitated by my outburst. He chose to ignore my statement. "Yeah, I suppose you could say Jesse has a bit of a reputation for being

insanely frustrating and sarcastic. He's about a year or two younger than me, so about your age. He can be nice at times, but he has to actually like you, which is rare. I personally have never seen it myself."
Jackiel's voice then dropped lower, as if he were worried Jesse might come around the corner. "There was one person he bonded well with however, her name was Scarah. Yet she died last year from an unknown disease, and Jesse hasn't exactly gotten over her like the rest of us. He blames the Royals for her death, saying that we didn't provide enough for her to survive." He sighed.
I paused, surprised. I hadn't expected the smug boy to have such a depressing backstory. I frowned. *But why he would let one simple death get the better of him is beyond me, but then again I was trained to be heartless and cunning. I've heard of ways of taking out your grief, yet he takes it out differently.*
I snapped out of my thoughts to see Jackiel looking at me inquiringly, clearly wanting me to say something to help continue the conversation. *I'm not good at this. I only really talk to people that I'm training with, and sometimes in this case I talk to my targets to gain their trust.* Other than the fact that I've never tried to have a conversation with him before.
"Huh."
I mentally slapped myself hard in the face.
Jackiel blinked, confused by my answer. Clearly this wasn't the answer he was expecting after talking about someone's life story. Then the uncomfortable silence came, us just staring at each other awkwardly. *Really Lexi? 'Huh'? What kind of answer is that?! It's a miracle if he doesn't report you for suspicious activities, plus lack of emotion. They'll think you're some psycho* I thought as I mentally punished myself for putting me in this position. "Uh anyway, who was

that guy who took Jesse to," I paused for a moment, trying to remember what he had told me and trying to hold onto whatever was left of my normality. "I think Combat 101? Something like that." I then quickly added. "You know just out of curiosity." *I'll be tracking him down almost definitely.*
Jackiel's face relaxed slightly, clearly he was as glad as I was to break the silence. "Oh? You mean Lord Draxis? He's pretty famous around here, I'm actually surprised you haven't heard of him already." I stared at him. "Not that that's bad of course! I meant that he is famous with the knights. Not everyone knows him, mainly just the people interested in taking combat classes makes it mandatory to know his story."
I nodded slowly, consciously searching my memory for someone called 'Lord Draxis'. No such luck. *Funny how someone as seemingly famous as him wouldn't show up in Analysing Enemy's Strengths And Weaknesses.* I found myself scrunching up my eyebrows in concentration. If he was as famous as Jackiel said and he was on the combat side of things, how could I not have heard of him? Perhaps it was because he was a teacher? That would make more sense.
"Lila was actually looking for you. But don't get the idea that I'm going to become everyone's messenger." He rolled his eyes at the words, a bit of the so-called 'bratty Prince' personality shining through. "She told me to tell you to meet her in the courtyard, which, I'm sure you have no idea where that is, do you?" He asked me, tilting his head.
Great Tien, how long was I wasting all that time? I shook my head quickly in response.
"Figured you wouldn't know; I can give you directions if you want. I have somewhere to be pretty soon so I can't exactly take you there myself. I'd also recommend you get changed into something more suitable." He shrugged, suddenly looking bored. *It's*

almost suspicious. Then again, he's a teenage Prince. He could be doing anything. He was certainly strange though, going from talkative to bored. There are many things about this Prince I need to find out. However, at the moment he isn't exactly a threat to my mission, not that he would be in a matter of weeks anyway. He's more of a book person, isn't he?

"Thank you! That would be greatly appreciated."

-Anasia Edwards-

CHAPTER 5: LILA

It didn't take as long as I expected for Lexi to arrive in the courtyard. Jackiel must've found her pretty quickly roaming the halls, to be fair she is the only person I know to wear an outfit like hers on a day like this. I was standing in an open passage just next to the courtyard. It had stone carvings running along it that looked like the flowers from the castle's garden, and it was open to the courtyard so I could see the boys in their combat classes. When you first enter the courtyard it is pretty much how everyone expects it. Freshly cut green grass everywhere, practice dummies located around the edges, and a massive fountain placed right in the middle. I sighed as I took a deep breath of the clean, outside air. Leaning against the fountain with her eyes darting from each side of the courtyard to the other was Lexi, and after a few seconds her grey eyes finally connected with mine and she smiled shyly. *She's finally coming along!* I thought, overjoyed. Lexi had pulled her pitch-black hair back in a five second bun with a strand or two whipping into her face as the late afternoon breeze swept through. She fiddled with a small blue bracelet on her wrist, as if she was waiting for something.

Lexi was the kind of teenage girl who always looked insanely smart with her shiny brown skin adorned with freckles, delicate tiny hands, and her nervously shy smile. She could hide any secret in the world, and no one would suspect a thing. But then again, why would she hide anything?

She'd changed outfits since I'd last seen her, going from a red Tiski to a dark blue tunic and a tight crimson skirt. She even wore black knee-high boots to go along with it. *Finally, her sense of style has improved*! I couldn't help but look down at my outfit for the day to see it darkened with drops of water. "Great." I muttered under my breath. "You just had to ruin it." I then rolled up my sleeves and stalked over to where Lexi was at the fountain, who was clearly hoping for an explanation. Funny, I just noticed. Jackiel isn't there.

"Hey Lexi! Is Jackiel not here with you?" I frowned, tilting my head to look past her as if Jackiel would simply appear out of nowhere behind her.

"No, he said he had a job he needed to do." she said, then looking at my puzzled expression and quickly added. "I don't know what though, he didn't mention anything else."

"Oh, well I'm sure he had a good reason. He always comes to these kinds of things and lets me watch them. Interesting he missed it, but I guess it's the first time for everything, right?" I chuckled.

"Yes. About that, why am I here? Why he didn't come wasn't the only thing he didn't mention."

"Oh? He also forgot to tell you that too? You must have been so confused on the way here!" I said with a laugh, still worried about Jackiel. *He usually takes these classes as seriously as he would with his life.* "Don't worry, I'll tell you. But first, you see those boys over

there at the training dummies?" I pointed just to the right of us where about ten boys were slashing swords and firing arrows at the training dummies with Lord Draxis critiquing each thing they did.
"Well, for about four days a week these guys always come out for training from 4pm to 6pm, including Jackiel. I visit a little too often. I've memorised the time at this point." I added sheepishly.
"So what? You just watch them the whole time? Do you even pay attention to what they do?" She asked genuinely, deciding to ignore my surprised expression. *She seems really interested in this.* I frowned, my mood dropping. *I was hoping she'd be more interested in other things, like I am.*
"No of course not! And keep your voice down!" I hissed at her, indicating with my eyes to the few boys who had stopped their training to stare at us. "They have no manners! Plus, you're making me sound weird in front of them!" I sighed. "I come here because Jackiel always asks me to. He always wants me to watch the others carefully for him, so when he's put up against them in tests he'll have an advantage."
"Wait but what would you know about fighting?" Lexi scrunched up her face in confusion. "You're a Princess. They aren't going to allow you to have any battle experience, you realise that?"
"Well," I began sheepishly, embarrassed. "I usually follow Jackiel to his training sessions, to cheer him on and things. I'm not actually very helpful for his tests. I just tell him what their faces look like when they are about to swing a certain move." I added with a shrug, tucking a strand of hair behind my ear. Jackiel wouldn't have missed this session for the world, especially since it would lower his perfect attendance score. I found myself fiddling with the fabric of my dress, letting the material weave

through my fingers in thought. *It must be something important for him to miss this.*
"So, are you sure Jackiel didn't tell you anything at all? Like where he might be instead maybe?" I pressed, watching Lexi with my best pleading damsel in distress. I saw a flicker of what I'm pretty sure was frustration covering her face for a moment, but it was gone so quickly I doubt I even saw it.
She sighed quietly before she answered. "No, no he didn't tell me anything else." Lexi then turned away and muttered something under her breath.
Something I couldn't quite hear.
I blinked for a moment, feeling awkward all of a sudden.
"Cal! Get over here and quit talking to your friends! Son of a Lord or not you signed up for this!" A deep masculine voice then rang out from the squadron of boys. I smiled at the voice. *Lord Draxis.*
"Sorry sir, I'll be there in a moment with Cal, Lord Draxis." I glanced at Cal's best friend Christian who then saluted Lord Draxis and turned his back to me, grabbing his best friend roughly by the arm and dragging him back over to the training dummies. I did my best to hold in a giggle as I watched Christian grinning at his best friend, his smile brighter than a thousand suns as he laughed. He was just so... perfect. Not that I'd ever tell Jackiel that, he'd torment me endlessly. But Lexi on the other hand? She's a lady too isn't she? A flash of jealousy flashed through me. She might think the same way, girls like us can be ruthless.
"Doesn't he look fabulous Lexi?" I sighed, putting as much dreaminess into my voice. "Christian, I mean. He looks like the one doesn't he?"
"Did he say Lord Draxis, Lila?" Lexi whispered to me as we watched Christian and Cal approach the group of boys holding in their laughter, completely, utterly ignoring me.

"Yes that's his name, why? And were you even paying attention to me?"

"It's just, that means--"

"Ah! Your Highness, My Lady." Boomed Lord Draxis ahead of us, causing us both to look up in his general direction. We both nodded in sync. "So that's The Lady who made Jesse lose his temper, again!" Lord Draxis gestured towards Lexi. *Well, it's not the first time that has happened. He loses it on a daily basis.* A wave of laughter swallowed the boys as everyone's attention was suddenly turned to one in particular. Lexi groaned. Jesse -possibly the most self-obsessed boy there- was standing awkwardly, his face bright red as the boys surrounding him laughed right in his face. I blinked. Lexi was becoming more and more strange by the minute for a Lady. Lord Draxis thumped the ground with his foot, and the boys stopped laughing.

The training session went on with the boys practising their aim while the others clashed their swords against each other, the sounds of whizzing arrows and metallic ringing flooded my ears continuously. Though of course none of them could compare to Christian. While the boys were busy with their task, Lord Draxis set onto creating a task that could actually challenge him. Which ironically mainly involved Lord Draxis trying to get Christian to teach the newbies how to properly punch, by stating over and over again about how if they kept punching like that their knuckles would never be the same. They definitely found it a little annoying but got the hang of it near the end and were punching at each other's protective pads without hesitation, causing Christian to earn a grin from Lord Draxis. Meanwhile Jesse was continuously shooting Lexi death looks whenever possible, especially when some of the boys would come up to him and one would say something making the others burst out laughing. I

couldn't help but smile to myself. It was a little evil, but to be fair Jesse deserved it. *Sort of.*
Once they'd neared the end of the training session, Lord Draxis had gathered them all together and discussed that next week the boys would be focusing on opponents weak spots and fighting techniques. I frowned. Maybe I heard that wrong? They'd already done that a few weeks ago, didn't they? I'll have to tell Jackiel, see what he thinks about that. No doubt he'll be surprised to hear it. I leaned forward from my viewing spot, trying to get a better look at the boy's faces to see if they were also confused, yet Lexi harshly tapping my shoulder made me turn around.
"Does Jesse keep secrets?" She asked absently, her gaze set on the red-faced Jesse.
"Not really, why?"
Her face froze, her eyes narrowing. *Was she okay? What even happened when she talked to Jesse before? She looks worried about something, but too stubborn to admit to it. She's zoning out, clearly stuck in her own thoughts. It looks like she is deciding about something.* "Hey, are you okay? I think there should be a seat in the courtyard." The words flew out of my mouth as she just kept staring, clearly concerned about something. *What could Jesse possibly have against her? This is only her first day at the castle, and it's not like there's a long list of things that he could have a vendetta for. Especially a Lady like her.* "Come on, let's just have a seat."
I grabbed her arm and wrapped my hand around it tightly, then was surprised by how she was holding her ground so well. It didn't matter how hard I pulled, she simply stayed still, not moving a muscle. *How strong is this girl?* She blinked, then turned her attention to me and she quickly relaxed. So fast I could've sworn nothing was wrong. She held up her hands, face apologetic.

"Oh! Sorry about that, I'm just lost in my thoughts. It happens sometimes." She said, smiling weakly.
I smiled warily at her in response, heavily aware of Lexi's sudden easiness. However just as we started to head to the courtyard, Lord Draxis called out something else. "Another thing, Your Highness! I would recommend coming again and bringing Jackiel this time. That boy's attendance has gone from unnaturally perfect to a normal human's score." He paused, grinning mischievously. "Good evening ladies! Hopefully I'll see you next week at four!"
I could see Lexi pulling on her best smile, unaware of just how fake it looked. *What in the name of the Celestial's was she doing? I'm not entirely sure if I want to know why Lexi is acting even weirder than she was before.*
I made a mental note to myself to find out what. Once we sat down on one of the benches facing the courtyard, I quickly noticed that there were still a handful of boys left from practice. I wrinkled my nose in disgust as I shuffled closer to Lexi. *Of course it's Jesse's group.* A group of five were gathered in front of us. Jesse with his back to us, and his four other minions swamped in front of him, a self-righteous smirk on their faces. The two redhead twins, Simon and Clarendon, stood next to each other to the left of Jesse, seemingly deep in discussion with him. Clarendon has terrible asthma, making him very sensitive to any strong smell. Which also means you can never quite fully understand him with the massive brown mask he has over his face that goes from his neck to his nose, like a bandit. Then we have Val and Terress, listening intently to the conversation. Some of the most good-looking boys here -except for Christian of course- yet some of the worst swordsmen of their age. Val with boring, blonde, straight hair and even more average hazel eyes to go along with it and Terress with the dark, matted hair and blue eyes. The one thing they bond

over except lacking fighting skills? Their love of unhealthy foods.

Absolute pigs, all of them I thought stubbornly, glaring at the group. It didn't take them long to realise we were still here. I didn't need to look at them to feel their stares ebbing into us. I could see Lexi's face tighten for what feels like the fifth time today.
"Let me guess, Jesse's friends?" She asked, clearly already knowing the answer. "Is this normal around here? To just have them, you know." Lexi gestured to the glaring group of boys, who seemed to now be staring and whispering. "Or did I really make such a bad impression?" I flicked my hair out of my face and turned to look at her.
"Don't worry, that group has a serious reputation that isn't exactly that positive. From what I can tell from just being around them? They hate everyone, especially people like us." I couldn't help but grin. "Especially Royals like us. They just, what's the word? Don't understand." Lexi nodded, catching on. I smiled, hoping I was giving off a 'so don't talk to them' look. This place takes some getting used to, but I'm determined to make sure she doesn't go down the wrong path. I flung my arm around her shoulder and beamed. *We're finally getting somewhere; I'd be brave enough to call us friends now.*
Lexi paused, then turned to face me with a question. "Hey, what exactly do you know about the war?"
"Oh?" I said, surprised. *I guess it makes sense for her to want to know more.* "Well, as you're probably aware our Alliance 'Unity', is facing off against Sorvia and Krinia in the Great War. Sorvia being the main enemy, and Krinia being the aid to Sorvia. I don't know too much more about it."
"Ah. I see." Lexi said, sounding a little annoyed. "How dangerous are they? Do they have some other way to communicate or dangerous weapons? Of

course, I'm only asking this for the sake of my people. I'm just curious on how cunning they may be."

I blinked at her. "Well, I have heard a rumour in one of my classes that Sorvia can communicate in sign language. I heard that it's one of the first things they learn. I'm actually in the middle of learning it right now."

"But wouldn't that be easy to notice?" Lexi asked, staring into my eyes with a look I couldn't comprehend.

"Yeah it would. I don't see why they do it, I mean how are you supposed to hide this?" I stretched my hands in front of me and started to sign random signs. Lexi laughed a little, looking almost relieved.

"Yeah." She said with a sly smile. "It would be difficult to hide it."

We were about to get up when a voice then called out from across the courtyard.

"Lady Wellfire!"

Both of our heads whipped around to see Jesse smirking, standing there with Simon, Clarendon, Val, and Terress staring back at us with arms crossed. "You seem pretty intent in coming into my castle, and trying to humiliate my reputation, are you not?"

I groaned, feeling ready to slap him hard round his face. "Your castle? Jesse, do I need to remind you of whose rule you live under? Because you seem very confused on the matter." I snapped from across the courtyard. "Or do I need to send the guards over to personally escort you to your room," I paused, smirking. "Again?"

Jesse's face went so red I could see it clearly from twenty metres away. Yet it quickly faded into a relaxed expression. "Terribly sorry, Your Highness. But if I'm correct, I asked the Lady a question here!"

I could see his cold eyes narrow in on his target.

"After all, she is the person who seems to think they

have all the power on their first day! Well, I think it's time for our Lady here to wake up to the real world. Us mainlanders know some form of respect, unlike our islander friends here! And there isn't a higher sign of disrespect than to embarrass one in front of their mentor is there? Regardless of status."
A resounding 'no' came from his followers as he fixed his eyes on me.
"And then we have our lovely Princess Lila over here, star and people's favourite. Also, the same person who helped organise the… incident. Wouldn't I like to get back at you for that? Don't you think that would be fair?"
Jesse sighed before taking some steps forward, advancing on us in an eerie way. I felt myself rolling my eyes at him. He was being so childish about the situation, and he was taking it way too far. The so-called incident as he calls it probably deserved a better name from how well it turned out. A handful of people from my circle and I got sick of Jesse's constant blatant remarks. So we found a way to expose his true nature to the Generals. Jesse had gone from one of the most popular knights-in-training in the castle to only being tolerated by a group of four. I smirked at the thought. The Great Truth as most of us liked to call it. I turned my eyes around for a second, searching for a guard I could call over to scare Jesse off. Yet there were… none? I frowned. Then it clicked. All the guards were attending the meeting with Mother and Father tonight, none of them would be too bothered about the courtyard and more on ensuring their safety during the meeting. *What an evil genius.* I thought, cursing myself for falling into his trap. I turned back to face him again, bracing myself to start a full rant about how childish and pathetic he's being. Yet the first thing I turn around to see is his face staring at me with the coldest snarl on his face and him shouting. "This is what you deserve, you brat!"

Yet before his fist could connect to my face, before I could even react, a burst of flame came from my side. It exploded the moment it came in contact with Jesse's fist, torpedoes of fire launching in all different directions. It propelled him backwards, blasting him away from the sheer force of it. The last thing I heard was someone screeching.
"What the-"
It was so quick. It was too quick for me to realise that it was my own voice speaking. It was also too quick for me to realise that everything was heating up. My eyes widened as the fire repelled off Jesse and back at me. But nothing could compare to how quick the pain in my head flared like a firework show.
And then it all went...
Black.

CHAPTER 6:
LEXI

One Month and One Day Earlier

"Lexi Ignei, your presence has been requested in the Councillors Chamber immediately." The short, hooded figure bellowed in front of my door. I knew it was one of my former classmates, one of the group who had been selected to be a Knight. No matter though, I would never find out who they were. Knights never had a happy ending. Nor could they show their real face. Instead, they wore a mask that represented how high ranked they were. Not that this one was very high, we were all only selected last month.

At least some of us were.

The Council threw out the weak, leaving only the champions to have the opportunity to strive. It didn't matter if you were number one and you lost your final battle. You'd be thrown out, try again the next year. It's a cruel but necessary practice. *I almost feel bad for Grady.*

I nodded at the knight, who had then guided me through the halls to the doors of the Councillor's Chamber. It was a large double door decorated beautifully, at least the Sorvian level of beauty. That door on its own could feed over a thousand people with the amount of gold and unique materials thrown at it. The knight nodded at the guards, who pushed open the door for us. I walked inside, carefully making my way through the small path laid out in front of me. The Chamber was pitch black and not to mention an abyss that led down thousands of metres in depth was on either side of the path I was walking on. The only things you could step on were illuminated by the light above, giving it a contrasted effect.

The path ended in the centre of the room, turning my attention to the five platforms emerging out of the darkness in front of me. One member of the Council sat on each, carefully observing me.

Here, the Council would observe me. From the left to the right, it went to Brain, Bravo, Mortal, Dagger, then Fox. Brain being the leader of the group, with the others following close behind.

"Lexi Ignei. Age: fifteen years old. Height, one hundred and sixty-two centimetres. Estimated IQ, one hundred and ninety-one." Brain said. "Does this sound like you, girl?"

I nodded, watching them with intent. "Hey, you're a pretty smart girl." Bravo said, her face lit up with a smile. "That's an unreasonably high IQ right there."

I bowed in response. "Thank you, Bravo."

Dagger watched quietly, as he normally does. He was always an observer rather than a talker. *I can relate.* His parrot sat on his shoulder, also watching. His parrot was reasonably intelligent for an animal, being a Councillor's companion. I knew this based on the research I had done on them.

Fox nodded. "Your smarts will definitely help out in the field we have selected for you, Ignei."

Mortal agreed with Fox, his bald head shining with the light. "The girl has talent. Yet I don't know if she'll be able to take on a job such as this, though Brain."

Brain shook his head at Mortal's suggestion. "She's ready. She's beyond mature for her age. Smart, talented, strong. She has all the attributes she needs."

Bravo hesitated, watching the other Council members exchange their thoughts on the conversation. "Should we really be talking about this, in front of her?" She said, pointing at me.

Fox shrugged. "Not like she hasn't experienced something like this before." He said, completely ignoring Bravo's question, his fiery red hair glowing even brighter. *A talented Flammous at work.*

Brain then held his hand up, silencing the group. All attention then turned back to me. "We have gathered you here because we believe your skills are perfect and essential for a highly skilled and rare profession."

I blinked, staring at them curiously. "What have you decided?" I asked them.

Brain narrowed his eyes at me, before finally answering my question. "You, Lexi Ignei, will be ranked the highest position we can offer. More information will be given to you tomorrow detailing your mission." He took a deep breath, before finalising his words. "With our Council's decree, it has been decided that you will become an Assassin. The leading pawn and key to winning the war."

I straightened my back. The assassin role? Was I really fit for that position?

"But of course, you won't be doing this on your own." Bravo stated, watching me curiously. "You'll be accompanied by a young woman who you are already acquainted with. She has moved up in ranks to Tactician, so she is more than perfect for the job. While she won't be there physically, she will be your

first and only person you can contact using this," she held up a square piece of red glass. "A CrysTalk, the latest version. With this, you will be able to communicate important information through her to us privately. The Tactician's alias is Granette."
Brain nodded at her words, before turning his attention back to me. "That is all for our meeting. You will receive more information soon through your Tactician. Good day to you, Ignei."

Present

It was necessary and unnecessary at the same time. I didn't need to protect the Princess. To be fair, my job would've been a quarter done if I'd left Jesse to punch in the direction he was going for. Her chest. It would've crushed her lungs with how quickly he launched his fist at her, and I wouldn't have to do anything. No suspicions. No nothing. Jesse would've been able to be sent to jail for murder, and I would've finally gotten that boy off my back temporarily. Probably permanently, now that I think about it. *He would've been executed.* But if Lila was dead, how could I possibly get close enough to the royal family then? They would've sent me back to my 'kingdom' so they could grieve in peace. No, Lila had to live, it was the only way. I was sort of proud of how I managed the situation. I managed to spread the fire around the two of them in a certain way to knock Lila unconscious and make it seem like Jesse had punched her, but then fell on the sword. *Hence the big scar along his waist.* It all made sense. It was all perfect. And with the lotion I keep with me, there were no traces of any burn marks. And now that Jesse is out of the picture temporarily, I won't lose my cool and he won't spoil the plan. *I was already wondering if he would become a problem, but at least*

that's one additional thing out of the way. Jesse's minions however were a little bit harder to dispose of. While one of them already fainted when he saw me shoot a fireball out of my hand, the others were getting ready to impale me with a sword. However, with a little bit of Snooze Memory in the air, they were out cold, and their memories wiped of the whole ordeal in seconds. It's not like it was too difficult to drag them off into an enclosed space, they were surprisingly light. *By the time people would've found them, they'd already be awake. It would look like they tried to escape from the situation like cowards.*
The sound of curtains whisking open interrupted my thoughts. One of the healers then rushed into the room, carrying a soggy towel and lots of different shaped pills close to her chest and headed towards the bed I was sitting next to. *Lila's recovery bed.* I honestly didn't quite understand the girl entirely, she was like a make-shift wooden doll that always looked perfect, even in a concussed state. And of course, with a massive bruise across her forehead. Her brown hair was laid out perfectly to showcase her new scar that she would probably have a heart attack when she saw it. Her eyes were closed peacefully, as if she truly had no idea her friend was plotting to kill her. Or that I was from an enemy kingdom. Though that should be the least of her problems. The healer quickly got to work, spreading all of her healing utensils on the table next to Lila and set to work, casually giving me glances that probably meant to show me she knew what she was doing. That, and try to reassure me that I didn't completely kill her.
"Her parents and brother will be here soon, to see how she's doing. Is it alright if when they come you can show them to where Her Highness is my Lady?" Asked the Healer, looking up at me after she'd wrapped a cool towel around Lila's head. "It'll be

easier than me having to leave her unattended while she's in the condition that she is."

"Don't worry! That's perfectly fine." I smiled sincerely, fiddling with my fingers as I added; "I'm still a bit shaken up about the whole incident before, is there any chance where you know where the boy-, Jesse is?" I asked, hoping I looked genuine enough. "I am wondering how he's doing as well."

"Ah. Jesse." The Healers face sagged at the name. "The boy who punched a Princess then fell on his own sword, yes. I'm afraid he's in critical condition at the moment on the other end of the hall. You won't be able to visit him I'm afraid. He lost too much blood, and he needs lots of fluid in him." She then raised an eyebrow at me, suspiciously. "But why exactly would you want to see him if I may ask? I understand a patient is a patient, but you just watched the whole nightmare unfold, didn't you? I would be pretty shook up at the thought of even looking at him."

"Oh, I'm just making sure everyone's okay. It was... rather disturbing when it all went downhill." I even shuddered for extra effect; my face twisted into discomfort.

The Healer nodded, clearly understanding my situation and then bent her head down to continue her healing process. I felt a little giddy on the inside that it actually worked to be honest. *Far too easy.* I was out the door in seconds after that, whipping the curtain around and peering down the hall to see more Healers panicking, running around carrying all sorts of medical tools I didn't recognise. Almost definitely where Jesse was. I was about to turn left to the entrance when the Healer's voice interrupted, "Oh! And My Lady?"

I stopped walking for a moment. "Yes?"

"Do you mind putting in a good word for me with the Royals? I desperately need a raise; my Father is too sick to get a job and I can't provide for him and a little sister with the income I'm getting. It would be… life changing."

That was awfully straight forward. Did I hear that right? I blinked slowly, turning my head around. She thinks that she needs help? She thinks that she is barely living? I forced a smile onto my face, an unsettling tingling sensation coursing through me. Sorvia is living in the dark compared to White Castle, relying on survival tactics. Most people are out on the streets. Yet here she is, working in a castle and clearly has fresh clothes to change into. The temptation to wrinkle my nose at her in disgust was unbearable.

"Of course I will." Echoed my hollow voice. "Anything to help someone in need."

And with that, I whipped my head around and stormed off in as much of a lady-like manner as I could.

It was only a matter of time waiting at the entrance before the sound of boots and high heels echoing quickly down the hall came. I repositioned myself from leaning against the entrance door to standing in a more formal position, with my arms folded over each other behind me as I waited for the Royals and their guards to appear around the corner. First came the Queen, unexpectedly quick in her high heels. I could see her squinting from afar, her make-up causing her to look what I honestly thought was an ugly Bracken Monkey. Her face relaxed as she recognised me, before turning her head back to the corner and calling out something which probably went along the lines of 'hurry up!'. *If I were her I wouldn't be so relieved if I saw myself* I thought silently. Before I knew it, a distinguished middle-aged man came waltzing round the corner wearing a purple cloak laced with gold and knee-high leather boots. His hair was a curly dark brown, similar to the royal siblings except with strands of grey peeking out from the edges. He had a reasonably thick neck and broad shoulders, with his face in the shape of a square combined with a goatee. One particular thing I noticed would be the fact that his eyebrows were so thick it was difficult to see his eyes. Finally, he wore a gold crown barely hanging on to the top of his head with one singular purple gem at its centre. He must be the King, Lila and Jackiel's Father. King Moralle of White Castle.

"Lexi dear! I was hoping I would meet you here. Is my darling okay? How bad is she?" Called out Queen Benice, struggling to maintain a proper posture as she strode over. I could've snorted at the sight, but no. I need to pretend that I truly am worried about Lila's position, that it truly is serious. *Like I didn't plan it perfectly. It's somewhat insulting that they all think she's seriously injured.*

"Oh, I'm so glad you're here! I've been so worried about Lila, it was terrifying! First her and Jesse were arguing, then he went to punch her and he- he fell- there was so much blood- I'm sorry I just-" I stuttered hugging myself as I widened my eyes in horror. "I'm sorry it was just truly terrible to witness. Lila just had a minor knock to the head but Jesse..." I let my voice falter at the name.

The Target looked at me with sympathy, half relieved that her daughter was okay and half anxious of my experience. Before I knew it, she was right in front of me, holding me tightly in a hug.

"That must have been terrifying for you dear, but I'm glad to hear Lila's alright." She bent down and smiled at me, face considerate. "If you're up to it, do you know which room she might be in? I feel it would be best if we could meet her in person."

I smiled lazily at her as I stepped aside and gestured for her to enter. "Of course, Your Highness! Just this way." King Moralle peeked over her shoulder and

held my gaze, staring intently. His bright blue eyes felt under exaggerated in the stories I had heard of him, they were both piercing and intimidating at the same time. He looks like the type of person who isn't easily fooled. *But that is to be seen later on.*
Guards swarmed to their sides instantly, nodding to me with expressionless faces as if to say, 'we can take it from here'. I resisted the urge to gulp at the sight of so many guards and important Royals in the same room as me, people who wouldn't hesitate to shove a sword through my chest if I let any of my true intentions show. I may be a trained assassin, but I'm only fifteen.
"Follow me, I'll show you where Lila is."

CHAPTER 7:
LILA

It was a funny dream.
Or was it a dream?
I can't quite remember.
On the contrary my head feels like it's on...
Fire.
Fire. That was it. Something really, really hot flew into my face. It hurt. A lot. Someone else was there though, who was it? Jackiel? I'm not entirely sure. All I know is that my eyes feel so... heavy. For the love of Tien, why can't I open them?
Think Lila. Who was with you? Focus on that instead of the piercing pain in your skull.
Damn it! I just can't remember. I tried to shout in frustration, but no sound came out, at least nothing I could hear. I focused harder as I tried to remember anything, something in this abyss I'm in. I think it was someone close to me who was there, but not a relative. I could've squealed in excitement if I could talk, it must be a

friend. That sounds right. A she. Her name... what was her name? It felt like a never-ending cycle at this point, with the only name I could spit out of my head being Jackiel, my....

Brother.

He wasn't there at the training. The combat training, that's right. But why would I go if Jackiel wasn't there?

Christian.

The name popped into my head immediately and I could feel the pain in my head easing slightly at the name. He was there at the training; I remember that much. He was teaching a group of beginners the basics during the whole session. Yet there was someone watching him with me, the person who had been by my side, watching patiently. Who was that girl? And why am I getting such nervous tingles? Is she... dangerous? No, I don't think she was.

Flashbacks flooded my vision of what I presume happened an hour, maybe more before whatever in the name of Tien happened to me. What felt like a swarm of bees invaded my mind as they peeked and prodded at the corners of my memory, rising events to the surface with a sharp touch of pain.

I was standing next to a doorway just outside of the courtyard, waiting for someone. I had been standing there for a while, boredom seeping through each of my supposedly perfect features. A group of boys were chatting to my left, also waiting for someone. Isn't that funny, Lord Draxis, is usually the first to be early to his sessions. I wonder what happened. I felt myself thinking without meaning to. That must be part of the memory-coming-back thing. I remember what I thought then too maybe? The boys had turned their attention to me at that point, heads swivelling in my direction as they had finally noticed I was there. One of the boys waved at me and ran over, face full of curiousity.

"Hey Lila! L-ila! Do you know where Jackiel-"

One of his friends came up behind him and gave him a large slap, not long before apologising to me, and not his friend, who was in fact rubbing his head as if he had been whacked with a saucepan.

"Princess Lila." He hissed at him, then knelt down and whispered to him, "Just because your Dad got you into the program doesn't mean you can just not show some respect for those higher up."

I remembered feeling uncomfortable at his words, knowing extremely well how much I hated being called that. The title 'Princess' had so much power and responsibility set upon the shoulders of whoever had claimed it. And this is before people will know I'm the Crown Princess. It was almost unbearable. Wait, what? But I love my title. Don't I?

The memory faded, along with the unsettling feeling. And instead, a new memory arose from the blankness of my mind, yet this one was far hazier and foggier. It also felt... Warm. I felt my whole body shake with fierce tingles, but not because I was cold. The warmth wasn't welcoming like it normally was, this time it was ferocious. Fire. I was terrified of this memory.

An argument had boiled out of control. Shouting, one from my side and one from the side across from me. The mysterious person was there again, I was sure of it. Yet the people on the other side had far more people. Multiple silhouettes of foggy figures had immersed into view, their features barely visible in the haziness of it all. I had felt frustrated at the one in front, frustration that led to surprise and shock. He had said something, something that had set me off guard. Whatever it was had caused the blurry bystanders behind them to back away slightly, arms crossed. I also noticed and felt the mystery person behind me getting closer almost as quickly as the person in front of me.

The person in front had a name. I wasn't sure of it, but I knew they had a name. The memory was getting even foggier now, as if I was reaching the end of it entirely. They had raised a fist towards me, aiming it at my chest and preparing to swing before something quicker than a flash came from behind me, a hand thrust out and a blast of fire exploded onto the person in front of me with a small majority of the blast rebounding off of their body to me, my head specifically. Then the memory cut to black, but my vision was growing brighter now.

I could hear voices, not ones from my memories or my imagination but real voices, getting louder and louder as my vision continued to brighten and a room and anxious faces came into view.

But that was also where one last detail of my memory came in, a better version of what I had just seen except focused on the fire.

I felt like screaming.

I recognise that hand, that little bracelet tucked around her wrist neatly.

The rich brown skin glowing beautifully in the light.

That was Lexi.

And she can control real fire.

I gasped for air.

CHAPTER 8:
LEXI

Lila ended up waking to a group of five standing over her bed, chanting her name and crying out meaningless words. I was a little surprised by her family's reaction. It must feel nice to have someone there all the time, anxious to watch you grow from each knockdown and care when you got hurt. I mentally slapped myself. What's all this talk for? I'll be the hero of Sorvia in a matter of days at this point. There was no room for forgiveness from these people. From my targets. There were two healers now, attempting to give Lila a swift and quick recovery. If I were in her position there wouldn't be anything left of the infirmary, nor the people in it. One of the Healers placed a pair of bunny slippers down next to her bed. *Ah, probably for when she wakes up.* When her eyes snapped open to see four people right in her face ·I was waiting calmly in a corner· she looked beyond terrified. *As expected.* Her eyes were wide and confused, her chest heaving for air as she took in deep, slow breaths. *For the love of Tien, I*

couldn't have hit her that hard I thought, genuinely concerned. It was only meant to be minor, and no trauma would be involved. The Healer I had talked to before attempted to calm the family down, trying to give Lila some space for everything to piece herself back together. I could see her assistant also examining the family closely, as if looking for something that was missing.
Jackiel.
The one missing member. I'll be honest, I wasn't suspicious of his movements and enquiries for the two times we had really communicated, but now I'm curious. What could possibly be more important than his only sister recovering from an unconscious state? What business did he need to attend to that was so important? *More importantly, what was he hiding*? I exhaled slowly. I can report my suspicions to Granette over CrysTalk. She'll report it to the Council about the potential backstep and they will decide whether I need to temporarily immobilise him as well.
I managed a worried expression, striding calmly over to where Lila was resting now fully conscious. "Lila! Are you alright? You took a really hard hit to the head before; I was worried you weren't going to wake up!" I told her, fear glistening in my eyes. I squeezed in between the two nurses and lent over to give her a quick but tight hug. "When Jesse fell I didn't know how to react and you- you were lying there unconscious, I wasn't sure on what to do."
She stared at me confused as if she couldn't quite recognise me.
Okay? usually they just have temporary fatigue when they wake up. She should recover properly in a few moments. However, I was not expecting her to scream and snatch the closest medical instrument -which ended up being a glass cup- and hurl it in my direction. I dodged it narrowly, letting the glass shatter against

the wall hard. I straightened up quickly, surprised and confused. *What did I do wrong?!*
What.
The.
Actual-
"Lila! My goodness! Lexi was the one to call the guards to get you to safety!" Shouted an outraged Queen Benice, clearly forgetting her daughter's current position.
Yet she had a point. Why did Lila just- does she know? My heart raced quicker than it should've.
Worse yet, does she remember anything? My head snapped around, scanning the room to see if anyone else had come to that conclusion while keeping an eye on Lila who was staring at me with a look of pure fear. I could see her far better now, as everyone had bolted out of the way and was now sticking to the walls of the room to not get hit by another flying glass cup projectile. With her chest thumping up and down at an increased rate, she looked like she was going to freak out and scream again.
The new healer took a few steps towards the Princess, wary of her every move.
"Your Highness, I can assure you it is recommended that you lie down for a moment and get fully rested before you start, ah, moving." The Healer said with a sly smile, waiting anxiously for Lila's response. Whether physical or not. Nothing happened for a few moments, Lila just blinking at the Healer with a puzzled expression instead of the one she wore for me. The Healer exhaled in relief.
"Now can we just-"
A glass plate went flying this time, but instead of dodging the plate the idiotic Healer stayed still. Their smooth face was soon replaced with shards of glass sticking out of their cheek and stains of blood dripping down them. A look of pure pain shone on their face as the Healer let out a guttural howl and fled the room, screeching in pain as they went.

Everyone in the room went dead silent, glances of horror shining in their eyes. The King's mouth dropped open, staring at his daughter who had quickly proceeded to lay down as if nothing had just happened. Which I found quite interesting. The great King of White Castle was afraid of his own daughter throwing glass around? *My mission might have just gotten easier.* Guards had rushed into the room almost immediately after Lila's head had touched the uncomfortable-looking pillow with swords pointed out in every direction.
Everyone seemed... confused. And horrified.
However, I knew better.
Lila knows something. I'm not sure how much, but she knows.
Her eyes connected with mine again. Staring a little saner into my own.
The way she looked me up and down, there was no denying it.
She knows.

By the time the guards had hustled the royal couple out of the room, I was already back at the staircase. The swarm of servants had returned once again, each hustling to get to finish their shifts to meet their families for the end of the day. This morning, I would've instantly thought that these moments of theirs would be short-lived. Now I'm not so sure. My meeting with Granette will change my mission because of this revelation, that I'm certain of. *Lila knows. Somehow she knows. Why else would she freak out like that?* I could feel my fists clenched tighter and tighter as I made my way up the steps. The Council might decide to jeopardise the mission if they find out, making the situation even messier than it was in the first place. All because of my one mistake. I could feel sweat dripping down my brow when I turned into the hallway. Each second felt like an hour, ticking by slowly as reality continued to set in. *Lila was going to tell her parents.* Guards would be at my door before the sun rose. I won't even be able to escape the castle in time before they order my head on a pole. Even if I do escape I will still have a massive bounty on my head. I took a sharp intake of air as I raised my hand to turn the door handle. *I'm dead. I'm deader than dead.*

It was a little disappointing to think about. Not that it wasn't expected. The most dangerous mission I could've possibly decided to embark on, and I thought I could just come back completely fine? I slammed the door shut a little harder than I would've preferred. So much for not caring. *But why do I care? Why? Everything dies eventually. It's just clear that this came a little... sooner than expected. At least the bed was comfy I suppose.* I wondered how they'd execute me. *Maybe the traditional guillotine, or maybe they'll get a little more creative and do the classic burn on a stake.* I frowned, then shrugged as if the idea was amusing to me. I'm all open to new ideas. *They may even surprise me, who knows. An arena would be something I'd prefer.*

Though before they barge through my door I do need to alert Granette so she can alert the Council. With a sigh I funnelled through one of my drawers and withdrew my CrysTalk, expecting an odd and short conversation.

"Coller, Granette."

My CrysTalk was the newest version compared to the others. It had a spotless rectangular face and was a shaded red see-through panel. The screen flickered for a moment, coming to life and glitching as it sent signals to Granette's device to make her pick up. After a moment the once red screen was

replaced with Granette's pale face. Her glasses looked like they were dropped onto her face, tilting on a funny angle that didn't match her serious expression. Her eyes were a pale blue combined with red hair and a circular face. I could see her sigh as she snatched her notebook and ink pen, slowly dipping it into the ink pot as she relaxed into her chair. We stared at each other for a few moments, both knowing something was amiss.
"So." Her brisk voice seemed to echo throughout my ears. "What happened?"
"It's… hard to explain but I think this might be my last night." Both our faces went stone cold at the words, proving our fears. G took a deep breath, before nodding at me to continue.
"I know it's only been one day, but it is way harder than I first thought. Everything was going fine at the start. I was given a room, people believed I was this mystical Lady Lexi of whatever-ville, then I met up with one of the targets an hour or so later, the Princess. We watched the knights-in-training complete their practice, and we were meant to leave right after that."
I stared absently at the window, marvelling at my last night sky.
"A group of other knights-in-training came up to us. Had some sort of rivalry with the Princess. Little did I know it would turn out to be them trying to punch the Target in her chest that would kill her instantly. It would've disrupted the plan, disrupted everything." I added quickly to my defence, noticing G's look of exasperation. "I threw a fireball at the offender, then quickly used some Snooze Memory to knock his friends. Some of the fire repelled back to the Princess but not enough to kill her, just knock her out."
"So let me get this straight," Granette said, looking beyond frustrated with me. "You used your cool-special powers to knock out the offender, and didn't

expect there to be burn marks? You're playing with fire, Lexi. Actual fire. What were you thinking?"
"But I did think about that!" I snapped, losing my calm fixture and surprising Granette. "I planned it all so perfectly. I used that special ointment Michelangelo gave me to remove any traces of burn marks. I dragged away the unconscious bodies of his friends. What I didn't plan was for Lila to somehow have eyes in the back of her head and see myself blast a fireball out of my hand!" I took a deep breath. "I am almost certain she saw me Granette. And somehow remembered me! She looked terrified when she saw me, her eyes were wide open, basically bulging and she even threw a glass at my head! It's only a matter of time before she rats me out to the guards. Now, I'm regretting giving her such a small dose of Snooze Memory."
Granette took a deep breath, intaking this new information. "Okay, but clearly since you don't have any guards banging on your door means she hasn't done anything yet. But to keep our mission alive and not have the Council make you eat that pill? You're gonna need to sneak back into that Treatment Bay they have her in and use your Snooze Memory. You have to wipe that girl's memories clean if you want to live another day."
She looked at me as if this was obvious. To be fair to her, it was. It's just the entire concept was beyond... What's the best word for it? Impossible. "You do know that you're asking me to sneak past every single personnel in this place, make sure that the Target is still in the place she was, and make sure she doesn't have a heart attack and call for guards when she sees me?"
"Well, it's either that or you take the path of a gambler and live your life on the fact that she might not fib to the guards. Which, by the way, is really unlikely." I grimaced, tempted to throw the tablet away and hope they just kill me in my sleep. "And

would you look at that? The face you make when you know I'm right." A smile lit up her face, one I haven't seen in a while. "If you follow this plan I might get to see it again." Granette's already pale blue eyes faded, seemingly right through the screen as she added quietly, "I don't want the Council to make me force you to take it. I can't. You're my best friend. My only friend."

I could only imagine what I looked like then. Face drenched in guilt and uncertainty. I rarely have this feeling. And I don't like it. I shouldn't let my feelings get the best of me. This decision legitimately affects whether I live or die. And there's only going to be one good choice. I groaned, massaging my forehead as I realised what I was thinking. "Okay. Fine. I'll do it. But I need some imprints on the castle layout before I even think about doing something drastic."

A slight smile peeked at the corners of Granette's mouth. "I swear if you were going to be stubborn like I thought you were going to be, then I would've taken the extreme to convince you." Her grin widened into a toothy smile. If she were in the same room as me I would've slapped her so hard, she wouldn't be able to smile without her jaw hurting. She just manipulated me, and I didn't even realise it. A little smile picked at the corners of my own mouth, almost matching Granette's, despite my unique situation. I taught her well.

"Alright, castle layouts coming up. Give me about five minutes to send to your CT. However, in the meantime," her grin widened to the point that it almost reached her ears. "Get ready to kick some butt and save the mission for me, eh?"

I'm glad that they don't check our bags like they do at Sorvia when we arrive. If they did they would've found a buttload of weapons and stealth armour. *Can only imagine how heavy it must've been for those servants.* Speaking of servants, I had to wait for them to send me dinner if I wanted to start the mission. It would affect it severely if a servant were to notice I was missing. The sun had set a few minutes ago, and the castle had gone quiet. Not long ago a servant finally served me dinner. *Finally*. Based on the imprints Granette had sent me, there was going to be no way I could get past any guards to make it to the infirmary. That is, only on the inside. Granette had an idea about the whole ordeal, however. Not one I'm particularly a fan of. Her idea was as bizarre and grand as any other Tacticians; scale the side of a four-storey castle. And what did my tactical saviour who was in charge of necessary items pack? Two sharp hooks to hook into solid stone blocks. If I won't die from getting shot by a crossbow or worse, I'll break my bones and then die from the guards after falling a length of thirty metres exactly. In G's words, better to go out like one of the fictional character spies we all read about growing up than being killed for existing while you sleep.

One particular imperfection in this perfect plan? My room is located on the third storey of the castle. The infirmary? The second storey.

"Isn't my life just fantastic?" I muttered to myself as I dressed into a pitch-black jumpsuit one and a half millimetres thick. The suit stuck to my skin like glue, designed to ensure that no squeaking sound would affect the wearer's mission. It was smart. Beyond uncomfortable, yet smart. It had attached wrist cuffs with small shards of silver hidden in them to sharpen and polish knives if need be. Shoes as snug and silent as socks. A belt wrapped tightly around my wrist bestowing spaces for pocketknives, katanas, even sedatives disguised as ugly pens. The best part? Firstly, it fits my small size. Secondly it holds my assassin's mark, an orange triangle with a flaming arrow crossed right down the middle with a line alongside it. An assassin's mark is a symbol that is designed to strike fear in the hearts of Targets.

Each line stands for a Target slain or beaten in battle. I only have one line, as the only battle I've won so far was against Grady in the Trials. *The incident from earlier could barely count as a battle.*
I gracefully glided to the door, resting my ear against it to hear if anyone was coming my way. Seconds ticked by.
Six.
Seven.
Eight.
Nine.
Nine. Lucky number. The second biggest, and most overlooked. Nine seconds of complete silence was all I needed. It took me far less than that to get to the window though. Maybe four. The cushions underneath my knees were comforting, yet not at the same time when I placed my hands on the cold window, looking out. I found myself admiring the beautiful night sky. A pitch-black blanket with splotches of glowing white embers of different sizes that swallows up the sky, only to spit it out after a few hours. A singular, white circle shaded with dark shapes is in charge of it all, and the one who shines the brightest. I slowly creaked the window open, a cool breeze blowing calmly past me sent shivers down my spine. My flames instinctively shone bright on my hand in response, warming myself up enough to feel the heat lingering in my veins. It was dawning on me now, as I glanced down to see the massive difference between me and the ground. *I might not come back after this. But it's worth trying.*
With a determined step forward, I landed evenly on both feet onto the building's edging which circled around the whole building. The breeze was stronger now I was outside, and I had to resist the urge to keep my flame shining bright. The guards would see it in an instant and my cover would be blown. I slowly turned around to hug the wall, heavily aware

of my heart rate quickening. I had never been one to like heights or crowds. I never thought I would need to worry about it. *I honestly don't like a lot of things.* The air was icy cold up here, even with my suit on the wind still found its way through the lining, tickling me with its frosty breath. An insatiable feeling. The feeling of warm flames had almost completely disappeared now, the only feeling of warmth coming from my chest, the flames waiting to be called upon again. Each movement of mine was small, the fear of taking one step too big lingering in my mind. I very quickly understood why I had better thoughts against the idea.

The feeling of the cold concrete complimented the cool breeze, brushing against my fingertips with each small shuffle of my feet. My ankles were almost hanging off the small ledge I was shuffling across. The two sharp hooks would lodge into the cracks, preventing me from falling off the edge. When I came across the first support beam I almost panicked. There were no tiny cracks or crevices on this massive, chunky beam that I could possibly hook into. No, I was forced to hug the beam and pray to all the Celestials in every single history book that they wouldn't let me fall to a very gruesome death.

Granette Coller, I love you and hate your guts at the same time for this stupidly, dangerously, frustratingly genius idea to make me live. I pushed myself against the wall hard, shaking slightly as I gently pulled my hooks from the wall. I would need them hooked on my belt, because hugging a wall does require hands.

"I hate this. I hate this. I hate this." I hissed under my breath.

My arms quickly wrapped around the insufferable beam that was separating my perfectly fine ledge from the next perfectly fine ledge. It had no grooves at all. Nothing for me to hang onto. I cursed under my breath. *Who designed this? It's horrible for scaling buildings.* My leg quickly whirled around the beam and landed on the ledge opposite. I took a deep breath. I was standing in an awkward position at this point, one leg on either side and both arms hugging the beam in the middle as if my life depended on it. *I still need to do this at least five more times.* The thought almost made me let go. My hands were slipping off the surface, my body heat finally doing something terrible for me for once. I needed to do something, and quickly, otherwise I would go down in history as the idiotic teenager who tried to play pretend assassin. With no thought into it whatsoever, one hand lunged for my hook on my belt as I launched myself to the opposite side, stabbing my singular hook as fast as possible into the cracked surface of the castle wall. I didn't waste any time snatching the second hook, and it didn't take long before it too was lodged in the castle's wall.

I took my time to steady myself after that. Just a few seconds, just to catch my breath. It was all I needed. All I could ever want in this living world. It didn't last long however, those precious seconds mattered to the last few potential hours of my life. One I could still save. Determination ran through me as I scaled the castle's wall, waiting patiently at windows for guards to turn away, dodging beams, and continuously picking at its foundation with my hooks before I almost made it to my destination. I was directly above the infirmary now, a faint light shining in the window below me. I frowned. That was just going to make everything far more difficult if someone is awake in there. I paused for a moment, thinking about what to do. If I killed whoever was there, someone would be sure to report a missing person and the castle would be on lockdown. Regardless of whatever form I used, an unconscious or dead person won't help my case.

So, the plan is now almost impossible. I have to avoid many people's eyes that are in there, with a light on when I'm wearing all black, and finally get to Lila's enclosed little room and get out. I feel like slamming my head against a brick wall. *No pun intended.* I slowly turned around to form a comfortable sitting position, overlooking the kingdom. Many home's lights were out, most had gone to sleep while some were up partying, or just having an enjoyable time. My legs kicked at the freezing air in front of me, drifting me from my thoughts. Helping me concentrate with a calmer mindset. The first step would be to get down that floor and analyse the situation, plan, then react. *It's funny to think that something I'd learnt from a young age could become so helpful.* Down below I could see outlines of guards wandering the outside areas with torches held in their hands. They won't expect anyone to be scaling the walls like some kind of ignorant buffoon.

With a deep breath, I twisted around to be in a good enough position to hop down onto the next ledge below gently, preferably with no sound. The wind howled through my ears when I leapt down to the ledge, catching myself quickly with the hook to steady myself. The only sound that echoed was the clinking of silver against concrete. Even if it was small it still made me wince and look back at the guards below to check if anyone was looking up.

Phew. No heads were looking in my direction. I turned back to the wall and shuffled closer to the window.

I stopped for a moment, listening to see if anyone was close to the window. I could hear about three faint voices in the distance, two of them seemed more high pitch, possibly female. While the other voice sounded deeper, and a little familiar. I frowned.

Is Jesse out of his bed already? Or is it someone else?
"Darn it, I hoped he would stay in his condition for a little bit longer." I muttered to myself, clenching up my fists and frustration. *That troubled teenager is*

going to be the death of me. The voices continued to fade, to the point where I couldn't even hear them anymore. Just ripples in the breeze. Feeling a bit safer, I turned my head to look into the window.
I was positioned on the far end of the infirmary, the light of the entrance hall lighting up the walls and floors with a faint yellow light. The wards were to my left, positioned in a single file line. There were three closed wards, one closer to me and two further down near the entrance. On the right was the Healer's area, with equipment neatly packed up in shelves and on tables. Lila's was the middle one from memory, a faint light peeking through her curtains to hint that she was awake.
I groaned. *The talkative brat was awake. Of course. Why wouldn't she be? She was born to the bane of my existence.* I shook my head and moved away from the mirror.
Calm thoughts Ignei, irrational ones are going to get you under more suspicion, or worse, dead. Analyse, plan, react. Plus, it's more likely that it's a Healer in there. Or, better yet, they just left the light on before they went to bed.
"Analyse, plan, react. Analyse, plan, react." I repeated to myself under my breath as I returned to the window.
My eyes narrowed as I took notice of something new. Boots, peeking out from behind one of the shelves near the entrance hall. *They're still here? I swore they left.* I slumped on the ledge, deep in thought. *I'll need to be far more stealth-like if I want to get past them.* I placed my hands on the windows, eyes scrunched in concentration as I searched for a way in. There were a few blockages to hide against on the way to Lila's ward. I took careful note of them and how much it would cover me. Which was a lot, one of the upsides of being short.
My hands caught on something thin and metal. My eyes followed to where my hands were, and I couldn't

help but grin. A latch. With one last glance at the now-missing boot, I flicked the latch outwards, and the window creaked slowly open. Warm air swallowed me up, giving me far more energy and strength than before. I crawled onto the window ledge, positioned like some unintelligent ape.
The boots were still missing, and the room was quiet.
No one's home. The freezing wind began to swarm the warm air, and if anyone was still here they'd be sure to notice the sudden change in temperature.
I landed gently onto the floorboards -which thankfully didn't creak- and silently shut the window behind me. The cool air faded, and the infirmary quickly returned to normal room temperature. With the last soft click of the window's latch closing, Lila's light went out.
Panic swelled up inside me. I stood still for a moment, urging myself desperately to move, to hide.
Someone was in there. Someone who was definitely awake.
I had a bad feeling that if I waited around here any longer then someone was going to come out and surprise me. *It wouldn't be pleasant either.* I backed up towards the wall, my palms placed on them firmly, ready for a push-off sprint to one of my hiding places when they may or may not open that curtain. My mouth pressed into a thin line. *I can't be caught. Certainly not like this.*
I shuffled a little to my left, kicking at a glass vase placed stupidly on the ground.
Crap.
 The moment it collided with the ground and made an ear-piercing smash, I had already dashed to the closest table, ducking behind it as the curtain was thrown back just in time. A small, shaky, possibly female voice echoed throughout the room.
"Hello? Is- is anyone there?"

My breath caught. *Whoever this was clearly wasn't going back to sleep anytime soon. Whether it was Lila or a Healer. For now, I'll go with the fact that I'm unsure of their identity, so I don't get too cocky.* They sounded far too terrified. I cursed silently in my head. *Whoever this was may have just ruined my chances at survival. And they don't even realise it.*

I could hear the girl's tiny footsteps wandering back far away, before coming back. An orange light flickered into view in front of me. Great. Now she's hunting me with a torch. How ironic.

"Please, whoever's there, I don't want to hurt you! B-but if you try to mess with me I'll have no choice!" The girl called out, sounding more frightened than confident.

If my life wasn't on the line I would've laughed at the words. This girl has no idea who she's dealing with. I'd bet my lunch on the fact that she'd run at the sight of a butter knife, let alone blood.

My hand instinctively went to my belt. Two silver hooks and multiple throwing stars and daggers hung in multiple areas of my suit. Yet it would only take one to remove this girl from the equation.

But no. Nothing in life is that simple.

Frustration rattled throughout me. *This girl probably won't give up so easily. It doesn't matter if it looks normal to the naked eye. The fear of the unknown is worse, and I doubt she'll be able to sleep tonight if she doesn't find out what that noise was about.*

"Clarein's vase?"

Her footsteps became clearer, louder. She was getting closer. I frantically swung my head around, searching desperately for a way out.

Perhaps I could disappear around the far end of the counter and continue crawling away? With one glance in its direction, I frowned. The counter I was hiding behind was longer than I thought it was. By the time I got to the end she would've already found me and called the guards.

Hope was falling out piece by piece. I could hear my normally steady heart rate quickening with each step. My hands felt around on the floor, hoping for some sort of secret, lost passage that could take me far, far away from here. They quickly moved to the counter feeling for anything, something that could save me. She was so close now, only a few more paces behind the counter I was hiding behind. I was about to give up and accept my fate when I felt something, something round. A knob for a cupboard. Excitement and relief devoured my past fears as I slowly crept the door open, willing myself to climb into the small, cramped space. There wasn't much in here, just cobwebs and probably spiders. It didn't matter though. *What matters is that I'm alive.* With a still beating heart, I creaked the door closed and settled into an uncomfortable sitting position.

It was pitch black in the little cupboard, that is until the girl's torch illuminated the edges.

"Hello? Oh, poor Clarein."

For a moment I assumed that she was about to leave it now that her curious hunger had been fulfilled. Yet the torch's light still shone through the cracks. Fear pulled up in my stomach, twisting and turning in a way even more uncomfortable than my current position. *Did I drop something? Did one of my daggers fall? Or worse, is she about to call the guards?* I could almost imagine her confused face when she spoke.

"Huh. The window isn't latched properly." A small thump came from the room, possibly a hand against thick glass colliding. "That's interesting, Scrinsun latched it just an hour ago?" She muttered to herself, wandering around the space. "Maybe it's just old."

The tension in the room slowly eased away as she dismissed her thoughts. The light slowly faded away as her footsteps receded. I waited to hear the swoop of a curtain being pulled back before creeping out of the cupboard.

My limbs were a tangled mess, one leg that way and one the other when I flopped out of the cupboard unprofessionally.

Fortunately, I landed quietly, not a sound to be heard. Without wasting any time, I shot to my feet, my body relieved to be out of the scrunched-up position. A smile creeped up into the corners of my mouth uncontrollably, not that I minded. It was a mere inconvenience that I didn't notice the cupboard.

Obviously I planned for that. I dusted myself off, flicking messy cobwebs out of my hair. The ward that the girl came from now had floppy bunny slippers in front of the curtain. Noticing the change made me stop for a moment. *Aren't those Lila's slippers?* It all made sense now. The familiar voice. The clear uneasiness in her tone. And most of all, cowardice. I should've already assumed that it would be Lila, she always had that unwavering curiousity. I'd already concluded that she was possibly awake. *That's just a little embarrassing. But I did guess it originally*? I snatched the Snooze Memory out of my pocket, holding the small woollen bag lazily. *This should be quick.*

With steps now filled with confidence, I strode over to the ward. The plan from here was simple. Lila obviously would still be awake, but that can be dealt with. I'll thrust the curtains open and dash over to her, blocking her mouth before she can scream. The Snooze Memory would then be released into the air - which she'll have no choice but to inhale- and all should be done within a short span of seven seconds. The best part? I'll be able to continue my mission, assassinate her bloodline, and return to Soriva as a legend. With no problems whatsoever. I fiddled with the bag's knot, loosening it enough to quickly open the bag when needed.

I stopped in front of Lila's ward, mentally and physically preparing myself to charge. My fingers closed around the curtain, its soft fabric ruffling under my touch. *I'll reminisce about this moment.* With a great burst of strength, the curtain swung back to reveal Lila standing directly in front of me. Startled, I jumped back, all the situations that I had imagined for this moment did not add up to this.

"Lexi! I was hoping that was you! Sorry I was really hoping I could get a moment to ask you something, you know after you kind of saved my life and stuff." Her grin almost reached her ears, pure excitement thrown across her face. "By the way, why didn't you tell me that you had super cool powers? That would've been an amazing conversation starter!"

I stared at her.

"Why are you… What are-." I stuttered, for once in my life lost for words.

"Okay, okay I get it. At least I'm pretty sure I do! You are here to ask if I wanted to join your super-secret mission! I mean I knew from the moment I saw you, 'I have never heard of that island' or 'that girl looks way too cool to be normal', and guess what? I was right!" She took a deep breath, eyes staring at me with the most idolised expression I had ever seen. "I know you were the one who saved my life, and the fact that someone as strong and- and powerful as you could've possibly cared about my measly life is amazing to me!"

I slapped myself in the face. *Great. Now she's some sort of superfan.* My hand hovered in front of my face for a moment, realisation shining through.

"Actually, I think I know what you can do, that is, if you want to join me on my quest." I lazily crossed my arms, staring at her with a slight smile. *This might actually work if she's as oblivious as I think she is.*

"Anything!"

"Fantastic! You see, I have this bag here," I held up the Snooze Memory. "And this bag is enchanted so only one of ancient descent can open it and reveal the secrets inside." I blabbed, basically lying through my teeth at this point. "I have been watching you for a while you know, and I think you might finally be the one to open it!" I sighed blissfully, fidgeting with the bag. *Please fall for it.*

Lila's face shone, determination and excitement fuelling her.

I held out the bag, letting her grab it carefully and examine it. Her hands trembled slightly, eyes wide. *Good grief she actually believes it. How pathetic.* If I weren't set out to kill her it might've been adorable.

"You- you really think I can? You know I always hoped there would be something special about me, something for people to remember me forever by. This'll be it!"

I watched with what I hoped was an excited expression as she twirled the knot around her fingers. Her mouth dropped slightly open, breathing in and out as she supposedly was about to help save the world. Honestly I don't know what she was thinking. *Clearly not straight.* I examined her features, hopeful and excited. Sure, she was beautiful. Yet clearly that did not assist her in the brains department. The knot loosened, the bag opened, and the idiotic Princess shoved her head right into the bag. *Well, that was unexpected.* Her head came back up in less than a second, her face covered from chin to hair in white powder.

"What do I do now?" Her voice slurred as she spoke, clearly trying to stay excited and calm at the same time. A real smile crawled up the corners of my mouth. This was perfect. She stood drowsily, eyes rolling to the back of her head as she muttered, "am I

worthy…?" Before collapsing onto her back on her bed, unconscious.
"Oh, don't worry," I grinned as I wiped the evidence off her face. "You're worthy alright."

CHAPTER 9:
LILA

"Lila? Lila!"

A voice called out, stirring me from my slumber. I woke peacefully, my head hurting a little but otherwise fine. The night felt like a blur, missing pieces wandering around my head like a maze I just can't quite figure out. My eyes opened to see Jackiel sitting next to me, holding my hand with his intense green eyes on mine. It's not like anyone can't call us siblings, we look almost identical if it weren't for the different genders. I straightened up a little, the only thing on my mind being breakfast. "Jackiel, what's for breakfast?" He blinked at me; his normal calm face confused. I repeated myself again, only now realising how much I was slurring. *Geez, I should go back to sleep.*

He chuckled at my realisation, very clearly enjoying this. "Would I kill to get Dad to see you like this!" His smile faded at the thought.

The atmosphere got a little darker at that. He sucked in a breath before talking again. "Doesn't really matter though, I got you breakfast anyway." He gestured to the tray to my left. "Unless that isn't what you want?"

"No! No, no it is, thank you Jackiel."

Jackiel laughed gingerly at that, plonking himself down on my bed. He breathed in a deep sigh. "The brightest flame always burns out the quickest, huh?"
"That's new, where'd you hear that one from? Another one of your books?"
"Trust me when I say you would never believe me if I told you."
"And what would I not believe exactly?"
"Nice try, I might tell you if you quit nagging me. Not that you ever will."
"Fine. I'll get it out of you eventually." I kicked him playfully in his side.
Relief flooded his face as he smiled and nodded. "Okay then, I'll leave you to it. Also, there's your favourite book just next to your bedside table that you can read while eating your breakfast, call a healer if you need them, basically stuff you already know." He was about to walk away before calling out; "Oh! That reminds me, don't injure yourself again, okay? Not a good look for you. Anyway, I'll see you at about lunchtime." He said with a grin.
"Hey Jackiel!" He raised his eyebrows. "Do you think you could get Lexi to come in?"
"Sure, I don't see why not. Might be a little while though, she's in the middle of a tour around the castle. They figured since yesterday was so traumatising," he eyes slanted at the words a little. "They would, you know, try to convince her and her kingdom not to just leave. It won't look good for us if they don't accept our Unity deal."
I nodded, understanding. *I really wanted to see Lexi again. It feels as if I'm missing something.* I blinked, trying to understand this brand-new connection. Maybe it was because she was the first person I'd met who was like me, a Princess destined to rule a kingdom. Maybe because she understood my struggles. My dreams. My fears. All of the above. I could list them all off like counting to one hundred.
"Do you want me to send someone else for you?

Maybe another friend, like Merridith." His words snapped me out of my thoughts.
"Oh! No, I think I'll be fine. You don't need to bring-"
And with that, he was already gone. I groaned, sinking into my covers and ignoring my breakfast, despite my growling stomach. Merridith was, how do I put it into words? Self-absorbed. *No Lila, think nicer, more polite. You're both pretty high up in the ladder. Self-regarding. That's better.* Merridith probably would take one look at my state then start ranting on about how she won some made-up event and that she has a trophy to prove it. My ward bed was fairly comfortable, stuffed with pillows to keep me at the correct height, toasty warm blankets, basically everything I need for the highest length of comfort. It is also big enough for me to sink into, drown out the world and hopefully Merridith when she comes by. I smiled to myself, if only.
My head felt heavy, unattached. I kept returning to that awkward feeling that I was missing something. Something I just can't quite put my finger on.
The smell of fresh bacon and eggs filled the air however, interrupting my thoughts with the growl of my stomach. I turned my head to take a look at what Jackiel had given me, no longer caring about the uncomfortable feeling. It was the usual. Bacon and eggs, served with orange juice that had an orange slice cut into the cup's rim. Next to it lay 'The History and Present of Mistlon; A Collector's Edition'. I snorted. *Jackiel's favourite. Definitely not mine.*
I positioned myself up, straightening my back into a comfy position before snatching the plate of food in a very unladylike manner.
At this point I couldn't care less if someone saw me eating like a pig, only Tien knows how long I'd slept in for. As I'd picked at some egg, I started thinking about the day before. Lexi more specifically.

When I first saw her, just two day ago now, when we'd picked her up originally, she seemed like the shyest girl in the world. Of course, Princess Jassai is also pretty amazing, her and her gift to shape shift. That's why everyone seems to be favouring Arcarlia, Princess Jassai has made such an impact on the world. Her being the only living magical being and all. I sighed blissfully as the egg yolk melted into my mouth. *Wouldn't that be amazing? To be... powerful?* My mind flickered back to yesterday, away from Jassai's hazel eyes. My mind still felt quite fuzzy about that. It felt like a swirl of emotions that I couldn't quite place a picture to. A voice without a face. A feeling of heat without a source. A pair of grey eyes.

It's almost like this isn't the first time my mind had a temporary reset.

Temporary.

Emphasis on temporary.

I munched on the bacon absently, the main thing on my mind being when Lexi would finish her tour. *That reminds me, the time, what was it?* My eyes flickered to the currently closed curtain; the clock hidden behind it. I groaned. I didn't exactly want to get up yet, it still felt so early. The covers felt like a rock sitting on top of me, unable to wrench away from it. *Except this rock was actually comfortable.*

Still, my curiosity overcame me, and it was enough to drag myself out of bed. Once my bare feet connected with the floor, a shiver ran through my entire body.

The floor was freezing, and now that I was out of the bed I quickly realised so was everywhere else. My hand landed firmly on one of the bed-side tables, surprising me when all of my weight leaned on it. My head felt woozy when I got up. Like someone was playing an orchestra in my head, yet I couldn't understand the strange words.

I shook my head profusely, shaking out the feeling in pure stubborn determination. With unsteady legs, I waddled over to the curtain, yanking it open with surprising strength. *To say I'm not confused would be an understatement. There is... no one outside?* I frowned. *You'd think that there would be at least one healer to check on me, yet no.* There was not a soul in sight. No signs of life.

That is except for the sound of clicking heels coming down from the entrance corridor to my left. The urge to slam my head into the metal pole holding up my privacy curtains was far too tempting. The sound of heels becoming louder and louder struck me with an unfortunate dilemma.

Jackiel was unfortunately right. The phoney girl who could have been convinced for some sort of obnoxious fake royal was approaching the infirmary, where I was.

The very thought made my blood boil. Not only did I have to live with the fact that I clearly can't leave the infirmary and there is no one here to properly dismiss me, I have to put up with this ignorant, sassy teenager too?!

Why did Jackiel send her to keep me company? She's possibly the worst person to accompany me when I already have a headache brewing.

The only option at this point was to fake sleep to make her leave me alone. Now not caring less about the time, I hobbled more quickly over to the bed. To which I attempted to set up the book and food the same as when Jackiel had originally set it up.

Speaking of Jackiel, I was going to enjoy our chat after this. After I torment him for sending her to me.
When I had finally settled for a false sleeping position, I could hear her heels in the infirmary now, her irritatingly soothing voice muttering about how she forgot which ward I was in.
I prayed silently she would give up.

My curtains rattled for a moment, hinting that she was right outside. *How in the name of Tien does she move that fast in heels*? I would've asked her if I wasn't so hellbent on hating her and wanting her to just give up and leave.

In possibly the most dramatic way possible, my curtains were swung open in a way that made it seem as if I were in the middle of a street performer's musical.

Her sweet yet conniving voice cut through the air. "Lila~ Your brother sent me, and I really want to make it so I truly did try to start a conversation with you even if you are ignoring me."

Pure silence. I squeezed my eyes shut tighter, hating every moment.

"You know it's rude to ignore people? I mean, I'm used to the cold 'hello' every now and then, but pretending you're asleep to ignore me? Ha! Good luck with that."

She's trying to bait me. *Come on Lila, just a few more seconds and then she'll get bored and walk away-*

"Look Princess. Quit it with the act. Your brother gave you breakfast then immediately went to get me because he felt bad he couldn't make time to stay with you. And would you look at that! Only five or so minutes later, your breakfast is almost done and you're asleep! Poor little Princess Sparkles." She basically spat out that last bit.

And with that, the last of my dignity and self-preservation gone.

I snapped my head up to look at her, mimicking the best glowering look I could on my face. "Are you done?"

With my eyes open, I could see how over-the-top she looked today. Wearing her normal pixie cut with large hanging pearls and red lipstick, you would've thought that she was planning on doing something special, like a date with someone. *I mean if ruining my day counts then yes, I suppose she was.* On top of that, she was sporting a far-too-short-to-be-real tight, purple dress that barely reached her knees matched with an animal fur coat.

"Is there something wrong, Your Highness? Oh, is it something I said? Or is it the fact that my style has outdated royalty? Not in an offensive way though," she sighed, almost sadly. "It is but the hard truth."

"Mhm." I sounded through a very tight-lipped smile. "What exactly brings you here on this lovely morning?" I said, my words dripping with sarcastic venom.

"Morning?" She burst into laughter. "My, my, my Princess! How long has it been since you've seen a clock? It's noon for crying out loud! Of course, the clock in the infirmary is rather rusted compared to my clock that was handmade from experts, don't you think?"

I blinked for a few moments. Noon? Then why on Mistlon would Jackiel give me breakfast at noon?

Confusing panic started to set in. *I've already missed the necessary hours of the morning! I could have been so productive in that time! Helping Lexi pick out her clothes for today as well as my own. Planning our first full day together, really getting to know each other.*

I've missed so much already. I'm meant to wake up at exactly seven thirty every morning! I'll have enough time to figure out what to wear, my schedule, all exactly thirty minutes before breakfast at eight. To have breakfast later on will end up ruining my schedule! I'll want breakfast later and later, far too many things will change. This simply cannot go by so easily!

"You know I could let you borrow my exquisite clock for a better understanding on the simple concept of time if you really want-"

"For goodness sake Merridith! We have the same clock! And thanks to all this, my schedule is never

returning to normal!" I shouted at her, finally losing it.
Merridith stared at me. For once she had actually shut up. That is before she burst into laughter again, that posh, obnoxious laughter I hate. "I'm sorry, your schedule? Dear, how is that your main priority? In case you haven't noticed, you are in the infirmary for a very nasty concussion. You were assaulted by a... peasant!" For a moment I thought that I was seeing her soft side, her more humane part of her that wasn't so self-absorbed. "Do you know how humiliating that is? Yet here I am, looking past all of that purely out of the goodness of my heart yet you are complaining about your schedule? I am putting my time aside for you! How could you not understand that?!" I threw a half-eaten piece of bacon at her head, smiling when it stuck in her hair, and she let out a shriek.
"Yes and you're such a lifesaver aren't you?" I snapped at her. "Excuse me for being knocked unconscious. And excuse me for not even caring in the first place if you even came to visit me or not! Honestly? You're only here because it makes you look better." At this point I was out of my bed, walking up to her with no stagger in my step and my finger pointing directly at her chest. "You have no heart, and all you care about is yourself and your perfect little image!"
She stared. Her eyes no longer had the sinister twist behind them. In fact, they had started watering up. She sniffled, turning around swiftly as to not dare look me in the eyes. Just another one of her performances. "I- I'm sorry. I'll just go then."
I should've felt triumphant at that moment. She had finally left me alone. *Yet I feel guilty*? My guilty conscience weighed on me, leaving me baffled and confused as I wanted to reach out towards her, call her to come back. I didn't know why. It just didn't feel right. It felt horrible.

However, I let these feelings go. Along with Merridith, as she stormed out of the room with no evidence that I had hurt her feelings in the slightest. She was probably about to go fib on me to the first person she sees who will actually listen. But as I plonked down on my bed again, soaking in the softness of the luxurious mattress I've become so accustomed to, I know what my current mission is. I'm not sure if I'm right, but Lexi was here last night. I feel like she must be here for a reason. I just know it. My fists clenched at the thought. She must need someone to help her.

And that someone is going to be me.

I had my nose in that book Jackiel gave me for a while.

I was determined to find something about magical beings that I hadn't noticed before.

Something that might be able to help understand Lexi's motives, and why she chose White Castle as her destination.

I'd flicked through the chapters with speed that surprised even me, and skimmed through unwanted words until I found the chapter I had been looking for.

A Ruthless Practice: Elemental Magic

My heart lit up with hope. My eyes skimmed down, looking for something to do with fire before latching onto something that caught my attention.

Ignei.

The word made me flinch. Something about it, I just couldn't quite put my finger on it. My fingers glided gently across the word, as if something magical were to happen. I wasn't sure what it was, but something about it seemed like it was the thing I was looking for. I followed the words down the page, reading aloud to myself softly.

"In the days of the old world, there were magical beings with abilities beyond mere mortal comprehension. Many believed that they were the descendants of the gods themselves. These beings had the power to manipulate the world around us, control the elements that are the foundation of our world. There were five different kinds of elements. Air, or the Aerials. Earth, the Terranines. Water, the Liquarn. Fire, the Flammous. And finally, the Nameless Lightning. The one singular element that had remained nameless for as long as our history books date back to. There was only one soul who had gained this ability, and the soul died along with it."

"In the olden days, Elementals were ones who weren't trifled with. Especially the descendants of the Ignei line." My brain did a double take. There it was again. *Ignei.* I kept reading. "The Ignei's were powerful beings whose powers quickly made them famous as the strongest Flammous line in history. The first Ignei to enter our world was Jaahn Ignei. Jaahn was a figure of power, with the ability to control even the toughest and largest of volcanoes. He had the power to halt a volcanic eruption and even create tornadoes made from fire. However, unlike the other Flammous, the Ignei's had a limit to their mind-bending abilities. They were prone to constant fainting after performing something no ordinary Flammous could do."

"It took the world by storm when they discovered they had disappeared. The most powerful Elementals disappeared in the blink of an eye one day. Many think they knew what was coming. The Rightful Purge. The day that all magical beings ceased to exist to the extent of one singular day. However powerful the Ignei's were, many believe that they knew that they stood no chance against the might of the humans."

I frowned as I stared at the book. Lexi's last name wasn't Ignei, it was Wellfire. *At least I'm pretty sure it is.* I flicked through the pages searching for a chapter just dedicated to the Flammous. There weren't many, and as annoyed as I was there were no further details to explain why Lexi is even here. I set the book down on my lap, staring at the piece of half-eaten bacon that I had thrown at Merridith's head lying on the floor. That was about the only accomplishment I had done today. Slightly irritated, I decided that I'll just have to find a way to get it out of Lexi then.

I placed the book onto the table. Boredom and the eagerness to talk to Lexi felt like the only two things on my mind. With a quick and not-very-thought-through decision, I decided to leave the infirmary to find Lexi.

Within seconds I was at the curtains, practically bouncing with so much excitement it surprised even me. With a swift yank, the curtain slid to the side noisily, clanking against the metal. Before walking out, I did a double take on what I was wearing, suddenly conscious of making a good impression. I mean I'm meeting someone with magic, actual magic!

Don't act too excited Lila, you'll seem too eager.

The healers had given me a silky white gown laced with purple lining. Something simple, nothing too extravagant. I felt like I was going to be sick. Here I was, wearing some pathetic little gown, wandering around barefoot and probably had my hair all fuzzy! I leant on the pole for support. That was when I felt something fuzzy touch my feet. Curious, I looked down to see a pair of bunny slippers positioned just next to me, probably for after I was cleared to leave my room. But let's be honest, I'm not taking any advice from some healer that we hired a few months ago.

After sliding my feet in, I quickly found a brush on one of the counters. Deciding to ignore the fact that it was very clearly used, I brushed my hair. It was fairly quick, but at least now I'll look somewhat presentable. With a bright smile adorned on my face that I know must look good, I waltzed out of the infirmary and into the hallway.

As I wandered the halls, I probably looked like I had come right out of the mental ward. *A stylish patient. The world's ran out of them.* The halls felt odd. It was a weird feeling, like everything was different from how it has always been. I found myself using the right wall to support me a few strides in. *It must be my head, there is just no other explanation for this feeling.* My arms feel heavy, as if I'm walking around with a boulder above my head.

Lexi might be able to help me. *Yes. Lexi seems to be my only answer at this point.*

I've never injured myself before. Not even a grazed knee, let alone a concussion. My thoughts wandered back to that sack of weird-looking dust that Lexi had given me. She'd said something before that, I'm sure of it. I just can't remember. It's weird. I'm pretty well-known for a good memory. A smile lit up my face as I recalled my fifth birthday. My parents couldn't make it, but Jackiel made it special. He'd always been a good brother to me, but that day is what bonded us both even more. He'd even baked me a cake with the help of our chefs. It didn't turn out very well, considering that he refused to let them help in any other way than give him instructions, but the thought counts.

Then the presents, oh, the presents! He had given me a-

"Gah!"

My head exploded with pain. It felt like every nerve in my body had just exploded as I collapsed to the floor. I squirmed and shrieked in pain, curling up into a ball onto the cold hard floor until I couldn't make a sound. My eyes were wide, and I panicked. My heart rate was accelerating way too fast. The air was knocked out of my lungs for a brief moment.

Shock coursed through my veins. The pain in my head was indescribable. I wanted my brother. I wanted to read his boring book. I wanted to talk to Lexi. The faint sound of boots coming closer filled the background. A voice cut through the pain.
"Your Highness? Your Highness?! What are you doing out of your ward?"
"I- I-"
The pain seared again, much stronger than before making me let out a high-pitched scream. But after that scream, after the stranger's hand clasped onto my shoulder, the pain stopped. My vision cleared. My breathing was shallow. And I felt a small click go off in my head.
"Your- Your Highness? My Lady, are you okay?"
I looked up slowly to see a kind, gentle face in front of me. She was dressed in the usual Healer attire -a white, flowy robe- that seemed to blend in with her pale skin. She had bright blue eyes, matched with white eyelashes. All the hair on her body seemed to be pure white. She was beautiful.
I cleared my throat.
"Y-yes, I mean yes! I'm sorry, I don't understand what happened then. I- oh, woah-"
I swayed on the spot with the world shifting around me. The woman seemed to appear duller than before, her once bright blue eyes darkening. She caught me as I swayed to the side, her eyebrows furrowed in worry. I looked her in the eyes drowsily. "If I may ask, who are you?"
She blinked for a moment, as if registering my question. She seemed to act like it was the most peculiar thing in the world. It was a normal question, wasn't it? She snapped back to reality, her pale cheeks-tinged red.
"Oh! Yes of course, my name. My Lady, don't you think there are more serious matters to attend to?" Her pretty face turned worried again. "I had rushed over here thinking you got stabbed! You were

screaming out in pain, Lila. That's not healthy." Her worriedness quickly turned into irritation. "And you should be lying in bed! Not walking around wanting an accident to happen! You should be working on making a full recovery, not wandering around without a Healer's permission! Goodness, what would your parents think? I bet that pain you were in before was because of your head, wasn't it?"
I felt my cheeks flush with embarrassment. "Well, yes. But I had thought that it had healed, and it would be okay! And I really need to talk to Lady Lexi." I added in a quiet voice, quickly second-guessing my decision. *Maybe it was a bit rash. I only needed to wait a little longer for Lexi to be able to visit and be done with her tour.* I suppose it was a reasonably dumb thing to do.
The Healer sighed. "My Lady, I understand you had felt better but that is no excuse! I won't inform your parents of this- incident." I breathed in a sigh of relief. "But never do anything like this again, otherwise I will be forced to inform them!" She then proceeded to help me up. "And my name is Elin. Elin Ewald." She added.
"Thank you Elin. But do you think you could do one more thing for me? I've been meaning to have a conversation with the new Lady Lexi, do you think you could let her know?"
"I will do my best, Your Highness. But no more trips! Your condition seems to be worse than I originally thought. You'll be staying in the infirmary for another two days minimum. Is that understood?"
"Yes, Elin. Thank you again."
And with that, we took our time to get back to the infirmary. It wasn't an awkward silence, more of a thinking time. *What I'll say to Lexi. What will happen next.*
What that strange click did to my head.

CHAPTER 10: LEXI

"-now for our final room. The Grand ballroom!"

It had been a pretty boring tour. Never would I have thought that my intelligence could be wasted on such a feeble thing. *Yet here I am. Wasting away.* Originally I had imagined that this tour would be helpful in figuring out the layout of the castle. Little did I know it would show me the places I have zero interest in for my mission. *No, Tour Guide. No, I do not care about the fact that this ballroom was created over five centuries ago. How is that information useful to anyone?*
At least now the servants of this castle have started to recognise me as the mythical 'Lady Lexi of Moralvelle'. I can finally walk around freely with them all giving me the space to move. I sighed. *If only the Royals had informed them of this earlier, then it could have made my adventures around the castle yesterday easier.* Speaking of yesterday, I haven't seen that servant who got wine spilt all over him. I wonder what happened to him.

The tour guide wore a rather peculiar suit for the occasion. A bright green suit decorated with industrial and floral patterns. It was tied with a pitch-black bow tie and a white-collar underneath. That, and his obnoxiously shiny boots made me want to puke all over him. The man had introduced himself to me as Ten Slouvin after he had stopped me after leaving breakfast. I still call him Tour Guide, he has yet to earn my approval with his ugly display. When I first saw him I had questioned the Royal's hiring decisions. *I still am.* He had later explained on the tour what the patterns on his suit meant. Something about how White Castle is spiritually connected to both Man-made creations and otherworldly ones. I couldn't quite tell, but it made the most sense.

During the tour I had mainly taken note of specific things. Good places for an ambush. Any statues with sharp objects. The most suspicious looking servants and knights. The castle seemed to be full of them. I almost wrinkled my nose in disgust. *How could such a perfect kingdom be so foolish? So ignorant of the world around them?* As if there were no dangers in their own little paradise. Certainly not the danger they let in with welcoming arms.

"The Grand ballroom has hosted hundreds, if not thousands of parties, galas, and balls! This room is sacred, as tradition is for every heir to the throne to be crowned King or Queen here!" Tour Guide then pointed to the back of the room, where two large chairs sat. One significantly bigger than the other.

"The King or Queen of royal blood is the one who claims the larger chair. That is tradition!"

I winced at his voice. It was scratchy and loud, and I had unfortunately been listening to it the past hour.

"Do you have any questions? Rumour around the castle says there will be a ball tomorrow night! Surely you have questions about that, people say it will be one of our biggest!" Inquired Tour Guide, his eyebrows raising up and down.

He's unique to say the least.
I fiddled with my wrist cuffs, curious. "We have a ball tomorrow night?" My voice was tinged with surprise and fear not even I could conceal. A ball with such a large number of people was not part of my training. I watched his eyes light up, as if he was just waiting for me to ask about it. *Maybe this man could be useful to me after all.*
"Yes you do! Oh, I can just imagine it! The last ball was spotless to say the least, but this one? A combination of three kingdoms all together! Why go small when you can go big? At least that's what everyone's saying." His hazel eyes tore away from me and to the empty ballroom. "Just imagine it! Streamers of all our kingdoms colours, banners, food, beautiful outfits! A beautiful symbolism of our kingdom's alliance! White Castle, Arcarlia, and Moralvelle!"
Confusion wouldn't quite cut how I was feeling at that point.

He was actually serious. I could see it in the look in his eyes.
But if this was truly going ahead, that would mean that the Arcarlian Royals would be arriving either today or tomorrow. *This changes things.*
That family has magic in their blood, more specifically their Princess, but who knows if that information is outdated? That's the entire point of why we targeted White Castle. Arcarlia with White Castle is far too powerful to deal with. And now, that same kingdom is coming far too soon. Why wasn't I informed of this earlier? Do they not trust me? Have they realised that Moralvelle isn't real?
No.
I closed my eyes for a moment, concentrating on my breath to regulate myself for a moment. Panic won't

do me any good. It will just make me more suspicious. Too many more complications and this whole mission will be a failure. And I won't be alive to see it.

I regained my composure, planting a smile on my face as I looked up at Tour Guide.

"Thank you for this information! I wasn't aware of it before, do you think you might know why?"

"You didn't? I'd assumed you already knew and just wanted my opinion on it! Well, honestly I don't see why you wouldn't know. If it makes you feel better I only found out yesterday when you had arrived. I haven't known about it for too long." He raised his hands in surrender, as if expecting me to be angry at him.

"Oh, that's fine. I'll see if I can ask the King or Queen when I meet them next." Tour Guide awkwardly put his hands down, nodding submissively.

"Well, that concludes our tour on the east wing!" His face lit up again, his hazel eyes shining in the light beautifully. "That is only if you don't have any other questions for me! I mean, do you?"

"Uh-"

I was saved by a servant hustling into the ballroom, who was clearly out of breath from running. He wore a more professional black and white suit, even if it was badly tied and a size too big. Unlike most of the servants, he had dyed blue hair and teal eyes noticeable from a few metres or so away. He was extremely flustered, attempting to wipe the sweat from his cheek with his napkin while breathing heavily. I tilted my head at him. *He must be here for a reason.* Looking at the skinny teen you'd think he'd never heard of exercise before in his life. After straightening his back and quickly realising he was in the presence of actual people, he cleared his throat.

"I'm- I'm guessing you're Lady Lexi?" He said, looking me up and down. I felt a blush creep up into my cheeks. *I look stupid.* I was wearing a sleek, white long-sleeve top with wrist cuffs tucked into a midnight skirt so long it almost touched my ankles. I'd never felt overly panicky about my looks. It must be the feeling of being discovered. That makes sense. *Right?*

"Yes, I'm Lady Lexi. But please, call me Lexi." I said, holding a hand to my chest.

The boy servant looked flustered again. "So sorry about that Lexi!" He chuckled. "I'm Terys. Just plain old Terys. I don't have a surname." He added.

"Very well then. Terys, what exactly are you doing here interrupting Lady Lexi's tour?" Tour Guide snapped, clearly annoyed. *Weren't we already done with our tour? And what does he mean he doesn't have a last name?*

"Right! Of course. His and Her Majesty have requested Lexi's presence immediately. Her Majesty says that she has important news to share and would like to talk to you in person." He said matter of factly, staring right at me in the last part. *He seems smart, Terys. If only we weren't on opposite sides, and I wasn't plotting his ruler's demise.* "She would like to meet her with the King on the west wing's highest tower. I am here to escort Lexi to her new destination Mr Slouvin."

Tour Guide's confidence and annoyance quickly faltered at the mention of the King and Queen. "Yes, well I suppose that would be appropriate for Lady Lexi to continue her tour later on if that is the Queen's wish." He turned to me with a hopeful smile. "I trust that we can continue later today or tomorrow?"

"Certainly!" I lied through my teeth. I was desperate to get away from this pathetic tour.

Terys grinned as he held out his hand. "Well then, shall we? It will be a long walk and we need to be there as quickly as possible. We need to leave now is the simple translation." He added with a laugh, which I had nodded at in return.

He held his hand out to me, a gesture I wasn't exactly expecting. *Lexi, you know their traditions are completely different to yours. Now suck it up and take his hand already otherwise you'll look suspicious!*

I nodded again, not quite knowing how else to respond before taking his hand. "Farewell, Lady Lexi. I hope we meet again soon." Called out Tour Guide.

"As do I, Sir." I replied, not bothering to cover my emotionless tone.

We were walking through an annoyingly beautifully decorated corridor when the boy stopped us. I didn't bother hiding my surprise at his sudden stop, which had of course led me to a very sudden halt. His blue hair flickered in the faint breeze. The only sound I could hear was a metal clinking against something. I straightened my back, refusing to look at him. I didn't have any metal on me. I was smart enough not to bring any weapons on the tour. My dress wasn't exactly fitting for hiding anything. There was only one pocket, and that could barely fit a small candy. Far too risky to bring any weapons today, even if I may need it.

If only the maids allowed me to choose what I wanted to wear, like at home. I'd pick a suitable outfit to fit all sorts of potions, weapons, and other trinkets I would ever need. Regardless, White Castle's sense of fashion is appalling. And I have never specialised in that area either.

Which left one option. The boy servant. *Terys.* A chill ran down my spine. *What could he possibly have in his possession?* Optimistic thinking would be a necklace. But Sorvia has never had time for Optimists.

Looking at him now, that suit looks like the Royals got it for him. His face? Not exactly the cleanest one

I've seen. I doubt he could afford a real necklace by the look of him.

So, I need to be ready for anything.

I hesitantly looked his way again, only to find him already looking back. There's that look in his eye. It doesn't look like malice. More like he wants to say something.

I waited patiently for him to say it, while calmly deciding what would be the best way to disarm him; pressure point or swift knock to the head? Eventually he finally spat it out. A question.

"I don't mean to offend you or anything, but I've never heard of Moralvelle. I haven't seen it on a map either. Do you know why that is?" His eyes. He's suspicious. *This isn't good.* His question is cleverly placed in grey waters. I can't tell if he's actually curious or up to something.

Smart.

I recalled the conversation I had gone over with Granette beforehand.

"Remember, 'Moralvelle' hasn't technically been in an alliance with anyone in the war. Not because it doesn't actually exist, but they think it does. Remember that. If they question that they haven't heard of it, you can point out that Moralvelle has attempted to hide itself from the war and the world. Especially remember that little info sheet I gave you about Moralvelle! I wrote all that stuff down for a reason you know? It has when Moralvelle began, the rulers, your own little language ·*that will be fun to say*·, your currency, your unique history, all sorts of stuff like that! And finally, in this little fantasy world your name is Lexi Wellfire. You are the proud successor of Konar and Aliah Wellfire. They had died in a terrible crash a few years back. Can you remember their names? Yes? Good. I think you're almost ready then."

I had reviewed that information sheet she had given me every night leading up to the mission. I've gone over this question close to a thousand times in my head. This should be simple. A smile lit up my face before I explained the reasoning behind it.
"Oh yes! You see, that's a question I get a lot of recently. My parents had felt strongly about keeping our island strong and safe from the war. We have actually been independent for centuries." I darkened my face a little, emphasising my sadness for the next part. "However, after my parents were killed in that horrific crash, I knew it was my duty to expand our kingdom. To help connect our people with different cultures and help save our world from this disgusting war by fighting on the right side." I returned to my big smile. "And that's it!"
I felt I had done rather well with my answer. Proud even. Terys however looked far from convinced. "That must have been hard for you. I'm deeply sorry about your parents." But at least the answer seemed to satisfy him. I took the opportunity to ask a question of my own. "I couldn't help but hear something weird when we'd stopped before you know." I tilted my head at him, eyes scanning his eyes curiously. "I don't mean to be invasive, but are you wearing some sort of metal necklace? Or a bracelet perhaps? I just found it a little odd is all." He looked offended at my question. "Are you- are you hinting that I stole this?" With a red face he pulled up a beautiful necklace with a ruby pendant hidden in his suit. "Because trust me! I did not steal this! I had waited a long time to get the money to even afford this thing! Not everyone can get whatever they want, you know." He finished with a huff.
"I am so sorry! I was just curious, that was all! I'm sorry if I offended you in any way Terys." I held my hands up in defence, displaying a look of horror on my face.

The reality was much different to how I imagined it to be. The boy wasn't armed with a weapon. It *was* just a necklace. Of course, it was something so simple, why wouldn't it be? *There I go again, getting suspicious of the smallest things.*
"Oh." He attempted to hide his face, clearly embarrassed. "That's fine then I guess…" His trailed off to the point where he was mumbling incoherent things under his breath.
I attempted to get us back on course again. "So, shall we continue, Terys? It wouldn't be wise to be late."
"Yes! We should definitely do that."

"Here we are, My Lady. The Royal Courtroom." Terys announced, his eyes off me and busy opening the massive double doors in front of us.
You could very clearly see that this room was different from the others. The doors were decorated with pure gold that was twisted into characters of an ancient language. *Interesting. This wretched place actually has culture. Or it's just some lazily drawn lines decorated to give off that impression.* I rolled my eyes at the thought. *Anything to make them look better.*
A few moments later the golden characters were splitting in half, folding to the side as the double doors slowly opened. Terys was clearly straining every muscle in his fragile body to heave the doors open. It was a unique experience to watch.
But as the doors stretched apart, a stunning room was bestowed in front of me. "Here we are! There. Do you see them?" Terys pointed at the Monarch, who were seated at the very back of the Courtroom in large chairs. *Didn't take him very long to point out the obvious.* "Now this is where I leave you‑"
"Yes, yes, yes I know. Thank you Terys." I completely ignored his last sentence, instead choosing to walk past him to get a better look of my surroundings. I

wasn't completely cruel though. I said thank you. And gave him a small, quick wave. That was about the limit of my generosity to the servant.

He had said something else, but I'd ignored him. I was more focused on the shocking beauty of the Royal Courtroom. Even if I hated this kingdom's guts, they had some sense of style. But only in architecture.

"Lady Lexi Wellfire of Moralvelle! It is a pleasure for you to be joining us this afternoon." Boomed the King from his highchair, his voice echoing around the large space.

The Royal Courtroom was made out of three materials. Marble, silk, and gold. Closest to the entrance at the front of the room were beautiful marble seats with purple silk cushioning fitted perfectly on each seat. The audience for each hearing. Today the seats were empty, abandoned. Closer to the sides were massive marble pillars lined with gold in each corner that were absolutely spotless. The pillars stretched across the entirety of the room on each side, establishing a parallel effect. At the very back of the wall was a large square table with chairs on three of the sides, excluding the side closest to the audience. There are four chairs at the back, one for each Royal of White Castle. The King, Queen, and Prince took up three of them. The Princess noticeably absent. To the left, another three chairs with a banner signifying that it was Arcarlia's side. One for each of the powerful kingdom's rulers. The final side had only one chair, which I assumed was for me. The fake banner of Moralvelle hung on its side. A single block of marble peeked up from the ground just in front of the table. Two hooks fit for holding chains were on opposite sides of it. The block for prisoners. *That could be me one day.*

"Please, take a seat." He beckoned, gesturing to the singular chair with the Moralvelle banner. I suddenly became aware of the number of guards in this singular room.

The hairs on the back of my neck shot up, the urge to set this room ablaze was intense. *But no. I need to keep my cool.* They won't attack if I don't give them a reason to. In fact, they are trying to protect me from danger at the moment. *Ironic.*

A soft smile spread on my face as I walked up to the chair a little more quickly, heavily aware of the eyes watching me do so.

I sat down in my seat gracefully. As if I was used to it. Granette would be laughing if she ever saw this. The Queen looked at me with sad eyes. Pity. I was the only one with a singular chair. In her eyes my family was dead. In my eyes I didn't know either of them. The fictional or the reality. The King looked bored, as if he didn't even want the meeting in the first place. He probably didn't. The Prince just looked at me with a look I couldn't decode. He was eerie to say the least. I may be able to easily beat him in a physical battle, but by the way he examines everything and everyone in that emotionless way he does he'd definitely win the battle of brains.

Queen Benice cleared her throat, breaking the silence. "I'm sure you're wondering why you were brought here?"

I nodded.

"Fantastic. No words and you're still more life-like than these two." She said in a tone that made me question most of the things I knew about her. It sounded forced. I wonder what kind of argument the family were in beforehand. It would explain the absence of acknowledging the other. Not that they'll admit that. "We had organised this meeting to clear some things up for you that will be happening in the next few days."

The King perked up a little at that. "Yes! Many different events and meetings will start in the follow up to the finalisation of our alliance between our three kingdoms. Which brings me to one of the main reasons for our meeting. To our knowledge, King Stafran will be arriving in White Castle's Capital tomorrow afternoon with the Prince and Princess, Jassai and Crimor. Tomorrow will also be the day of our Royal Alliance ball to commemorate day one of our new alliance." The King paused, before chuckling softly. "The townsfolk will be joining in on the parade that has been highly requested for the opening of the ball. It will essentially be a quick parade throughout the capital. Giving each of our Kingdom's the opportunity to showcase what we can provide to the people."

Interesting. It's as if they've completely forgotten about Lila already, the incident was only yesterday. I wonder what they're thinking.

The Queen's eyes locked with mine. "It wouldn't be wise to come empty-handed. I'd suggest sending out an invite to some of your most trusted individuals today to prepare. The people won't appreciate the bare minimum. Please do well to remember that. We can provide a quicker transport for your selected to arrive closer on time if you wish. It would be the least we can do for Moralvelle."

Crap. How am I supposed to get anyone from Soriva in that short amount of time? I can't even accept their offer for the transport. *Wait.*

"That would be lovely, thank you! But our island is focused on independence and privacy, so I would prefer to request a meeting place where my individuals can meet with the transport away from my island. I cannot fully trust White Castle until the alliance is signed and official for precautionary measures. Surely you understand, don't you?" I put on my best smile, showing I was truly grateful for their support.

They looked uncertain by my answer. Even a little suspicious. But as the words sunk in, the suspicious looks faded. Jackiel just nodded at my response, making no effort to join in the conversation. That was fine. I knew he was just there to show the Royals as a united front without Lila. It was the King who accepted my proposal.

"Ah, you truly are content with your independence and privacy then. I suppose there's no arguing with that." He glanced back at his wife, who then nodded her approval. Both see no wrong in it. *That was a close call.* "White Castle accepts your request as long as you can provide a meeting place within two hours after this meeting. If not, no transport will be sent to assist your individuals and they must attempt to arrive here on their own. Fair?"

I nodded again. "Thank you, King Moralle. Your generosity is much appreciated."

"As is your participation in our alliance, Lady Lexi. Now for our next question, how will you present your kingdom? The people will be looking for who they will put their trust in, and who will be potentially walking their streets in a few weeks' time. Impressions matter deeply." The King looked me up and down. "They'll be looking for something different. Unique. A special connection to Moralvelle and their people. Surely you have a tradition of some sorts that you can emphasise into a spectacle?"

The Queen had then interjected with her thoughts. "Arcarlia normally emphasises their Princess and the Lost Era Of Magic. Always a spectacle for the people, that Princess. Doesn't surprise me that they don't want her to be Queen. Far too much pressure on such a young girl already and she isn't even an adult. Plus, being Queen would just make her more of a target." She sighed. "Anyway, White Castle focuses on appearance. Emphasis on our beauty and style. It is our tradition."

There was a momentary pause, as if they were all anxiously waiting for my response. It's funny that the people I was sent here to kill are the ones asking the questions. And they don't even know it yet. To keep up my charade, I need to think of something unique. And fast. Or at least make a good excuse about not having one. I blinked, suddenly agitated with myself. *No Lexi. Quit it with the excuses. Give them an answer. Come on! Think fast.*

Come on Lexi.

It's not that hard.

Just think of something.

That's all.

Something close to you.

Something that can make it seem like true passion to them.

Aha.

"We do have a rather unique tradition. It was passed down through many generations. Moralvelle has a strong connection with fire. Each year a festival is hosted, a celebration to the Celestials that gave us warmth and flames. The power to help and destroy. There are many performers that specialise in breathing fire. Almost like they can control it with the tricks they do."

The Queen had a look of surprise on her face. "Oh really? That sounds rather exquisite. Definitely unique. The people would love to see such tricks. As long as they are safe of course."

"Yes, they are completely safe. Only professionals who have been practising their whole lives participate."

"Very good then. I'd expect you to be dressed in warm colours then?" The King wondered aloud. "Very unique, fire tricks."

"Yes, warm colours will fit. I'll add that in my invite. Expect around seven to ten individuals, your Highnesses."

Wait. The realisation of what I had just said suddenly sunk in. I just broke the most obvious rule in the book. Fire has too much of a relation to me, why did I say that?! That's just more information to link back to me. How in the name of Tien am I supposed to get a large group of Flammous to magically breathe fire in one day? That's not even possible. I mentally slapped myself in the face. *Well, there's no going back now. I just have to deal with it.*

"Lovely to see that settled." The Queen said loudly, before switching the conversation. "Now for our next topic; our alliance and what it will entail. We will not force you to sign a scroll that has any outrageous expectancies in your kingdom's eyes. This would only damage our alliance. We would like you to read through this scroll and highlight any concerns you may have that affect your kingdom. Please, take your time." The Queen smiled warmly, as she pushed a scroll that was lying on the table in front of her toward me. "Please feel free to ask us any questions you may have, and we will gladly answer them." I could tell by the look in the Queen's eyes they weren't going to alter it in any way. The King seemed like he had the same perspective.

I caught Jackiel staring at me for a brief moment, as if screaming 'don't waste any more of my time with your stupid questions'. I ignored the spoiled Prince and laid the scroll out in front of me, eyes trailing down its contents. It read:

Dear current ruler of (Moralvelle),
It has come to our attention that your kingdom wishes to join the Alliance of (Arcarlia) and White Castle. Another common name for this alliance you may come across would be Peace Bringers (more commonly used by the

people) or Unity (more commonly used by higher-ups and will be used for the rest of this passage).

If you have received this scroll, we have accepted your inquiry for joining Unity. To fully become a member in our alliance however, you will need to adhere to these essential requirements. Failure to do so will result in your immediate exclusion out of Unity. Depending on the magnitude of consequence in your actions will depend on whether Unity will use force against your kingdom. Please read through these requirements carefully if you truly wish to join.

Requirement One: Assist.
Your first requirement is assisting other allied kingdoms. Depending on the task that needs assistance will depend on the number of resources (or soldiers) your kingdom will/can provide. It will also determine whether your assistance is needed and may come down to the allied kingdom with the required resources at the ready and is closest. This requirement is the most important one to follow. Failure to cohere with this requirement could very well result in brutal force.

Requirement Two: Trade.
Your second requirement will involve the rotation of gold and food. This rotation of resources between kingdoms will occur once every month. Potential resources that may be rotated are:
-Food
-Ores
-Weapons
-Gold
-Silver
Other resources may be required for the rotation. Please be prepared. Failure to cohere with this requirement will result in a warning. If a kingdom is unable to provide these materials however, resources will be sent to said kingdom instead and they will not need to provide

resources for the next few months. All will depend on the current situation of the kingdom.

Requirement Three: Meetings.
During each rotation of resources there will always be a meeting occurring at the same time each month. This meeting will take place in a new location each month and information on the whereabouts of this meeting will be sent out by the host kingdom on the day for safety reasons. There should be no reason your kingdom is unable to attend a meeting. If you yourself are unable to attend, please send your closest advisor to take notes and spread information.

Requirement Four: Loyalty.
The final requirement is loyalty to the cause. Any sign of fraying behind will be taken as treason and result in your immediate exclusion from Unity. To be loyal to the cause you will have yourself (or a trusted other) attend all meetings, always be prepared for anything that other allied kingdoms may need assistance with, assist in your part of rotations, and be willing to sacrifice your kingdom for the others to rise if necessary. Unity must be able to live on to win the war, even if that means you and your kingdom are annihilated.

These requirements are completely necessary, and it is recommended that you revise them for the future.

By signing this scroll, you place you and your kingdom's lives and trust into Unity. If you happen to pass during this alliance, you will be remembered in the stories of Unity's great victory. A valuable, powerful ally who died fighting for the cause. To rid our world of Sorvian and Krinian filth.

Your signature:

____

-Anasia Edwards-

I stared at the scroll in disbelief.
They really think that having your pretty little name in some history book is good enough? *Anyone who signs this outrageous trash is either stupid or just thinks they can be protected by these fools.* I thought, wondering why Arcarlia could've ever possibly signed this. They probably didn't look through it properly. Or they did and just thought they were invincible. They all think that. But in the end it's them who scream the loudest. And first.
I forced myself to nod, hating the movement.
The Queen clapped her hands together with joy. "Ah! Perfect. I think that's all we needed to settle in this meeting, isn't it?" Her eyes glazed over to the King, menacingly. It made me question who was truly in charge of this castle. Let alone the kingdom.
"Yes, yes I believe we are done here now." I stared deep into the King's eyes. All he was doing was repeating the Queen's words. There was no point in that. He knows it. I can tell. Something about her seems to frighten him. *It's interesting.* I smiled, not bothering to hide it. *I can use this to my advantage. Lovely.* "That is if the Lady has no questions that is?" His eyes poured into me. They were a soulless type of green. So dull it was like all life had been sucked out of them. I can't believe I hadn't noticed it before. *So very unique.*
"Yes actually, I do have a question. Who exactly is in charge of the ball planning? I'd love to have a chat with them." *And get all the information I need out of them to be done with your horrendous bloodline.* "I might see if I can add a Moralvelle twist on it, you see."
The Queen's eyes lit up at my suggestion. "That would be so wonderful! Wouldn't it be dear?" She looked at the King as if wanting his approval. *What a*

~130~

unique relationship. Is she even aware of the power she holds on him? Or is she doing it to show them as a more united front? "Yes, that would be wonderful. His name is Ghen Grey, I'll get one of the servants to find him for you."
"Thank you so much, Your Highnesses!"
"No, thank you Lady Lexi of Moralvelle. Your cooperation has just made Unity a far more powerful alliance than it was before! Now, to conclude our meeting I would like to-"

"Your Highnesses! My Lady!" An exhausted but eager voice called out.
I turned my head to see a servant sprinting towards the table, only to stop and realise it would be unwise to go any further. I would've called them somewhat intelligent if it weren't for the fact that they just interrupted a potentially classified meeting between four higher up individuals. *What kind of idiot is she? Doesn't she know the consequences for such an act?* I sighed, rubbing against my temples. No wonder White Castle was so simple to infiltrate.
Looking at the tall, albino female servant I could see that she felt the need to be here. I frowned for a moment, taking in her attire. She wasn't a servant. A Healer instead. What was a Healer doing so far from the Infirmary? She must've been sent by someone. Why else would she abandon her position and potentially get fired, or worse, executed? Judging by the way White Castle described their allies in that letter it wouldn't surprise me if they executed one of their own for such a simple matter. But the question still lies in my mind. Who sent her? And why is she here?
"Healer. You have exactly fifteen seconds to explain yourself about why you just interrupted a confidential meeting." Boomed the King, his eyes narrowing in irritation. The unspoken words lay

heavy in the air. Or there will be consequences. *It's not that confidential. Personally I don't see the reason why they felt the need to make it so.*
At this point Jackiel has sat up in his chair, clearly amused by this new form of entertainment presented right at his feet.
"Y-yes King Moralle. I was under the impression that the meeting was over already, I am deeply sorry. Princess Lila has sent me to collect Lady Lexi to meet her in the Infirmary. She has been rather... persistent to say the least." Her surprisingly bright blue eyes dared to look at the table I sat upon. Fear was clearly evident in her entire posture. She was practically shaking in her boots quite literally. "I am so sorry, I- I can go and come back later if you wish." The King sighed. "Of course, Lila would want to see the Lady. I suppose I can forgive you for Lila's impeccable timing." He groaned, as if recalling other events similar to this one. "She's rather impatient. Not one of her best qualities. Healer, come back in five minutes to collect Lady Lexi for her new appointment with Lexi. However, if this happens again, I will not let it go so easily. You would do well to remember that."
"Thank you sir!" She nodded and bowed with such ferocity that I couldn't piece her together with the scared girl I had seen before. I smiled. *What an interesting switch up.*
As I watched her run away, I thought back to what she said. *Lila wants to see me?* I relaxed all possible thoughts of discovery away. Lila had inhaled an entire bag of Snooze Memory. She'll be lucky if she remembers yesterday at all. For the future though I clearly need to give her a higher amount if another incident like this happens again. Though to do that, I'll need to smuggle some more back in when the others come. That won't be much of a problem though, I can just tell the Royals the materials they

bring will be a surprise. They don't seem to be overly suspicious of me.

The King's attention returned back to me. "Now, as I was saying, to conclude our meeting we would like to make one final request. When we collect your selected few for the parade from the meeting point, we will allow a squadron to accompany them for protection. However, we will not allow anyone with supernatural abilities to join your party."

I stared at them, surprised. They don't trust me enough to bring someone who could possibly have more power than them. I scanned them for a moment before coming to a conclusion. *The only reason they even let Princess Jassai come and go as she pleases is because they have power over her parents. They're scared they don't have that level of trust in me.* In that moment I felt a small pang of sympathy for the Arcarlian Princess. She's not yet of mature age, so she feels she has no power over her family. The assassination of her Ally kingdom's Royals might make her realise how easily she can overpower them.

I nodded submissively. "That is a reasonable request. As far as I am concerned there is not a single citizen in Moralvelle that has possession of a supernatural ability. Our traditional fire breathers can only do so through trained talent."

The Queen looked me up and down, clearly trying to decide whether I was telling the truth or not. Little does she know I'm trained in the art of lying. She relaxed and smiled. "Lovely to hear! Thank you, My Lady, for your cooperation. Our meeting is finalised." She called out loudly, signalling for the servant to come back.

The King and Queen of White Castle along with their son stood up briskly after that, before bowing towards me. I returned the gesture.

CHAPTER 11:
LEXI

The meeting had been confronting to say the least. An unease had settled in my stomach when I was escorted out. The family had such a unique and uncomfortable family dynamic it seemed like each move was unpredictable. It was clear the Queen had authority over her husband. Whether this meant she was manipulative or purely strong enough to overwhelm the beast of a King was beyond me. Jackiel didn't seem like he was that large of a threat, more like a mere inconvenience. If he was aware of his Mother's power or not was something I wasn't certain of. He clearly had a talent for concealing things. The Healer had hurried me along, frantically apologising for interrupting the meeting so consistently it had given me a headache. "I am so sorry again for the inconvenience, My Lady. I didn't mean to pry on your meeting. Please understand it was Lila's wish for me to collect you to her-"
She stopped short, face flustered. I exhaled, relieved. Is she finally done with her pathetic rant? "I'm talking too much aren't I? And I'm repeating

everything I'm saying," she looked at me as if she was disappointed with herself. "For the love of Tien, I'm hopeless. Ah, sorry I have a habit of repeating everything when I'm nervous."

And she did it again. Her eyes searched mine for some recognition, something that could show her I related to her issue. It just made me wonder how stupid this kingdom is, expecting some sort of relation between two people over a simple quirk. I didn't bother to hide the fact that I couldn't care less. Instead, I filled her need with disappointment.

"If you think that a few apologies and excuses are going to hide the fact that you have broken a law, then you should be ashamed of yourself. You're lucky you didn't receive any harsh punishment." I snapped at her instead. Her face immediately fell, her head whipped forward quickly to tear away from my gaze. I knew how intimidating it could be, I have that evidence from my competitors in the trials. We continued walking after that, with a notably large gap in-between us. It gave me time to think about that healer. The only information I was given about her is that they just call her Healer, with the information I've then gathered concludes that she wasn't exactly worth keeping around. Certainly not information-wise. No real point in making a real effort to befriend her.

It probably would've felt like a longer walk if I had been stressed. Yet my thoughts were more settled now. There was no possible way that the Princess could resist such a high amount of Snooze Memory. It was physically impossible. And from the whispers echoing throughout the castle, I can assume Jesse's followers couldn't remember a thing. Which wasn't exactly that surprising. They didn't appear all too bright. Regardless, the entrance doorway to the infirmary was just in front of me. I poked my head in to survey the room, choosing to ignore the Healer. It was the same compared to last night, not too many large differences aside from one of the ward's curtains being wide open. It was far less stressful to walk into a place casually instead of sneaking in. The Healer mumbled some words about our talk 'only being quick, as I'm worried about her being involved too much'. Not that I was interested in a long conversation anyway. My main priority at the moment was finishing this up as quickly as possible so I could pass this new information over to Granette to get something organised quickly. I nodded and thanked the Healer for accompanying me before striding over to Lila's ward, one I had become particularly familiar with. Especially considering it was me who put her in here. Sort of.

"Lexi? Is that you?" Called out a weary voice as I came into Lila's view. That Snooze Memory must have taken a real toll on her. Makes sense though, the amount she had was equivalent to the amount that could put a small army unconscious for a good few hours.

"Yes, it's me. Hello Lila," I smiled at her. "Are you feeling any better?"

Judging from the bags under her eyes she certainly isn't.

"Honestly?" She sighed, sinking into the pillows. "I feel like my head hit a brick wall." Her eyes were slanted, her body limp in the comfort of the mattress. It looked like she tried to brush her hair. Tried. It was quite possibly the most defeated I'd ever seen her. She groaned, her eyes rolling back into her head. "I couldn't even have a nice shower! Worse, I slept in this morning! My day is going so badly right now." She whined loudly.

For the love of Tien, she's acting like a whiny brat. *Is it that hard to be grateful? For once?*

"Oh! That reminds me." She suddenly perked up again. Her switch-ups are even more confusing than mine. "I wanted to ask you about something. Something important. I wanted to tell you, like an hour ago, but I kind of almost fainted trying to find you and everything got really weird and- oh my goodness you're glowing!" Her mouth dropped open, staring at me. I looked down at myself immediately, did some of my fire break through my hold? But no. There was nothing.

"Do you want me to call that Healer over here? I think you're hallucinating." This was different. *Did she actually get some severe neurological damage*? I've done something similar to this before and there's never been an outcome like this. Maybe I misinterpreted my calculations. I must've put too much force into the outburst. *If that was the case though, wouldn't Jesse be dead*? I frowned, bewildered by my own abilities. Maybe Lila is just weak. That seems to be the only logical thing behind it.

"No! I'm not hallucinating! I'm not joking you're- wait no. It's gone now."

"R-right." I left the conversation there. The Healer's would deal with whatever this is. "Now, what exactly did you want to talk to me about? Because if it's not a need to know right now, then I should probably get going because I'm pretty busy today." I tried to put it as gently as I could, but her face still fell. I groaned. I'm meant to be getting closer with her not pushing her away. But it is necessary to get the message through to Granette though. I have to sacrifice at least one thing.

"Ah! I'm sorry if I'm wasting your time. It's just getting lonely here, you know?" She looked like she wanted to say something but didn't. "I want to talk to people, but I'm just worried I don't have a clear enough head for it. I mean, everything had seemed so dull since like, an hour ago until you came. But I suppose that's the boredom talking, huh?" She sighed, looking almost sad. I hadn't seen her so down before. Not that it mattered. *Why would it matter?*

She'll get over it. But I suppose she needs my recognition.

"You're not crazy. And you're not wasting my time."

Yes, yes you are. "Honestly! If I was in your position I probably would have lost it ages ago. I cannot stay in the same spot for too long." I let out a small laugh. "Plus, I was only joking when I said you were hallucinating. It was most likely the reflection of some light behind me. You're just tired, so please quit worrying!"

That got a smile out of her. I was right. As per normal. A giggle escaped her lips as she propped herself higher up. "You know what? You're right. I think I've become bored enough I'm seeing things. I don't know what I'd do without you, Lady Lexi." She said, her last words hinted with a teasing tone.

"Hah! I don't even want to know the answer to that one." We shared a small laugh, something you'd think old friends would do when they'd shared a joke. Except we weren't old friends. Or even actual, real friends for that matter. The truth is that Lila Camhok only has a maximum of two weeks to live, if our mission goes according to plan. *May as well cut some sympathy for the girl and give her somewhat of a friend. It's nothing personal, just the real world.*

The Healer walked in then. "Ladies, that is plenty of chit-chat for today. One of you needs to be on bedrest!" She then remembered that she was also talking to me, and quickly changed her tone. "I- I think you should organise your plans for tomorrow is all." She then muttered under her breath in my direction. Lila looked at the Healer, then me sceptically. *What? Did she actually like this lunatic of a Healer?* I didn't know whether to be impressed or ashamed.

Instead, I nodded and smiled like the Lady I was. "Of course! It was lovely catching up with you Lila, I really hope we can do it again. I'll bring you

something next time, oh! Let me know if you want me to get you some food or something to do from somewhere?" I asked, eagerly. Lila beckoned me closer with a dastardly grin before whispering, "If you could bribe one of the Baker's to make me a vanilla croissant, that would be fantastic."
I mouthed 'I got you' before wandering out of the ward with my smile completely diminished.
Once I was out of earshot of Lila, the Healer hurried up to me. "Excuse me, Lady Lexi? I just wanted to thank you for not telling the Princess about my, uh, technical error from before. I also wanted to apologise again for that. At Moralvelle you must be very considerate of your laws, and I apologise if I offended you in any way or set a bad example for White Castle staff." She took a deep breath. "My actions should have been punished, as I should have waited outside instead of telling the guards I had permission to go and intrude on your meeting."
Her words caught me off guard. *Is she joking*? Did she actually convince the guards to let her in? "You- you did what?" I stumbled over my words, actually surprised by her lack of intelligence. "Why would you admit to that?!"
"To... telling the guards I had permission to enter the meeting room?"
"Yes! That's even worse than just wandering in!" I hissed in her face. This one idiotic servant just gave more reason to see this kingdom crumble. "Let me get this straight. You lied to a guard to intrude on a potentially classified meeting because a girl who almost fainted told you she wanted to share her hallucinations with me?"
The Healer went red in the face.
"I- I, uh..."
"Save it." I shooed her away before giving her a deadly glare. "You know what? I don't care anymore. Save your excuses for when the King and Queen find out about how you got in. You'll definitely need them

then. Now get out of my sight and do your job, but who knows? You might not have that at the end of the day if we're being honest." She'll be lucky if she has her head actually, her job should be the least of her troubles. War can make the simplest mistake into a death sentence nowadays.
She gulped; her face even paler than it was before. She bowed before hurrying back to where Lila is, finally taking my wording of 'hallucinations' into account. I know for certain that I couldn't care less of what becomes of that Healer. I walked past a guard on my way out of the Infirmary.
"Your Highness." He nodded at me. "Allow my partner Mateo to join you on your way out for security measures." The guard gestured to the man on the other side of the entrance.
"My Lady." He bowed. "Where to?"
"My room, thank you. Second floor."
Even without me, this kingdom is doomed.

I collapsed onto my bed the moment I came in. I'd gotten almost no sleep last night and it was finally catching up to me. My CrysTalk was hidden under my mattress from this morning, and it was a difficult task to pull it out. When I held the once shiny crystal tablet up high, letting it analyse my face as its owner I started questioning my own life decisions. And the Councils. Surely there was a more qualified adult for the job? Someone with more expertise and experience than a fifteen-year-old girl? At this point I was barely getting by unnoticed. The story they had given me was a difficult one to continue and emphasise. A young girl below the age of eighteen as some far-off kingdom's orphan Queen? A hardly believable story. It was an honest miracle they had accepted me and not just thought of me as some fake. Thinking about it more, I'm pretty sure they only put me here to test how gullible and oblivious the Royals were and what the limits of their suspicions were to then send a more trained individual to replace me. It feels like the only thing that makes sense in this cursed world. A young girl wouldn't be too much of a loss. I sighed. "Coller, Granette." I told the CrysTalk, slightly more confident than last time. G's face popped up a few seconds later, this time she was sitting in a concealed stone room with Sorvian guards stationed behind her. *So, she's moved to a more confidential area for our meetings. Smart.* I'm guessing that the guards are pretty high up then to overhear our conversation. Then again so is G.

"So, she still breathes! You had us worried for a few hours you know. Glad to see you survived the night." Granette grinned as wide as she could at the words. The guards behind her nodded her approval. "There's no listening device or someone else in the room with you, is there?"

Well, that was pretty straightforward.

"There are no other individuals in the room besides me. As for listening devices, no one has gotten close enough to me to plant one. Plus, I've pre-searched the room on my first day. No devices of any sort." I let out a sly chuckle. "I honestly don't even think they are capable of making one anyway from what I've seen."

"Well, that's good to know. Or not. They might have other ways; you never really know. But I'll take your word for it Lexi. You were always the perceptive type." Granette then changed to a more serious expression, finally getting down to business. "Now, I trust you have some information for us? If not, you wouldn't have that look on your face. You didn't almost get busted again, did you?"

"Yes, to the first question and no, they aren't suspicious of me yet."

"But didn't you say that one of the targets had seen you? Did you deal with her?" She questioned, her eyes narrowing in concern. "You did have some spare Snooze Memory to do that, didn't you?"

"I did have spare Snooze Memory and she doesn't seem to have any memories of last night or yesterday's incident. But-"

"But? Lexi what do you mean but? And what do you mean last night? She saw you again?" The guards were leaning in now, suddenly intrigued by the conversation.

I took a deep breath before answering. Only about two weeks in and G is already amazing at her new field. Impressive. "Yes, it was apparent that she was awake during my raid of the Infirmary, and she did view me. But I had managed to trick her into taking the Snooze Memory herself. The only downside to this is that she may have taken the entire bag."

"Lexi, I want definitive answers right now."

"Right. She took an entire bag's worth of Snooze Memory."

The sound of Granette slapping the table was loud enough to make me wince even from the other side of a screen. She's scarier than me at times. The guards turned to look at each other, a deep groan coming from one of them. I could only imagine their faces behind the mask. *It's a fair reaction, but I wasn't expecting Lila to just snatch it like that.*

"Are you telling me that that girl took an entire bag's worth of Snooze Memory, not to mention your only bag of Snooze Memory, and is still alive?" She leaned back in her chair, rubbing her temples. "For the love of Tien, I actually feel bad for the poor girl. She's probably in a hell of a coma right now." Her attention then returned to me. "Now, how exactly do you expect us to supply you with any more of that stuff? Not to mention that it's incredibly hard to come across and crazy expensive! You can't just go dishing Snooze Memory out like that as if we have unlimited stock! I cannot believe this..." She groaned loudly and ran a hand through her hair. "It's fine. We can find a loophole around this. You know what? Just tell me the other important stuff, I'm sure you've got some by now."

I imagined myself sinking into my bed and never coming out. Come to think of it, it would've been smarter to just give her a smaller dose instead of the whole bag. I panicked way too much. *Damn it! I can't do that again.* Next time it might totally sabotage this mission. I gritted my teeth as I thought of what to tell her next.

"Earlier today I was given a tour that didn't show me many places of interest. Safe to say none at all. Near the end I was informed that I was to attend a meeting with three members of the royal family." Granette looked surprised at that.

"They already had an important meeting with you? That was quick." She seemed almost suspicious.

"That's what I thought." I nodded along. "The meeting was about tomorrow and this alliance that they think we're joining. According to them tomorrow afternoon or evening they will be hosting a parade throughout the Kingdom where each allied Kingdom shows off their uniqueness to the townsfolk. Basically, a display of their power, culture, and richness. I was told I had to come up with something connected to the culture of my kingdom." I then glared at G. "They had the idea that I already knew something that could go well with the parade already because of how I described my fairytale kingdom too. I had to come up with something on the spot otherwise it would've seemed too suspicious because of how cultured and sophisticated 'Moralvelle' sounds like."

Granette face went beet red. "Ah. Right. I thought that would've come to our advantage with a more believable story, but I guess that worked too much." Her face cooled down after a little bit. "What exactly did you tell them?"

Now it was my turn to go red. "Well, I had to make it seem like I was passionate about the topic. So, at the

time, I thought it would be best to think of something I was close to in order to be more believable." Granette stared at me with pure disappointment on her face. *Yeah, I know what you're thinking, Granette.*
"Lexi, did you seriously just break the most obvious rule in the book? Please tell me you're joking. Lexi."
Almost got it right. She sank back into her chair again. Her face fell when mine only shifted to show a small hint of embarrassment. "Oh. My. God. Lexi, what in the name of Tien did you tell them?"
"I told them Moralvelle had a long-lasting tradition of... fire breathers." I was surprised when she looked relieved. "That wasn't the result I was expecting." I blinked at her, surprised by her answer.
"Yeah well what you just said wasn't what I was expecting either. From the way you put it I thought you'd done something more elaborate and more connected to you. Don't think you're off the hook just yet, however. That was still stupid. *Very* stupid. You should be grateful it's me on the receiving end of all this and not some random from the trials. They would've lost it ages ago." She caught my eyes looking past her at the guards. "Yeah well they don't count as 'random'. This isn't even the dumbest thing they've heard of. That I'm certain of. Please, continue."
"Ah. Fair enough. Well regardless of everything, they seemed to like the idea. They said I need to bring about five to ten to participate. I managed to convince them to organise a meet up spot further away from Sorvia, so they don't suspect where you're from. No obvious use of powers either. I told them we don't have any supernatural beings and that will need to stay that way if we want them to trust us."
G frowned, confused. "Why?"
"If they think we have anyone with supernatural abilities then they'll attempt to add more rules to

their already lengthy alliance papers and find some way to manipulate us. It's the same thing they are doing with Arcarlia. Plus, they personally told me not to bring anyone with abilities either. Regardless, I'll need a handful of Flammous who think they'll be capable enough to mimic breathing fire without making it seem like they are using their abilities."
"Wouldn't be Lexi if you weren't asking for so much in such a little amount of time. I suppose we can bring another bag or two of Snooze Memory while we're at it. When did you say this parade was?"
"I wasn't given a specific time, only before the ball. So, I'll assume the parade will be hosted at around four to seven in the afternoon. It would be a logical time to have it considering most balls are hosted after your average dinner time." I said, rubbing my temples. "I'll also require a, uh," I fumbled over the word. "Dress for the ball as well. Something with warm colours and just screams royalty and ignorance should do."
Granette snorted in amusement. "Don't worry, I'll get you a dress. In fact, I might take charge in that area." A dastardly grin lit up her face. "In fact, I'll see if I can get a quick CrysPic of you wearing that dress. Oh! The frizzles and puffiness will make you look, what's a good word for it? Extravagant." She said the word while motioning with her hands a vast space. I groaned.
"Of course you will." I muttered under my breath.
"Anyways, I'll need to organise a meeting spot with you all first and assist in making preparations for the parade. That is if I'll be included in the organisation of it all." I raised an eyebrow at G, who shook her head.
"No, we'll be doing that on our own. You need to stay on mission and continue gathering useful information. Leave the planning to us Ms Assassin."
"And the meeting point? I'll need to tell the targets about it as soon as possible so they can send out a

team to bring you here. They have quicker transport, and if we use ours, they'll recognise the workmanship of a Sorvian."

"True. I'll get some of our scouts on it. Hey Seven?" She called to the guard on her left. "Meet up with the Head of the Scouts, Michelangelo. Tell him to get some of the best scouts to map out the safest spot to meet. Make sure he gets a safe location that can be used as an ambush if things don't go according to plan. And tell him to get it a few kilometres away from the shoreline closer to the healthier lands to help prove our point. Make sure we can get there quickly though and map out the best path for us too." She then nodded and gave him a thumbs up.

"Affirmative, Red Two." The guard then hurried out of the room, with a new guard swift to replace him.

"See? I told you to leave the planning to us. We've got this. You just sit back and stay low until they arrive." My eyes narrowed slightly; a new question popped up in my mind. "With that small group you're going to send over, be sure to add someone with some experience in combat. Preferably someone who can do both long range and close distance just in case things do go south. The more people we can get away from their clutches the better."

She almost laughed my question off. "Don't worry Lexi. I'm not that stupid to not bring at least one person who can pack a punch. That'll be part of the requirements for the team who will be joining you of course. Now, is that all the information you've acquired today?"

"There was the mock Alliance scroll they showed me as well. Stupidest thing I've ever read. One thing to take into consideration though is that they do all sorts of material exchanges and meetings each month. So, the next one should be in a week's time. Could do well to intercept one of those and get more info out of the transporters don't you think?"

G hesitated, looking to the guards behind her as if for help. "Well, if everything goes according to plan there won't be much need to do that."
"If what goes according to plan? Granette? What are you guys planning over there?" I straightened my back, suddenly more invested in the conversation. Were they going to be planning a surprise raid sometime this week? Why wasn't I informed of this before?
"I'm not sure if it is my place to tell you if I'm going to be honest Lexi. I think they should instead."
"They? Who's they?"
Granette tensed slightly, before spinning her CrysTalk around so I faced the opposite side of the room. There sat the five members of the Council, staring at me with mixed looks of disappointment, excitement, and blankness. From left to right there was Bravo, Mortal, Fox, Dagger, and finally Brain. Dagger and Mortal shared an annoyed and bored expression, with Bravo being the complete opposite. She was quite possibly the only person who could keep the Council sane. Fox looked mildly impressed. Brain was the only one whose face I couldn't read. A blank stare, as if he was looking right into my soul. Foreboding can't even begin to describe it. What was more concerning was that the Council had overheard everything. All my mistakes. My errors. Not like they could come over here right now and scold me while teaching me a painful lesson, but the embarrassment was there, just the same. I swallowed back my gulp. I can't let them see my fear.
"High Council." I addressed them as respectively as I could, suddenly heavily aware that I was attending a meeting in the comfort of my bed. "To what do I owe this gracious pleasure? I wasn't expecting to see your faces. At least not so soon."
Brain replied first, taking the lead as he normally does. "Cut the formalities. There's no need. The quicker we get this done, the quicker Ms Coller can

assist with preparations. We are here to assess how you properly handle a meeting by handing out information without you knowing that we are watching. The things we have learnt are… interesting to say the least." I tried my best to prevent a blush from flushing up my cheeks. "Please remember the next batch of Snooze Memory we send you will be your last. Unless you are in complete dire need to the point where the entirety of Sorvia is on the line, then you will be receiving no replacements after this. This action of yours was careless, and if you happen to return to Sorvia again you will be punished within reason. Regardless of whether you have completed your mission or not, this act cannot go unnoticed."

He paused, as if waiting for me to nod for my understanding. Which I did. "Now to one of our new advancements. To start, our timeline has been moved up. Your assassination of White Castle's royal family will be occurring tomorrow night." He held up his hand to stop my protests. "To help explain this, let me fill you in on something. At first, we were uncertain of when we should send in this elite team, but now we know when. Tomorrow, during the ball, an extremely high ranked team of specially trained individuals will be ambushing White Castle's Capital. This shock will give you the time to slit the throats of the family during the panic and our team will forge a quick and efficient way out of the kingdom almost immediately. The backups arriving tomorrow to participate in this 'parade' will provide you with more information regarding the situation. At the moment, this is all the information you will be given until our plan is certain."

I sat there in shock. I didn't even hear a whisper on how I was going to be escaping the kingdom after the job was done. I had assumed I would be told during the mission. Maybe a good four or five days after the mission officially began. Not to have the assassination be pushed up to night three. Certainly not to have some 'elite' team to come in either. I grimaced at the thought of having to rush things. What confused me more is why they felt the need to rush this instead of biding our time. *What threat could this kingdom possibly pose that was greater than it was a few days before?* It didn't make sense. But I knew better than to ask that question. They also knew that too.

"I understand, High Council. I will ensure I am prepared for tomorrow then. I will be ready for whatever time we will strike. Thank you for passing this information onto me early."

Bravo spoke up next after that. "Lexi Ignei. Your last name holds so much strength and power, and you, doing this for your kingdom, better yet, the *world* proves how much you deserve the title." I imagined her kind hand on my cold shoulder at that moment. "Remember, Ignei. Patience in this is key. Despite the panic, you can't immediately lash out and expect good results. Use your wits, make it quick and clean. Represent your kingdom for our future."

Then Fox spoke. "Remember what's at stake right now. The victory of this war relies on you and how you cooperate. Don't let us down." I think his words were meant to inspire me. Instead, they came across as a threat. I shrugged it off anyway, letting all their words flow through me while knowing their true meaning. They aren't actually trying to support me. Bravo might, in her own little way. The others? Not so much. They are testing me. I can see it in their eyes. The hint of a smile peeked at the corners of my mouth.

"Your advice is all appreciated, High Council. But I am no amateur to the art of war. I understand the stakes and will not repeat any past mistakes. That I can guarantee to you all."

Dagger nodded his approval at my words, silent as always. Mortal did the same. As did the others before standing up. I then quickly realised what was happening and fumbled with the CrysTalk before I mimicked their movement. I set the screen down on a table before saluting and bowing to the miniature High Council tucked behind the screen. They saluted back.

"For the glory and pride of the Forgotten Lands."

With that, I ended the meeting with more questions than answers.

The screen then went black.

I have a feeling this mission is going to be more trouble than I first imagined.

CHAPTER 12:
LILA

I had dinner what felt like ages ago. And I was hungry again, already. But I can tell by the fact that the only light in the entire Infirmary is coming from my room means it is way too late to eat anything. *Disappointing.* I sagged into my bed, trying to figure out whether I was tired enough to go to sleep or not. My head was brimming with thoughts, mainly regret. Why didn't I just ask Lexi then? I mean I wouldn't have had enough time to ask her everything, nor did I have the willpower to do it. But it still would've been worth it to ease my mind. *Wouldn't it?* Maybe I'm just overreacting. Maybe I did dream about everything. I mean Lexi seems to be acting like nothing happened, so maybe nothing did happen. My thoughts had kept going in circles like that for the past hour. My eyes had begun to hurt from staring at the ceiling too hard. It wasn't this hard to fall asleep the other nights. But then again, I'm usually exhausted going to sleep. This time though, it's different. A different kind of tired, one that's incredibly draining. So draining that I thought I was imagining the sounds of footsteps entering the Infirmary. It was way too late for anyone to actually be up. That is if they were sane enough. That just almost confirmed my suspicions of me going crazy, I desperately wanted to sleep at this point.

The supposedly imaginary footsteps stopped just outside my ward. *Must be another Healer, hopefully it's Elin.* I thought to myself, smiling at the thought. She was so sweet when she gave me my dinner. I promptly sat up, tilting my head to see if I could peep through the curtain. But I feel bad if she's awake so late just to catch up on me. I suppose I did give her a pretty big scare today, so it makes some sense. *Ooh!* I gasped, excited at my newest thought.

Maybe she brought me some cute pyjamas! Hopefully those pastel purple ones with the cotton trimming. Or better yet! Newer and fancier clothes! *That would be amazing!*

The curtains parted to reveal my mystery visitor. To my surprise, it wasn't Elin. In fact, the boy standing in front of me was so unrecognisable that it took me a while to piece him together. "Jackiel? What are you doing here?"

Jackiel looked almost startled by my voice. He looked completely diffcrent from how I usually see him. His hair was a living mess, curls that used to be carefully brushed down were now sticking up. His eyes looked darker in the candlelight, which was weird. His eyes weren't even close to looking like that during the day.

Must be the lighting. His clothes also had darker stains on them, like he was climbing through the chimney system and got soot all over him. It was funny to see, Jackiel normally prides himself on looking his best. I guess he doesn't care as much when he's walking the halls with almost no one around except for guards. He's pretty unique at times. "Lila? I thought you were asleep. I mean, you should be asleep." His tone quickly changed to a

more protective one. "Considering your current physical condition, you should be resting for as many hours as you can. Don't think I don't know about that little incident with you disobeying Healer orders."
I gasped. "And how do you know anything about that? That was strictly between E-, I mean one of the Healers and me!" I crossed my arms, feeling defensive over my own mistake. "So, what if something happened? Now we know that I can't go for walks for a little while longer, that's all. We learnt something from it, so that doesn't make it that bad of a thing you know."
He started to laugh, looking away to try and hold it back. Which made me feel even more defensive. "Why are you laughing?"
He snorted, before bringing his eyes back to mine with a dastardly grin. "So, you did do something then, huh? I wasn't sure if you disobeyed orders in the first place, but now I suppose our Crown Princess isn't that angelic now, is she?"
I blinked for a moment, letting his words sink in. When they finally did, my expression turned sour. "Shut up Jackiel." I snapped at him. "Don't tell Mother and Father about that though, they'll never let me hear the end of it." I turned my attention to his outfit again. "But it's a bit difficult to take you seriously when you look like a chimney sweeper who hasn't slept a wink in his life."
"I'm wounded Lila. I really am. And don't worry, your secret is safe with me. You're my sister, so obviously. But there's no telling I won't take advantage of this though."
I groaned, half relieved and half annoyed at his words. I decided to switch the topic back to him. "Why are you here anyway? Is there something you want from me? It's pretty late, as you said yourself."
"Ah, right. Well to be completely honest with you, I wasn't expecting to see you awake." He said, scratching the back of his head. "I had originally

planned to just come in and see how you were doing. I was going to ask the Healers before, but I was pretty busy with that meeting and everything. And I can't exactly ask them at eleven o'clock at night now, can I? So, I decided to come check on you myself." He shrugged, then a smile returned to his face. "But I guess now I can give you a midnight chat."

"Midnight chat? Yeah, I'm technically not allowed to hold a conversation for too long. I couldn't even walk that far past the Infirmary without collapsing, so one of the Healer's told me to limit as much interaction as I could." I said, looking at him disappointed. "Especially at this late of night."

I sank back into the bed, staring up at the ceiling. I sighed, and I could hear him do the same. I assumed he'd just leave after that and wish me good night. But no. He made no movement of leaving, at least none that I was aware of. He then began to speak again.

"That's fine. You don't need to talk. Just listen. I've got some stuff I want to tell you, and I don't mind if you forget most of it in the morning."

I sighed again, before looking back at him. Jackiel looked at me anxiously, as if waiting for an answer.

Aw. I really wanted to try going back to sleep. Well, he looks somewhat serious, so I guess I'll hear him out. I mean he's my brother after all. I reluctantly nodded, gesturing for him to continue.

"Perfect. I don't mind if you fall asleep sometime during this, so I'll get to the point now and drag it out later. Tomorrow at the ball, I'll make sure we get our own little area away from everyone. But don't worry, I have it all planned out perfectly." I frowned at his words. *Don't worry? What plans?* But I said nothing. I felt compelled to say nothing. "Yeah, I see your face. Again, don't worry. I have it under control and you'll be completely safe. You'll just have to trust me, okay?" He waited until I nodded. "Excellent. Glad that parts out of the way. But I do have a

question for you. You can just nod or shake your head to it if you want. How would you react if, hypothetically, Mother and Father... died?"
I blinked. Stunned. This was not the question I'd expect someone like him to ask. *Why was he even thinking about that kind of stuff?* It's not like Mother and Father aren't basically invincible from all the bad things in the world. They've got a whole other kingdom backing them up, and soon to be Lexi's too. *Why would Jackiel be worried?* It felt as if the temperature in the room shifted to an icy cold breeze. I felt trapped by new fears.
"Huh. Not the question you were expecting? Well, I've got a follow-up. Again, remember this is all hypothetical. Would you be sad if something did happen to them?" His expression had turned harder with each word. It was unsettling to say the least. I felt unsafe. "Well then?" He tilted his head again. He wants an answer. I was left with my own thoughts.
How would I feel? I'd never thought about it before. I nodded. Of course I would. Who wouldn't? Everyone loves their family. *But where is he going with this?*
"I figured that would be your answer." He let out a crooked smile, then exhaled sharply. "Here's another food for thought, Lila. We both know that everyone is expecting you to be White Castle's next Queen, right? But I've been wondering for a while now. What if I was King? What would I do?" He slowly became lost in thought, gazing at nothing in particular as a sluggish smile spread across his face. "That power. Wouldn't it be amazing? I'd have an entire kingdom in the palm of my mind. And a whole alliance. That's half the world under my control, isn't it? What a funny thing to think about. I mean I've been to all of Mother's and Father's meetings, haven't I? Surely that makes me somewhat qualified."
He said the words as if he was a child trying to bribe someone to give him a toffee. It was almost cute. But

if he wanted to be King in waiting so badly, why not voice it? *Why stay in the dark?* I don't mind him gaining that title. As much as I'd love it, I have to admit. He's five times the ruler I'll ever be. Jackiel is so calculating, calm, observant. He's perfect for the role. So, why'd they pick me instead? Because I'm pretty, popular, easy to talk to? I mean, I guess I do have those qualities, but Jackiel is still amazing at everything he does. Some of the tutors here think he'll have an IQ well over two hundred by the time he's older. Yet here he is. A forever Prince.
"But maybe I don't just need to be King of White Castle to have power. If I was King of the world, everyone would listen to me. Even that Krinian and Sorvian scum. Imagine that! The war over, all because of me. Jackiel Camhok, the teen who fixed all our world's problems. But if you really think about it though Lila, it was mankind that created these problems." He frowned at that. One of the rare occasions that he had done so. "All those other beings from long ago, were they really all that bad? Maybe if they existed again instead of people then our world would be better. After all, there were no recorded wars of any sorts before humans took over the world. It's funny how all these little things can impact our world. Imagine the minerals and architecture we could've learnt from the dwarves. The patience and life lessons from the elves. The wisdom and power from the wizards. Maybe even the unique aspect of life from the elementals. Just think about it, Lila. Think about it."
I felt weird to say he was onto something after all the random and strange things he had said before. I wasn't sure exactly how to feel about it all.
"You never know Lila. We could've outlived the world, as brother and sister. We still can if we find a way." His eyes returned back to me. "I think I'll leave you for now. You look pretty tired. Get some rest, Lila." He said with a smile.

I didn't need much more incentive after that. It didn't take long before I felt myself drifting off. I couldn't help but imagine the world Jackiel was picturing. It was strange, yet peaceful enough to ease me into a heavy sleep. However, Jackiel never left my side. I felt his eyes on me the whole time. Then I succumbed to the tiredness and drifted into unconsciousness.

I woke up to lots of hustling in the Infirmary. Jackiel was gone by the time I'd opened my eyes. It took me a while to work out whether I had imagined him last night or if it had actually happened. I still can't decide. Trusting my instincts to ignore it anyways, I yawned, and stretched my arms out wide. Today was the day of the parade, then my favourite part. A big, glamorous ball. A ball I could only attend if the Healer's deem me fit to leave on my own. Which is something I definitely need to prove after yesterday. Let's just hope Elin is feeling rather generous and reckless at the same time today.
Not that I actually looked forward to getting out of my bed, I knew that I needed to eventually. It looked like my curtain was a quarter open, giving me a perfect view of how many Healers were rushing past. I overheard some words about Jesse, stuff that went along the lines of, 'he's finally awake!', 'it's been so long, I thought he was dead', and 'do we seriously need to tend to this disaster of a boy?'. I counted around twenty Healers running back and forth. I recognised none of them. Plus, it looks like most of their attention was currently fixated on Jesse and his apparent waking. I groaned. I was hoping that brat would stay unconscious a little longer. He better not be attending the ball. Not that I think that he is anyway, by the sounds of it he only woke up an hour or so ago. Maybe less.
I frowned, staring up at the ceiling. My head felt a bit clearer this morning, so that was good. Hopefully that meant I'd have a better chance at joining the

ball, or at least just the parade. I sagged into the bed, I was looking forward to that ball, it was going to be the highlight of the year. One I got to share with Lexi for the first time ever. Another yawn came up from inside me. Jesse wasn't exactly the nicest person ever; most would call him one of the worst. And I'll give them points, he's pretty close to the one of the worst people I've met. Either way, no one deserves to fall on a sword. Certainly not in the way he did. I even grimaced at the thought.

I forced my mind back to the upcoming ball. I'd wear a beautiful dress. No one would think twice about me not being a Princess. Both men and women would marvel at my beauty! I'd be the star of the night! Everyone would want to talk to me! And best of all, I'd have to tell them I was off limits. I had my own amazing friend to hang with, Lexi! I'd reject them all!

"Hello? Your Highness? Ah! You're finally awake!" I was surprised to hear a familiar, sweet voice calling from the peek in between the curtains. Elin's kind face brought a smile of my own.

"Elin! Hi! How are you this morning? Good, I hope?" I beamed at her.

"Oh! Thank you for asking. Yes, I am alright. But I think the bigger question here Lila, is are you alright? You're the one in the bed." She said, smiling softly, a hint of worry in her eyes.

"I'm fine! In fact, far better than yesterday. So fine I think I might be able to, you know, attend the ball tonight?"

"Of course that's your intention. The ball. I should've known." She said with a little laugh. Elin then proceeded to look me up and down, evaluating me.

"Well, I can't quite give you a proper diagnosis. I'm pretty busy right now with uh," she hesitated, clearly choosing her words carefully. "Jesse waking up and all. But you do sound better, but that's about it. I can't give you any promises though, remember that.

You were really bad yesterday; I hope you know that."

Aw. Should've been expected though. "Fair enough. Do you think you could bring me some breakfast at least? Or get someone to bring it for me?" She smiled and nodded at my request. I breathed a sigh of relief and sank back into my bed. At least one thing was going to go right today. Ironic how that thing was breakfast.

Elin left shortly after that. Around twenty minutes later, a new Healer arrived in my room with breakfast. The same thing as the day before. It was rather repetitive, and I wondered if I stayed here any longer whether I would eat the same meal over and over again. It merely fuelled my determination to leave the infirmary more. I had asked that Healer about Lexi when he gave me my food. He'd told me that from what he'd heard Lexi was busy planning for the big night tonight, and that was all. He said that he wished he knew more so he could tell me. An hour flew by, to which I dedicated my nose in that book Jackiel gave me. Another flew by, to which I finally learnt the time of the parade from one of the Healers. Six o'clock. I'd barely started the day and the parade itself started in eight hours. For the next two hours, I had multiple conversations with some of the other Healers and myself. I had a reasonably boring experience. It was after I'd had my lunch I finally decided to do something worthwhile. That entire morning Healers were running to and from Jesse's ward. Barely anyone could be spared to check up on me, excepting giving me meals. It was lonely to say the least.

When I set my plate down, I felt the uncontrollable urge to move my legs. I'd been sitting in my bed for far longer than normal. Usually, I get a decent walk around the castle. But recently, I haven't been able to do that. I haven't even been allowed to leave my bed. Let alone move properly. I tilted my head to check if anyone was coming in. They usually give me an hour or so to eat, then come in and grab my plate. Since everything has died down since this morning however, I might get less time. Regardless, I took the opportunity and crawled out of bed. When I stood up, I had a similar feeling to yesterday. The dizziness and numbness in my legs were the same, just a little less unbearable from before. I waltzed over to the curtain, heavily aware of my awkward walking position as I did so. I probably looked like some drunk coming out of the bar. I winced as I peeked my head out, observing the passing Healers. None of them took much notice of me. Some of them probably didn't even know about Elin's conditions. They probably thought it was fine for me to be out of bed without their permission. I smiled as I swiftly shut the curtain, closing the gap fully. Let's keep it that way.

For the next two hours, I had a streak going. For five minutes, I would walk around my small, confined space and occasionally stretch out some of my muscles that were still asleep. Then I would take a break for ten minutes doing whatever I could with moving the littlest bit. I repeated this constantly. Balls are incredibly important to me. They allow me to shine where others sometimes don't. Dance to beautiful music while showing off spectacularly. Meet new people, and most importantly; wear my own jaw dropping dress! I giggled at the thought. I was in the middle of one of my walks, and slowly losing my thoughts to the ball. *How could someone not enjoy something so spectacular*? Honestly, they are some of the best things that humanity ever created! Plus, I'll get to share the experience with Lexi! Which makes it even better than it was before! Her first ball! What a special moment.

I flinched as my head flared up again. The painkillers they had given me with my food hadn't exactly been working as I could tell. My head had been flaring up pretty frequently, but I was getting used to it. It was as if my head was in a war against something each time it flared. I'd imagined that it had gotten better considering how peaceful I'd woken up, but I guess it was just a cover. I wonder if Lexi meant for that fire to hit me. I don't see why she would though. I mean, what could her motive possibly be? We're friends. Best friends, some might say. She was just trying to protect me of course! So much that she had to use her power to save me! I smiled at the thought. She put her own safety on the line for me. Now, to return the favour, I physically have to be there for her first ball. *If I can push through my pain, then I'm a worthy friend of hers*! I thought confidently to myself. I winced again as the pain in my head escalated. Actually, maybe now's a good time for a break.

I sank into my bed, to where an unwavering feeling of sleep washed over me. Did I tire myself out that much? Yawning, I succumbed to the feeling and blacked out little less than a few seconds later.

Time was flying by, and I couldn't properly make sense of it, stuck in this room all day. I woke to someone gently tapping my shoulder. It was Elin again. I groaned, and turned away, mumbling about something I myself didn't even fully understand. She continued tapping my shoulder, trying to get my attention.

"Lila? I thought you wanted me to test you for tonight?" She said, her voice tinged with a teasing tone.

Her words made me spin round to face her within seconds. *Ah, yes. I'd forgotten about that.* Well, I almost forgot about that. She smiled softly, tilting her head at me. She just had some sort of aura about her now. As if she was happier than before, I wasn't exactly sure what it was. I yawned, rubbing my eyes at the same time. It was always a pleasure to see her. Even

if it was when she caught me napping. "I hope this little nap of yours means you were saving up your energy, right?"
"I, uh, yeah. That was the plan, definitely." I replied, stretching out my arms as far as they would go. "What time is it again?"
"About three hours till the Alliance Parade starts, so it's a little after three in the afternoon. Well," she turned around and looked through the now-open curtain to where the clock was. "Technically three ten, but that's just the specifics."
"Three hours until the parade starts? I thought I was only asleep for like, ten minutes. That's close to an hour! Probably more!" I whined, sitting up in my bed. "Lexi's probably having a blast getting ready for that parade, isn't she? I wish I could join her!"
Elin sighed at that. "You can join her once you prove to me that you can actually do that. But first, I'd recommend waking up first because I'm only giving you one shot at this. If I don't see any improvement the first time I evaluate you, then it's right back to this room! No parade, no ball. Understood?"
I nodded lazily; my head awake but my body still asleep. "Yeah, I understand. Just give me, let's say, five minutes. I should be all ready by then."
"You sure that's all the time you need?" She said, surprised. I nodded at her in response. I'm pretty quick at waking up. "Okay. Well, if you end up the same as yesterday's incident, then I guess I'll have a nice talking buddy for tonight. Don't worry! If you're not going to any of the festivities, then I won't either. I'll keep you company, how does that sound?"
"That would be nice if I actually end up needing it."
"Ha! Confident now, are we?"
She spun on her heel and trudged out of the room immediately after that. She really doesn't mind whether I exceed her expectations or not, she's content with whatever. I cannot understand this woman, but she's nice. She left me alone for a little

while longer, giving me time to get out of bed and stretch. Since I didn't have a whole twelve-hour sleep, it was pretty easy to wake up properly. In fact, the five minutes might have been a bit of a stretch considering everything. Regardless, I took advantage of the time I had. Elin came in a little while later, wearing a hopeful look on her face.
"Now, are we ready?"

CHAPTER 13: LEXI

Twenty minutes until the parade.
Seventeen minutes.
Eleven.
Nine.
Five.
Three.
The minutes ticked by faster than I could possibly
count. The moment I had been dreading had arrived.
We had only one singular night to prepare, where
what felt like the entirety of Sorvia joined in to assist
in my mission. It should've felt a little bit
supporting. But the feeling was replaced with the
worry that I had to trust them with something I
should've been taking care of myself. Instead, I hated
that feeling. Granette would've come with the group
if it weren't for the fact that she was so intelligent
and valuable in the investigative and negotiation
fields. Even though I hated to admit it, I kind of
missed her. I find it hard to trust a group of
strangers who had been thrown together just for this
one festival. How could I trust them with my secrets?
How could I possibly trust that they'll do their part

correctly? In the hour counting till they arrived, I was given no description of appearance or personality wise of the arrivals. For safety reasons of course, which I found extremely frustrating. All I knew was that those escorts of the Royals had been successful in collecting them and would be arriving in the hour. What a painfully tense hour that was. Here I was in my room, pacing circles around it anxiously. I was never one to get nervous, or even get close to breaking down. But the reality of my position, the fact that I had to pass some of my responsibilities to others, was unbearable. It still is. I turned around to get one more good look at the group I had been paired with. Out of ten, I knew one person. A young Flammous boy who passed eleventh out of a hundred. His name was Adrian, he had blonde hair with dark ends that covered his eyes, and he had freckles. His personality? Quiet, timid. The complete opposite of your average Flammous. They are normally outgoing and aggressive, the urge to use their power only fuels that rage. It took me ages to control it. I suppose I had to give him points for self-control. There were seven other Flammous, all adults and varied from the ages of twenty-two to forty. The final other two were the stylists. Two female teens who should be on their scouting duties. They were picked because they were the only Scouts who were capable of making professional level clothing from a small number of materials. The one thing they all had in common was the fact that they could all kill if they wanted to.

Which definitely makes me feel better about the whole ordeal I thought sarcastically.

The other kingdoms had already left to go on their journey throughout the Kingdom, showing off what they could do. Ours was the final kingdom to leave, and our scheduled time to go was coming up quicker than I would've liked. The first Kingdom to go was this year's host, White Castle. Their float consisted of a rather large carriage missing its roof disguised as a cloud. The cloud had mini buildings sticking out of it with an architecture similar to the buildings you'd see everywhere here. Then there were the mini wooden citizens dotted everywhere. Guards riding horses in pure gold armour were in front and behind the float. The Royal family sat in the middle of it, all four of them. I was surprised to see Lila there among them. The message they'd tried to put across was simple. Together, as a kingdom, we will rise to the clouds. Simple, but symbiotic. Then there was Arcarlia. They had guards wearing gold armour like White Castle's, but they didn't waste any time getting to the main part of their presentation. Their float had no eye-catching qualities, but that was on purpose. While it was a see-through carriage with banners of Arcarlia everywhere, that was about the limit of their creativity. So they could present their

real spectacle, the Princess Jassai. *Shapeshifter.* When she arrived at the castle a few hours ago, I knew her very presence could complicate things. A shapeshifter within such close proximity with an assassin, it just didn't work. If she got the slightest bit of suspicion about me, she could turn into something as simple as an insect and overhear every word I say without me ever knowing she was there.

One more minute. I had overheard them talking about how she was going to morph into a massive falcon and fly over the crowd, drawing their eyes to the sky. Smart, so no one would really notice their lack of effort in their float. No one would question it with the Princess around.

Then there was our float. I also had a design somewhat similar to White Castle's. There was a roofless carriage, except there were no walls either. Just floorboard, wheels, a fancy-looking chair, and me. However, on both sides of the float, there were four hovering pedestals. This is where the fire breathing Flammous were stationed. On these pedestals they would perform their tricks and inspire the crowd on the same level as their heads. Then I sit in the middle on my throne-like chair, smiling and waving the crowd like any other Royal would. This is where I was now, gripping the sides of my chair tightly and practising my smile. Hopefully it looks real enough.

All the floats were lined up inside of a tunnel in the order they would leave in. The tunnel had massive doors at the front that seemed to open on their own when it was time, revealing the Kingdom's Royals to the crowd eagerly awaiting them. The sound of cheering was deafening to my ears, the last time I had heard a sound even close to that was when I was in the arena. Yet this crowd seemed bigger and louder than that one, and I hadn't even seen them yet. One of the workers blew some sort of horn, signalling for the doors to open once again for the last time. I braced myself, and as the natural sunlight peeked through and the crowd roared, I heard a voice come from my left.

"It's fine. We've got this." I turned to see Adrian, mentally bracing himself for the crowd while repeating those words over and over again. His words faded out quickly and were replaced by the sound of a massive gathering of cheering people laying just in front of us. The golden guards in front of us began to pull our float forward, dragging us out of the tunnel and into the sunlight. It was only here when I realised how big this crowd was. Our path was set out clearly, lines painted into the ground marked where the carriages and people went. Unfortunately for the people of White Castle, there wasn't enough space for them all to fit into the space provided for them. As I looked up, people were hanging out of higher levels of buildings to get a good look at the parade. I smiled and waved at them. *Hey, they are pretty persistent.*

A sudden blast of heat came from both of my sides, telling me the Flammous had started their show, much to the appreciation of the crowd who roared in approval. Pieces of colourful paper were thrown in front of me, and I was stunned. It's not that often I see that many colours at once, and they were just throwing them away? I shrugged off my thoughts and continued the act. *Smile and wave. Smile and wave.* I turned to see the Flammous doing an excellent job at making it seem like they were breathing the flames. To only be quickly taught in one night and have that much skill was impressive. But monitoring both of the sides closely, it looked like the older Flammous excelled at it much better than the younger ones. This I frowned at. Age shouldn't have much to do with skill, this was disappointing to watch. To my knowledge, they all learnt the art together as one, so they'd be equal instead of an unbalanced group. Yet the younger ones were grouped with the younger ones and the oldest with the oldest. Which in turn made a very noticeable difference in skill. But as I became worried about the sudden fear, I took in the crowd's faces. It isn't perfect. It isn't even close to being perfect. *But...* I looked into the eyes of an elderly woman, whose eyes had lit up at the sight of the group. She looked like she hadn't felt that much joy in a while. *Why are they so happy?* They should be disappointed in our lack of organisation. *So why aren't they? Why aren't they all?*

The path set out for us had many curves and turns, yet with each one more Whienans came into view. Who knew such a dense Royal line could have such a massive population? I turned to look at Adrian, who had seemed nervous beforehand. His expression had changed from worry to surprise. No one here had seen so many people in one day. Not one. Especially not such a large group of people so happy. It was... overwhelming to witness. Nevertheless, I continued smiling and waving. *The quicker we get this over with, the better.* A large gust of wind flew by, followed by a big shadow. *So, they weren't kidding when they said Princess Jassai was going to turn into a massive hawk then, huh?* I looked up to see a hawk with a beautiful feather pattern of hazel, brown, and black with lines of gold. Its wingspan was equivalent to two full grown men. At one point, the Princess flew so she was right in front of the sun, making her hawk figurine a black shadow with the light reflecting off her back. She looked like a star, and from the cheers and shouts from the crowd they shared the same thought. The Princess then started to do flips in the air. The flips started off incredibly fast before slowing down tremendously. So she does get tired pretty easily in her form then, at least the giant hawk one. *I'll keep that noted.*

The massive bird then descended a hundred metres or so in front of us, probably to where her family's carriage was.

"Wow! Did you see that, Le- I mean My Lady?" Adrian shouted over the roaring crowd, with a few of the others nodding along. "I didn't know the Princess could do something so big! She must've been holding out for this moment."

"I didn't either, if I'm being honest. I heard a rumour that she was doing something like this, but I didn't think she would." I would've smiled and tried to congratulate her if we were actually on the same side. "She does seem to tire easily though, doesn't she?" I hinted, glancing at Adrian and then the older Flammous. They all nodded; they saw where I was going with this. Some useful information to pass on to that squad later on. Not that Arcarlia will send their Princess out into the front lines, they'll probably use her for a tactical retreat when our plan comes into focus. The crowd's cheers seemed to ring in my ears like a deafening drum. It was quite possibly one of the loudest things I'd ever heard. To tune it out, I returned to my thoughts. My happy place. I thought about the events earlier today, more specifically when this group arrived and all the pain that came afterwards.

I was pacing in my room again when someone knocked on my door. I had been thinking about this group all night, so much so that I had been up since four in the morning. I only got about five hours of sleep last night. I'd opened the door, surprised and suspicious as to why two guards stood there with stoic looks on their faces.
"We have been sent to inform you that the individuals you had requested have arrived with all their belongings." Said the guard to the left.
"If you like we can take you to their current location, My Lady. It would be a good idea for them to get more familiar with how things are going to be planned out." Said the other guard to my right.
I'd let them take me to a new area of the castle. It was a wide and vast room that clearly used to be empty, but now had Moralvelle banners hanging on the walls. Around ten or so people had stood in the centre, surrounded by crates and boxes that they were busy unloading.
"I take these are the individuals you had requested us to transport?" One of the guards had said, their brisk voice one I wouldn't be able to forget.
"Yes, yes, they are. Thank you for your kindness." I nodded to them to leave, to which they had taken guard just outside the doors to the room.
Once they had left, the group's eyes had turned onto me immediately. From a quick analysis, I had found three teenagers and seven adults among the group. Eight of them were easily recognisable as Flammous by their faces and clothing style. I had frowned at their attire. "Couldn't you have all picked something a little less obvious to wear?"

One of the adults had snorted, whose name I had later found out to be Fraug. "It's not like any delinquent here knows the difference between a Snautwest and a Nat. The idiots couldn't care less what we were wearing. The Council was fine with it as well, considering this clothing has none of Sorvia's unique trademarks. Only a Flammous could know the difference, or, I suppose, an Ignei like yourself." Eventually, for the next hour while they were setting up, the ten were split into three uneven groups. One for critiquing everything they saw in all of White Castle, another trying to get them to act somewhat normal, and the smallest group of two just trying to ignore it all and unload everything. Meanwhile I barked out orders for where to organise everything. I had to sometimes shout it out a little louder, so the guards would think we were still unloading and wouldn't walk in on a very specific group of Flammous criticising the very ground we stand on. This was around where I learnt all their roles. The Flammous who were going to become fire breathers, and the two Scout-turned costume designers. The eldest Flammous had assisted in keeping everyone in line. I found out soon enough that his name was Uragus, an interesting name. One I never forgot. The designers had brought with them two crates' worth of costumes and had two different designs for everyone. Meanwhile I had received four. Two choices for the parade, two choices for the ball.

Time had flown, to the point where I had to leave them for a surprise afternoon tea I had been invited to in the Palace gardens. Nothing of interest had happened there, besides the fact that Lila had appeared again. Not that we got a chance to talk, she was busy talking with her parents. When I returned, the group had split again. This time more evenly. Half of them continued manufacturing the float for the parade while the others worked up a battle plan in case things went south beforehand. Regardless of any minor inconvenience, things had gone well. I had planted some listening devices in popular spots in the castle so Granette and the others could listen in to some potentially important information while I got this parade out of the way. As far as I was concerned, no information has been leaked yet. But then again it would be foolish of them to try and contact me at this time and place.

The parade continued, time almost flying by as we arrived at the end of the line. The other kingdoms had already finished and were waiting on us as they unpacked their intricate floats. More like a waste of resources. Our float alone took a massive chunk out of our already limited wood supply. The crowd dispersed once we'd reached the end, instead regrouping behind us and forming a large circle around an intersection where the floats lay. In the middle of the circle was a massive stage with people hurrying around all over it, desperately trying to put it together in time. I frowned. But why? What could they possibly need that stage for? A speech? I panicked. *I'm not prepared to do a speech. And certainly not first.* But if they wanted their people's attention through a parade and ball, they wouldn't then have people walk away from some speech they'd heard every year, wouldn't they? *No. No they wouldn't. They are planning something else.* I looked over at White Castle's Royal family, who were now approaching the stage with astonishing speed. I was surprised to see Lila being able to catch up with them. She was wearing heels and technically meant to be on bed rest, so what was possibly driving her? She turned and saw me looking her way and gave me a cheesy wave. I returned the favour.
My attention then turned to the Arcarlian family, who looked as confused as I was. The King had his eyebrows scrunched up confused. It was the first

time I had seen him in person. Any of the Arcarlian family for that matter. The King had tanned skin and short, dark brown hair patched with hazel eyes. His beard was well trimmed and in the form of a goatee. His clothes were a long, blue robe matched with diamonds stuck all over the robe's design. He wore heavy, leather armour underneath with a crown made out of pure Silver that reflected in the sun. His offspring had similar features. Same tanned skin and brown hair, except Princess Jassai's eyes were a raving gold instead of hazel, shining bright against everything else.

The family were exceptionally stunning in beauty. As expected from the Royal Arcarlian bloodline.

King Moralle and Queen Benice took the stage, with their children standing idly at the steps. The King's voice boomed out loud to the crowd.

"Loyal citizens of both White Castle and Arcarlia! Today marks the twentieth anniversary of Unity, the alliance between our kingdoms. For twenty long years we have worked diligently together against the evil of Sorvia and Krinia, and the fact that we, us, you, are still standing is because of our teamwork and perseverance in the face of evil!" He shouted, raising his fist high in the air to which the entire crowd repeated the same notion. "However, today does not just celebrate the coming together of two kingdoms. In our parade, our kingdoms have celebrated our most powerful and unique aspects that make us strong! But today, a new ally has joined us! Please welcome the island of Moralvelle, coming together to help fight for all that is good and join the alliance of Unity! Moralvelle, the fiery island of bravery and heroics!"

The entire crowd cheered, throwing that same colourful paper into the air as before. A chant soon rippled throughout the crowd.

"Moralvelle!"

"Moralvelle!"

"Moralvelle!"
"MORALVELLE!"
The chant continued until the Queen raised her hand, to which the crowd then fell silent within moments. "Now, as our yearly tradition, we typically have honourable battles between our two kingdoms to determine who's will to defeat all that is bad is stronger! However, this year we feel the need to do something different, something we have never done before!" The Queen paused, letting her words sink into the crowd, who responded with quiet murmurs rippling all around. "This year, we have decided to do a more unique dance inspired by our new partner, Moralvelle! As you have all seen, their unique float had everything to do with traditional fire dances, correct?" The crowd murmured in agreement, intrigued. "Well, we have collected dancers and magicians of our own to pull off this amazing spectacle we have to show you now!" The Queen whirled around to the King, who nodded solemnly. They raised both arms and gave a resounding clap which echoed around.
It was quiet for a few moments, before around a hundred people from the crowd dressed from head to toe in black gear came to the centre of the circle, much to the surprise of both the crowd and me. *Why are they- They're trying to impress us? But why? There's no point in doing so when they should believe I already have their trust.* The men and women in the circle all then lit a unique looking match, with blue flame flickering above it. The audience awed in admiration. The King gestured out with his arms as wide as he could. "And here, new member of Unity, is our gift to you!" The black-geared members then began to break out into a series of beautiful movements while using the larger-than-normal match. Blue flame streaked across the air as the performers soon evolved into a dance.

I pretended to enjoy it. Sure, the average person would find it entertaining. But as I looked deeper into the Royal family, more cracks appeared on the surface. The Queen and King looked bored, as if they couldn't have thought of anything else to possibly do. Lila and Jackiel both looked heavy in a conversation, ignoring the so-called spectacle happening just in front of them. Lila actually looked uncomfortable for once in her life. I frowned, wondering what their conversation was about. I was too far away to read their lips, unfortunately. The Arcarlian family merely stayed in their float, quietly watching the dance continue with tiny blue sparks flying into the air, causing the crowd to shout in excitement. Funny how such a small and pathetic thing can really make someone feel excited. The Royals know what's happening. A mere front for them to hide their insecurities underneath, that's all it ever is. It's never truly earnest in this world. No one in the entirety of Mistlon doesn't have at least a small drop of 'bad' in them.

Urugas tapped me on the shoulder, shooting me a look like he wanted to talk about something. I nodded at him, allowing him to speak. "This sure is something, huh? Those Royals went all out." *The Council doesn't want me to tell you this.* He's using that old trick that we were taught at a young age, all of us Sorvians. You say a cover up sentence and use sign language as you say it, while masking it as gesturing with your hands. It works when you're trying to sign to someone but not make it too obvious that you are doing so. It's a good trick to know.

"Yeah, definitely. Can't believe some of the stuff they have access to too." *How can I trust what you say? Prove it to me, Urugas.*

"It's almost unreal sometimes. Back when I was younger, they didn't have nearly as much as they do

now." *I'm one of the oldest Flammous you're going to see alive. Trust my words, Ignei.*
"Though I feel like their choreography could have been better though, look, they are a bit lazy when they do their dip there." *That doesn't change anything. I'm not saying I'll trust you, but I'll listen.*
"Yes, I see it now. They could also probably get some better matches, so they don't burn through them so fast, but otherwise a good performance." *Good, that's all I need. That elite team they are sending in. They're wizards. A whole group of them.*
"Yeah, I wonder if they teach. But I'm also curious on how they get some parts so perfect. It's almost inhumane, you know." *Wizards? That's impossible. They died out ages ago. Any word you hear of them is a rumour, and that's it.*
"It is sometimes. But then you see those little mishaps we saw earlier and then it all makes sense, doesn't it? But I suppose we should probably just watch and not talk though, to get the whole experience. Not that you should have any problem with that." *I don't care if you believe me or not. There's a reason that the team is classified. And that is why, whether you believe me or not. Wizards exist today and are working with us right now. That is the truth.*
"Yes, we should. Thanks for reminding me!" *I still don't trust you. At least I don't think I do.*
And the conversation was left at that, our gaze now finally returned to the dance that was already almost over. Wizards? What kind of idiot does he take me for? They just disappeared. They don't exist. No one even knows if they did in the first place. I shook my head. *No, Lexi. Don't let a crazy old man's words invade your thoughts. He probably misheard it anyway. The elite group probably just calls themselves that.* I sighed,

before returning my attention back to the performance, which was seemingly almost over already. The masked performer closest to me was watching me closely, before giving me a little wave mid-dance. I was surprised. Does this one know me? I mean I guess it's not like this whole new kingdom arriving thing is a secret to them. I shrugged it off, trying to find any enjoyment in the final moments of its performance. You could tell they'd just thrown random ideas together to get the finished product. Considering I'd only told the King and Queen that lie about fire breathing yesterday, I'm guessing they had very little time to prepare. I could see Lila and her brother on the other side of the performance, watching it closely as if they were actually interested. *I didn't know they were such good liars.* I watched the Royal family with a realisation dawning on me. This would be their last afternoon, their last taste of sunshine. Yet they waste it on this ludicrous performance. Now that I think about it, since the Council are sending in an elite team at the ball, wouldn't that just make me a cover for their own team? I frowned. This promise of getting the glory of eliminating one of Sorvia's greatest enemies, would it actually come true? Or would I be lucky enough to get just one swift strike at a singular target? The very least that would do is inflict a little bit of pain.

I gritted my teeth. *How could I not have not noticed this before? Am I really a pawn in their game? Are they even going to help me escape? No, of course they will. I'm a loyal assassin of the Council. Plus, I'm the only known surviving Ignei.* Even if they don't mean for me to have this mission, surely when they are more certain of my skills, they'll allow me to finish the job? 'Trust the Council'. 'The Council is always right'. That's the saying. So, who am I kidding? Brain probably has some genius plan cooked up, one that will shatter Unity even more. One that I'm a part of. The dance ended with the performers shooting flames into the sky, letting the audience watch in awe as they exploded into fireworks. It was followed by a large cheer from the crowd, clapping, whistling, chanting, as if they were really engaged by that pointless performance. The Arcarlian Royalty also clapped to which I quickly realised how close I actually was to them. The gap between us was barely a metre distance. Yet as I surveyed the group, they didn't seem the slightest bit interested in it. At least they didn't come across that way. *They're probably thinking of all the better things they could be doing.*

Once the crowd died down, the King proceeded to speak again. "A lovely performance created by some of White Castle's most creative minds! We give this display as a gift to Moralvelle, something to represent our newfound understanding of each other." He clasped his hands together before taking a deep breath. The King clearly couldn't care less. The Queen being the same. *A corrupt couple.* "Now, for our final part in our parade for this year. Speeches! As many of you know, we always end our parades with a thank you to all of our assisting kingdoms, which has now gone from two, to three! Today we welcome and celebrate Moralvelle's new arrival into the Alliance of Unity. We also celebrate Lady Lexi's commitment as ruler of Moralvelle. Just only two years ago, the original King and Queen of Moralvelle were killed in a horrific accident." The crowd gasped at that, eyes sneaking each other glances I couldn't decode. It's either they are putting on a show or genuinely sorry. I can't decide. "So, for her third year as ruler, we present Lady Lexi to the stage! A young, mature ruler who wishes to take her kingdom to the next stage in the new world!"

The crowd erupted into cheers, finally realising who this 'Lady Lexi' was. As all eyes turned to me, the Sorvian group ushered me forward. I felt like staying there, still as a statue. I hadn't prepared for this. There wasn't a single part of it that required me to think of a speech. So, I need to think of as many topics as I can to cover, use the information I already have and turn it into something else people will believe, all while still presenting the information I have told others as well. And people wonder why there is such a shortage of assassins in Sorvia. I gulped, I was truly nervous as I approached the stage. *Did I mention I don't particularly like crowds?* Each step felt like a hundred new pairs of eyes were on me, which they probably were. A single mishap in this could result in my immediate imprisonment and execution. I forced a smile onto my face regardless of the consequences. I stepped out onto the stage, prepared for anything. *Well, maybe not everything but- Shut. Up. This isn't the stuff you want to be thinking right now. Present the information in your head, then put it into words.*

I walked past Lila, who gave me a big cheesy grin and a thumbs up. Jackiel simply gave me a slight nod. That's the thing I like about him. He doesn't mind if he shows that he doesn't care about something. Like how he couldn't care less about how this will turn out. *I definitely prefer him over his sister.* I nodded at them both. The King and Queen then invited me onto the stage. The Queen then whispered into my ear as I got close enough; "They'll want a speech. Tell them about your kingdom's hardships and how you overcame them. And tell them how proud you feel to be here." Her breath so close to my face made my blood run cold. I nodded slowly, putting my focus on the crowd in front of me, which seemed to have grown bigger in the last few seconds. I cleared my throat, making sure I had all the dot points in my head before I began to speak.

-Anasia Edwards-

CHAPTER 14:
LEXI

"I failed, didn't I?"
I groaned, standing in the dressing room I had been assigned to after the speech. The two Sorvian fashion experts were with me, whose names I had personally assigned to them. One and Two. One had blonde hair and green eyes, which was unique for a Sorvian. And Two had the stereotypical dark brown hair and boring brown eyes. Both winced at my words.
"No, no, no! If I was in that crowd, I would've thought you were legit for sure!" Said Two, as she flocked through dress designs she had sketched up. Turns out she didn't like the dress designs she bought with her, so she and One were going to change it. Not that I really cared.
"Don't lie to me. I stuttered twice. It would've been good if I wanted them to think I was some heartbroken teen who was still holding onto their parents' memories. But no. I turned out looking like an idiot." I buried my face in my hands, mentally slapping myself for not thinking that they would make me say a speech sooner. "People like me don't mess up. And that group you two came with?

Probably going to blab to some high-up about me messing up." I groaned. "I can say goodbye to being an Assassin, that's for sure. Maybe even my life if they get too suspicious."

Two groaned at my response. "Do you not hear yourself Lexi? Do you not hear how stupid you sound? Your problem can easily be fixed! Don't you see?" Two stopped double checking my measurements to look me dead in the eyes. "You have seemed all bubbly but business-like the whole way through in their eyes, right?" I nodded, suddenly seeing where this was going. "So why don't you just-"

"-Act as if I was just holding it together? Get the sympathy of all the higher ups?" I cut in, scolding myself for not thinking of it immediately.

Two laughed, circling multiples things in her book before showing it to One. "Yep, at least that's what I was thinking. Now come on, it'll only take us a good five minutes to add these extra stitches to your dress so get ready for us, okay?"

I nodded. "Just checking, it does have hidden pockets, correct? Because I'll need those for the finale in just an hour." I said, wondering about where I'll be able to store my weapons without having one of my bags checked and my weapons discovered. *They might be more cautious during the ball.*

Both of them nodded again, before swiftly leaving the changing room to a different one. It left me wondering about things. The walls and ceiling of these rooms were beyond modern art. Each wall was made of stylised marble with stunning gold patterns. Paintings adorned each and every wall of some old and important man or woman or a notable moment in history. Where I was standing in the centre, was a large pedestal. It was made of smooth concrete and was clearly designed so stylists didn't need to bend down to attend to the lower parts of someone's attire. There are mirrors almost everywhere. It was essentially impossible to not see your reflection at least once in this room. The ceiling had a massive chandelier hanging by a very thin yet strong thread. The light reflected in and out of each of the crystals, making a beautiful display. My thoughts took me back to that speech. I tried to remember people's reactions, hoping that might help future decisions. Yet no, I was too focused on not messing up that I had completely forgotten about that. I just had to go in with the same attitude as that speech then.

One and Two arrived back less than five minutes later, even quicker than their original time. They had bright smiles on their faces, which I hoped meant they had done a good job on at least hiding the pockets. I couldn't fully trust their skills after all. I didn't even know their real names. They walked up to me, handing me a dull red dress and walked off, closing the door behind them. I took the hint and began to change into the dress, marvelling at how well it fit. The dress was made out of a similar fabric to some of my armour, so it could withstand some damage to it. The fabric was strong while disguised as something delicate and weak. How fitting. The colour was a dull, maroon shade of red to ensure any bloodstains wouldn't stand out indefinitely. It had the appearance of a tight dress around the body but oversized and flowy around the arms. After a quick glance in the mirror, I confirmed that it surprisingly turned out well.

"Finished." I called out.

One and Two re-entered the room, clearly anticipating the big reveal. I could see with the way their faces lit up that they thought they had done well. Even I had to admit they had. *Phew. I was worried I couldn't rely on them for a while*. One had her hands behind her back and brought them out in front of her to reveal a white pair of heels. I groaned at the sight of them. "You couldn't have done something else with boots maybe? Heels won't do me any good, you know." Two shrugged.

"They aren't just any heels. They've been made especially for you. Disguised as heels, there's a button in each of its sides that transitions it into somewhat of a, well, a boot for easier mobility."

"Ah. Smart." I nodded, deciding not to ask how something like that even exists. *The Council must be putting a lot into this mission.* "Where are the pockets?" One handed Two the heels and walked up to me. "Well, there should be five pockets in total. One here-"She poked under one of the layers of frill in one of my arms. I flinched instinctively away at her touch. "Oh. Right." She blushed, then continued to list off the rest of the locations with no physical connection. "Uh, the others are here, here, here, and there." She finished pointing to all the separate places, which I had to admit were expertly hidden. Despite the fact that I had barely been able to resist the urge to snap her wrist in two after poking me.

I nodded in approval at her. This will come in handy for sure. Two then handed over the heels, to which I reluctantly put on. Once it had slid onto both feet, I tried to stand up. I'd never had a problem with balance, but now I certainly did. "Woah!" I tilted to the side almost immediately, staggering on the platform. Two let out a yelp and threw her arms out to catch me before I fell. I glared at her, to which she snorted in response, as if humoured by my reaction. *I can do this on my own. Just give me a second, that's all I need to work out how these ludicrous heels work. How women walk around in these is beyond me. Actually, here's a better question. Why even wear them? They must have some sort of intensive training before wearing them.* I shook her off, attempting to retain my balance again. The heels they had given me were extremely high, a good estimated eight centimetres. I mean, I'm pretty sure they're high.

"How do they feel?" Asked One, her green eyes completely focused on my new heels. "I'm pretty sure you'll need some practise in them, but I'm sure you'll get it in time. You're Lexi Ignei after all." She said with a hopeful sigh, her eyes returning to me. "Should we get started on ball customs? We only have fifty minutes until the ball starts, and you'll need to be ready to go ten minutes before."

"Ball customs? Come on." I groaned, adjusting my flowy sleeves. "It shouldn't be that hard to act decently at a ball. How hard could it be?"

Two burst out into laughter, tilting her head back as she did so. "Lexi, you're a child of war. Okay? War. Not a child of frilly pink dresses. Or fashion. Or anything even related to a ball. You wouldn't know the first thing."

I straightened my back, visibly offended. Of course, I know something about balls. Even back in Sorvia where we have nothing of the sort, the books tell us everything we'd want to know about them. Important people dress up, dance, and listen to awful music. That basically concludes it. I didn't bother to hide my annoyance. "Of course, I know something about them. We both had the same upbringing, did we not? How would you know any more than me?"

"Well, to start it off I wasn't put through extensive training and forced to become number one. Plus, before this mission we were required to do research about previous White Castle and Arcarlian crossover balls to come up with designs for your dress. So yes, I do know quite a large amount about it. You, on the other hand have just gotten your information from either your head, or some fairytale book. Am I correct?"

My face went bright red.

My thoughts went back to snapping someone's wrist in half all of a sudden.

"I, uh-"

"And our valiant assassin is lost for words. Again. Honestly, I really hoped you had done your research." She crossed her arms. "So much for the Council's pride and joy, huh?"

I clenched my fists, knowing very well that attacking another member of the same side for personal reasons was against the Law. *Oh, but she's making it ever so tempting.* I sighed, then relaxed. But I suppose I do need her and One's intellect in the whole situation. These people might do it differently from the books I've read. I grimaced and swallowed my pride. "Please, tell me. What are the ball customs? I'll need this information, since I currently do not have it." I said through gritted teeth.

One smiled, glad to see that I'd come around. Two just smirked at her victory. A short-lived one, but I suppose that was worth something to her. "Glad to hear it. How about let's start by walking down from that pedestal in heels, huh?"

"Easy enough." *No, not easy enough.*

I put on a smile and staggered forward. My legs crossed each other awkwardly, and each step downwards felt like a torturous device pulling my ankle apart, but I'd made it down without falling flat on my face. It's the small things that count.

"Would you look at that? The same smiling mask hides the pain every woman bears. Beautiful work, Lexi. I knew you'd be a fast learner." Two said, clasping her hands together. "Now, for some simple etiquette for you. Rule number one at a ball, a Lady such as yourself should never be without a partner during the ball. In other words, you need to find a distinguished gentleman who can pretend to be your partner for the ball." She said, in her poshest voice possible. She's really playing the part, but she still needs to take this seriously. This is a life-or-death mission. I paused, suddenly realising what she just said. I need a partner for this? Who am I going to get in such short notice? Who would even want to take that role?

"Oh, but that should be the least of your worries! We can just set you up to be with, uh, oh! I know! We'll get Adrian to be your partner!" One exclaimed, eyes lighting up. "It'll be handy too; you'll be able to pass information to each other without worrying about the other finding out about tonight's plan."

"Yes, yes, yes. We'll get Adrian a fancy little suit, but I got to move on to the next thing. Next, you'll need proper manners. And when I say that I mean if you breathe incorrectly you will have to apologise. I'm not kidding. The balls are a way of the other Royals testing to see if you fit in with them. Until the elite team crashes the party at exactly ten o'clock tonight, you'll have to try your hardest to fit in. They'll all be looking to see your weakest areas. Think of it as the trials, except you actually have to be overly polite to win." She grinned for the next part. "Now, how about we test it? I'll ask you a question, and I want you to answer how you would to the Queen of White Castle, okay?"

I nodded bluntly. This should be easy enough, right?

"Okay, then." She cleared her throat. "Oh, hello Lady Lexi! What a wonderful pleasure it is to be in your acquaintance. I just have a small request for you. Would you mind answering this question of mine?" I nodded again. Two's face fell. "No. That is not what you are meant to do. What kind of Royal is so high up like they think you are just nods? Give me a full answer. Try again."

She tried again.

"Okay, now try being less passive aggressive towards me and more polite."

And again.

"I feel like you didn't hear what I just said before."

Again.

"That is... not the answer I was expecting."

I hate this.
"Try again, this time put more authority in your face. You got the right words, just the wrong voice. It's intimidating."

Fine.
"Okay. Well now you just sound like some old geezer King on his deathbed saying his dying wishes. Try again."

Two held her hands out in defeat after ten more failed attempts. "You know what? Do whatever you want, just try to avoid people. Act somewhat normal for the last three hours, will you? I give up on trying to educate the unteachable. Good luck."
One's face went into a full panic. "B-but Two! You can't give up on her now! Her mission isn't yet over, you know that!"
Two looked me dead in the face, before uttering these words. "She's confident enough to look past all this, that I can count on. Her last name is Ignei, after all. We'll see if she can live up to it then, won't we?"

-Anasia Edwards-

CHAPTER 15:
LILA

I'd finally worked up the courage to ask Christian to go with me to the ball after that parade. My heart had been brimming with excitement and anxiety in the following moments, but I'd finally done it. *And he'd said yes*! My heart had practically skipped a beat. Christian, the boy I had been idolising forever, said yes! Now here I was, standing outside the ballroom, watching couples go in while still waiting for Lexi. I could feel my palm getting sweaty in Christian's. It had been a good five minutes since the ball had started, so that made her five minutes late. Which was funny. Lexi didn't seem like the kind of person who was late to things. In fact, she came across as the complete opposite of that. *What if she doesn't come? What if I'm left here, with no Lexi to talk to when I get too nervous to talk to Christian?* She's like my anchor, Lexi. She better be coming soon. Especially after all the trouble I went through to get my outfit done. I looked down at myself, proud of the reminder. I'd organised the tailors the moment after I got clearance to come to the ball to make the most amazing dress they'd ever created before. With a few of my own adjustments, of course. My outfit was a beautiful, pastel purple tight dress that snaked down past my knees. It was even sleeveless to give it that extra effect. The design was a two-dimensional flame shape coming out the side sticking above the base of the dress. Everything was a beautiful shade of purple, my favourite colour. Even my heels were that colour. I'd tried my best to mix a little bit of me and Lexi's personality into the dress, so she'd really notice me. Maybe we'd finally have a discussion about her powers tonight. I felt giddy just thinking about it. But of course, that all depended on if she was even coming. I was worried she'd decided to skip out on it. "So, Lila. Why aren't we going in yet?" Asked Christian, waving his hand in front of my face to get my attention. "Or are we just going to stand here all night and miss out on the fun?"

"Oh, right. Just a few more minutes. I want to make sure Lexi is definitely coming before I do anything. I've been looking forward to her first ball all day, you know." I said, keeping my eyes fixated on the pairs walking into the room. "I just really hope she isn't going to miss it."

Christian sighed, before laughing softly. "Okay, fine. We'll wait another five minutes, but then we're going inside and having some fun! I do want to show you some of the new dance moves my friends taught me for this."

I turned to face him, beaming at his face. "Thank you, Christian!" Before returning my attention back to the crowd.

Two minutes went by, with unfamiliar faces wandering into the ball with gleeful smiles on their faces. No Lexi to be found so far. Time was ticking, the doors would close eventually. *Come on, Lexi! I am totally going to scold you for being late.*

Another few minutes went by, to the point where we went over Christian's time limit. I sagged in disappointment but let him drag me into the ballroom anyway. To my amazement, it was even more grand than last time. Instead of two banners, three banners hung at the end of the room, symbolising each kingdom under the name of Unity. There were ice sculptures of mythical animals and people, and diamond statues to be seen in each corner. The once bland roof was now covered in many colours ranging from every one of the rainbow, they were reflecting off a chandelier with multi-coloured paper stuck onto each of its lights to give off the effect. There were tables filled with luxurious desserts and drinks for the guests. There was also a massive space in the middle for dancing, with a whole orchestra located at the back of the room. I was about to walk over to the food table when someone tapped on my shoulder, to which I spun around and saw none other than Lexi with a boy I didn't recognise. My entire face lit up when I saw her.

"Lexi! I thought you weren't coming at one point, why were you so late? I was worried!" I said, all at once.

"Oh, uh," she tilted her head, as if trying to remember something. "We were unfortunately busy trying to get Aidan's suit here tailored faster. His original one accidentally got a stain in it, so we had to get a new one."

The boy next to her -who I assume is named Aidan- nodded slowly. "Y-yes. I mean right. Still don't remember where that stain came from, huh." He stuttered. *He probably isn't used to talking to people that much.* I looked the two of them up and down. Aidan and Lexi. What an interesting pair. I heard Christian gasp from next to me.

"Wait a minute, I recognise you guys from the parade! You're that guy who could do those amazing fire tricks while standing on a small platform." He pointed at Aidan. "And you're, well, you're Lady Lexi. Ruler of Moralvelle." He then pointed to Lexi, and hurriedly bowed. He then arched his brow at me, before whispering into my ear. "I didn't realise when you said 'Lexi', you meant this Lexi. That's crazy how noble your friendship circle is."

I blushed, before nodding. How did I only realise it now? Lexi is technically Queen of Moralvelle. I stared at her. Well, that's a scary thought. *She's already Queen before me.* "Well, she is! I'm so proud to call her my friend!" I beamed at her. *I'm best friends with a Queen*! Christian then tilted his head at Lexi. "I'm sorry My Lady, but can I ask you a question? Why does everyone call you 'Lady Lexi', and not 'Queen Lexi'? Forgive me if I'm intruding too much, I'm just curious."

"Oh! Right." She cleared her throat, before a gentle smile spread across her face. "Well since I have yet to legally become an adult, I can't fully inherit my family's throne. So therefore, I am labelled 'Lady Lexi of Moralvelle." She said with a small laugh. *Oh, well that makes sense.* She's just so perfect. I'd strive to be on the same level as her.

"Ah, that makes sense! Thank you, Lady Lexi."

We were all quiet for a moment, not that I really noticed. I was amazed by Lexi's beautiful dress, which fit her perfectly. She looked every bit of the Lady she was. I clasped my hands together, careful not to bang my two gold rings together. "Okay, how about we give each other a proper introduction? I'm Lila Camhok, Princess and heir to the throne of White Castle. This is my partner," I gestured to where Christian stood beside me. "Christian Dale, a very loyal soldier-in-training. He's one of the best there is!" I watched Lexi take her eyes off me and onto Christian. *She isn't thinking about taking Christian for herself, is she? No! Of course not. Why would she? We're friends after all.* "Now, you guys?"

"Oh! Right." She cast Adrian a sideways glance, one with a certain amount of intensity I couldn't piece together. "Well, as you already know," she said with a shy laugh. "I'm Lexi Wellfire, Lady of Moralvelle and soon-to-be Ally of Unity. And here is my partner." She gestured towards Adrian, mouthing words to him I couldn't quite hear.

"Right! I am Adrian Blaughwater, uh, Duke of..." He looked to Lexi for hope. She just stared at him in disbelief. I looked between the two of them, confused.

Does he- does he really not know where he lives? I looked over at Christian, who was staring at Adrian suspiciously. He must think Adrian is lying about him being a Duke to be with Lexi. Now that I think about it, he might be onto something. Who forgets where they were born? My eyes widened in shock. If I don't do something about it, Lexi might be falling into a trap! My head swerved around, looking for something I could distract Adrian with. I need to talk to Lexi and tell her Adrian seems like bad news! "I'm so sorry about that!" Adrian squeaked. "I'm uh, really bad around people you see. I-" He looked back to Lexi, desperately wanting help.

"Don't worry! This is your first ball here at White Castle, there are way more people here than your average ball back home. It's totally fine!" I waved it off, smiling. I still don't trust him. As if he gets nervous around people, he's meant to be a Duke! He'd have to talk to countless people all the time, I don't buy it. "But I do have a question for you though, Duke Baughwater. What region of Moralvelle do you come from-"

"Lila! There you are! Can you come with me?" I turned around to see Jackiel's warm face staring at me intently.

"Oh, hi Jackiel! I would love to, but I'm just talking to Lexi and Adrian right now, maybe another time?"

I could see him tense slightly at my words. He looked almost… worried? Worried myself now, I leaned closer to whisper into his ear. "I'm sorry, is there something going on? Do you need my help?"
"Lila, you should probably go with your brother. I need to talk with your Mother and Father and King Stafran, please, have fun. I hope we can talk again tonight." Lexi smiled, and bowed towards me, before walking away while tugging Adrian along like a dog on a leash without even giving me a chance to say goodbye.
Christian then turned to me next. "Is it okay if I go too? I want to meet up with some of my friends. But don't worry, I'll definitely come back for the dance. Bye!" He too walked away before I could say goodbye back.
I turned back to Jackiel, exasperated. "Well, I suppose there's no excuses now. Please, take me." Jackiel smiled at that, before grabbing my hand and leading me to a small table in the corner of the room. It was nothing fancy, just one of the spare tables that they had decided to set out just in case. He pulled the chair out for me, motioning for me to sit down. I did. He then sat opposite me in the other chair. I wasn't entirely sure why I was just picking up these details. Maybe it was because I was so anxious about what he might be about to say? I got into a more comfortable position, before looking at him. He didn't look at me, instead he looked around, checking to see if anyone was close enough. They weren't. He stretched his arms out, before returning his gaze onto me. "Alright then." His smile slowly dissipated. "Do you remember what I told you last night? About, well, everything?"
"Uh, yes. What is it? Are you okay?"
He nodded at that, completely ignoring my question. "Good, now for another question. Do you trust me? Completely? With all your heart?" His questions began to make me feel uneasy, similar to last night.

"Jackiel, what is this about? You're my brother. Of course I trust you."

"Okay then. Since you trust me, I first want you to listen to everything I have to say. No interruptions. Your interruptions aren't going to change the future. And," he paused, looking down to check his watch. "I have five minutes to do so. Lovely."

"Um, okay?"

"Uh uh. That counts as an interruption." He smiled darkly. I nodded slowly. What is he thinking right now?

"In about five minutes, I am going to take you with me, and we will exit the ballroom before it explodes."

He said simply, as if it was a matter of fact. *Explode?* I stared at him, suddenly questioning my own big brother's sanity. "Good. You didn't interrupt, I thought you would. Anyway, Mother and Father and everyone else in this room is going to die. That is a fact." I tried to get up from the table and leave, wanting none of his nonsense. He appeared beside me in seconds, pushing me back down. "Since you're my little sister, I'm going to let you live, of course. But I doubt you wouldn't let me just save you though. To settle it, I'll let you pick someone in this room right now. One person. That is all. They will also get to live." He paused for a moment. "You can speak now."

"What the hell are you talking about-"

"Pick a person before I change my mind." His voice was so cold it sent shivers down my spine. "Look around, who do you want to let live? I'll give you a hint of who not to pick, though. That guy you brought with you. Christian? Look over there." He pointed to the far side of the ballroom, where I saw Christian talking to a number of girls. I covered my mouth with my hand. *But I thought he was going to his friends from training?* "As your big brother, I'll make sure if he somehow survives the explosion he won't

survive the aftermath. Now come on, Lila. Pick wisely. It could be a servant if you want."
It suddenly dawned on me. For the love of Tien, he's actually serious. My eyes widened in terror. My own brother is a terrorist. A traitor. And he's going to kill everyone. "I, uh, uh." I frantically glanced around the room. He's going to kill Mum and Dad, so he won't let me pick them. He wants the crown for himself. And he's going to commit a heinous crime to do it. My eyes finally found Lexi. "L-Lexi. Right there. Lexi Wellfire." I pointed in her direction. He laughed at my choice.
"Well, I suppose that would've been your choice anyway. But do you want me to tell you something, Lila?" *Oh no. Is she on his kill list*? I swallowed back a scream. "Lexi Wellfire, doesn't exist." He cackled softly to himself.
It felt like all time just stopped. "What do you mean, she doesn't exist?"
He patted my head with a woeful look on his face. "Well, I hate to be the one to tell you, but Moralvelle doesn't exist either." Another bombshell. Dropped right in my face. "But I'll tell you a place that does exist. Sorvia. Your 'friend' Lexi? She's a Sorvian spy. Better yet, she's an assassin who was sent to kill us. She only pretended to be your friend. She wanted to get close to us, kill us. I had intercepted a call between her and her Masters using a special device of mine. When you guys went to that training session? I snuck into her room and planted a listening device. They planned to get rid of us tonight. Don't you see?" He raised his voice a little, agitating himself. "The world is against us. There is no such thing as friends. Don't get me started on family. Just because you have a blood tie doesn't mean you have a bond. I mean," he stopped himself. "We have a bond. Yet our parents don't. They're selfish, controlling, power-hungry. We can't trust anyone. Don't you get that?"

I stared forward. He was lying. He had to be lying. Lexi is my friend. The only one I can relate to. I can't do that with Princess Jassai, what is there to relate to? She's our generation's goddess. A girl with powers. I'm just- I'm just-
Tears slid down my cheeks silently.
I have no one to trust.
I'm just a teenage girl who got lucky, that's all. Jackiel sighed. "Yeah, I guess that was a lot. I didn't mean to make you cry, though. At least we have each other, right?" I nodded quietly. I didn't see what his reaction was. I couldn't look at him. "Now then, back to who you're going to pick. Do you have an answer?" I paused, thinking. I don't want Jackiel to kill anyone. I want to save everyone. I don't care if Lexi wants me dead. She gave me something I'd never had before. Something that felt like a real friendship. The tears stopped rolling down my cheeks. I don't want to save everyone. I *need* to save everyone. I turned to look at Jackiel, who was waiting patiently. Jackiel lost his mind. He's going to try to kill everyone and I'm the only one who can stop it. All for some stupid crown. He won't say it out loud, but judging from what he told me last night, he wants to rule the world. This is just step one. I straightened my back, feeling more confident. He said it himself. He doesn't want to kill me. So, if I refuse to leave, maybe he'll give the people more time to get out of here. But how can I tell them without alerting him? An idea crossed my mind. I looked back to where Lexi was. If she was really from Sorvia and she had Sorvians here ready to kill me when the time came, wouldn't that mean she knows sign language? I recalled a conversation we had back at Mr Draxis's training session. The one where we were talking about the war. *Is that why she asked me those questions? Because she wanted information? Was everything really a lie?* I widened my eyes in surprise.

It would only make sense, considering all the rumours I'd heard about them communicating in sign language. I just needed her to look at me, then I could sign it. Who knew my classes could actually come in handy? An announcement was delivered then.

"Hello distinguished Ladies and Gentlemen, I would like to welcome you all to our Twentieth Unity ball!" A cheer went up in the crowd, and all the attention in the room went to the speaker.

And by some act of the Celestials themselves, the speaker happened to be right next to my table. I could feel my heartrate accelerating. Everyone's eyes were to the speaker who was standing just a metre away from me, so wouldn't that mean I would get noticed? I saw Lexi, who's eyes were drifting past the man and to my table. I gave her a small wave, hands rushing to make the word. I put my hands into fists, placing them on top of each other, then imitated an explosion. Bomb is what it meant. Her eyes widened, clearly surprised that I knew sign language. *Does that mean Jackiel was telling the truth?* Then I could see her mouth drop open in fear as she realised what it meant. I saw her mouth some words and excused herself from my parents and Adrian. I could only hope that she was getting back-up. After all, it was either that or everyone in this room would die. I didn't care if she was from an enemy kingdom. She values her own life as well, and me just signing 'bomb' doesn't give her too much information, so she won't just leave with Adrian. At least, I don't think she will.

Moments later, I heard Jackiel's voice again. "Oh? Hey Lexi. What are you doing over here?" I could hear his voice laced with delicate venom to it.

"Me? I was just wondering if I could talk to Lila for a moment, is that okay?"

I turned my head to see Lexi standing there, and Jackiel looking uneasy by her question. *She was so fast!* The five minutes is getting close to being up, and I wonder if he's realised that yet. He probably has, Jackiel's a child genius. I mentally prayed that Lexi would take me away from him, assassin or not. If I left Jackiel, he'd be forced to either let Lexi live or postpone the explosion. *Come on Lexi, please. I don't want the people I care about to die.*

"Ah, do you think I could keep her for just a few more minutes?" Jackiel asked, with a happy smile on his face. "I just need to finish talking to her if you don't mind."

I looked at Lexi with a pleading look on my face. *Please Lexi, take me away from him. If you managed to convince a whole kingdom you were a completely different person in a matter of days, surely you can do this, right?* She looked at Jackiel with a determined expression. I exhaled a breath of relief. She wasn't going to give up.

"True, but you can always continue your conversation later, can't you?" Lexi said sternly, giving up her charade. She snatched my arm and yanked me up and away from Jackiel. She wasn't going to take no for an answer, nor was she going to wait for Jackiel. "You can talk to her after this, okay?"

I looked back at Jackiel, who was looking at me expectantly. He thinks I'll break away from her since I know the truth. Little does he know I'd rather follow an assassin to my death than lead everyone else here to their own. I turned to face forward, ignoring Jackiel. I could only imagine his face. Fear flooded through me, was he going to kill me now? I shook my head. No, he isn't. I mean, he shouldn't. There's no real point in killing me if he's so determined that I'll join him. And with that, Lexi led me through the crowd and exited through the door, pulling me behind her while quickening her pace.

I could only imagine Jackiel's face.

Once we were out, I sighed, relieved. "Lexi, you have no idea how glad I am that-"

"What in the name of Tien is 'bomb' meant to mean? Huh?"

CHAPTER 16:
LEXI

"What in the name of Tien is 'bomb' meant to mean? Huh? Explain yourself." I said sternly, trying to make sense of the conversation.

There were only a few minutes until the elite squad arrived, and this was my first-time hearing of a bomb. There was zero mention of it from Adrian, One, Two, or Urugas and the others. So, this was either one of three things. One, a mishap from Lila and she was just throwing her hands around at me with no thought about what she was saying. Two, the Council had actually organised a bomb without any of our knowledge. *Which was unlikely, considering how dangerous and outright stupid that is.* Or three, there was a psychotic outsider who was trying to eliminate three kingdoms at once. Either way, I was on the verge of losing it at this girl. At least it was probably going to be my last conversation with her. Not that I would exactly miss it, certainly not if she really just signed 'bomb' at me for no apparent reason. In fact, I might end up disposing of her right here and now. *They'll all die in a couple more minutes anyway.* My hand rested on one of my secret pockets, already ready to swing a dagger out and end the Princess in front of me.

"I- I'm sorry! But Lexi, you have to understand, this is serious!" She narrowed her eyes at me, trying to look like the bigger person when she knew she wasn't. "I know everything, okay? I mean, not everything. I still don't know what your real name is, but that isn't important right now. What's important is that everyone in that room is going to die in like, three minutes!" She said, almost out of breath. She looked terrified. *Wait, she knows that? I didn't think the Council was going to issue an all-out kill order.* My hand faltered away from the pocket. *What exactly does she know?*

"What do you mean you don't know what my real name is? It's Lexi Wellfire, don't you know that?" I chose my words carefully; in case she was bluffing. However, her face never changed.

"I know you were sent here to kill me as an assassin for Sorvia."

It felt like everything had just stopped at that moment. *How long had she known?* I mean, she doesn't seem like she's bluffing now.

"And I'm guessing by your silence that Jackiel was right then, huh?" She kicked the wall, as if mad with herself. "I should've known, you were way too perfect to be royal in this day and era." She then looked me dead in the eyes. "But that doesn't matter now. Right now, I need you to tell me exactly when that team of yours is going to strike. So, you can- you can-" She stared off into the distance, as if she didn't know what to do with her words. She shook her head again. "So, they can target Jackiel, but not kill him. Just, ugh! I don't know anymore! He's the one who knew about you all this time, he is also the one with the bomb. I don't know where it is, I don't know if he can

stop it, all I know is that he wants everyone in that room dead."
"Okay then. Okay." I said, massaging my temples. "Let me get this straight. You told me this because you think I can help, right? Help you?"
Lila nodded, confident. "You're the only one with the means to stop him, aren't you?" I tried to stop myself from laughing at the insanity of what she just proposed. It didn't work. "What?" She said, crossing her arms. "You got that cool fire power, don't you? Plus, you are always glowing each time I see you."
"You're still hallucinating? Lila, I'm not glowing. And- wait. 'Cool fire power'? What would you know about that?" I was left stuttering for words. How can she possibly remember that? She had an entire bag's worth of Snooze Memory. How could she remember? It was a miracle that she wasn't in a coma, but not that much of a miracle. No, Jackiel must have told her that along with everything else. *Of course, the Prince.* I had a feeling he would be a problem at some point, just didn't expect him to blab about everything if he found out. *That's what I get for underestimating him, maybe I was right to be so suspicious of everyone in the beginning.* "I'm guessing Jackiel told you about that too, huh?" My hands lit up with flames, releasing the constant urge. Heat filled the air around us. I waved my hand around, twinkling flames between my fingertips. "So, you do realise how easily I could end my mission now, then? With just a little push, these flames could travel to the air," I thrust out my hand, the stream of fire narrowly missing her, only singing a few hairs before disappearing. "And burn you. You realise that don't you?"
Lila crossed her arms, surprisingly not threatened by me at all. However, as I rose the temperature to an almost lethal range, sweat began to trickle down her forehead. "You don't scare me. But yes, I do

realise that. So therefore, Jackiel must realise it too. If you could threaten him to deactivate the bomb, then both your comrades and the people I care about won't die."

"Comrades?" I raised an eyebrow at her. I then smiled. She thinks the team is already here, hiding amongst the servants. Maybe Jackiel thinks that too. If he knew there were only one of us in there at the moment, he probably wouldn't make this outrageous demand. Still, I decided to test the waters. "How many do you think there are of us? Because to tell you the truth, I only know a certain number. So please, elaborate."

Lila paused, uncertain. She was scanning my face for clues, not that I was planning on giving any away. Unless she gave me a real reason to work with her, then I wouldn't bother. Even if Adrian gets caught in the crossfire, the only reason he was placed eleventh was because of his strength. Not his bravery. Probably why they sent him, not much of a loss if he dies. Even if he is a Flammous. "I... don't know for certain. But please, Lexi. I know you're only doing this because you've been ordered to. I get that it would probably be better for you and Sorvia if these people die but think about it. You're going to be letting innocent people die."

I frowned. Sure, some of them are innocent. That's not my fault anyway if they die. It's her own psychotic brother's fault. "You know, so far, you're just listing off stuff that profits you. What about me? Would any of this benefit me enough?"

Lila looked me dead in the eyes. "I can get you some important information, Lexi. Information about battle plans, future renovations, classified documents, whatever you want from me. But only if the people in that room live." She crossed her arms. "There you go, now we both can profit from this."

"Wait, really?" *Is this girl serious? She's just going to give away information?* If she does this, her parents could just die later on, but I guess all she wants is for them to live a little longer. I groaned, tilting my head up to face the ceiling. I guess she has a point. "Fine. But if I get the smallest hint that you're going to be unfaithful to that, you can guess who's about to become a human barbecue."

She saluted me. *Man is she childish.* "Thank you Lexi! But I have a question for you. If we're doing this-"

"Are you really adding more conditions to this already fragile, temporary truce?"

"No! I'm just asking for your real name. I'll need it so when I get you the documents I can get the name right." She's a really bad liar. She won't need my name for that, everyone knows me by my first name anyway. Not that it'll put me at a large disadvantage, my surname is fairly famous regardless. Might even teach her a bit of respect.

I snorted at her. "My name? Eh, fine."

"Oh? I thought you were going to point blank refuse that, and I'd need to spend the rest of these people's lives trying to get it out of you."

"You were honestly going to sacrifice their lives for my name? You know what? Never mind. My name is Lexi, Lexi Ignei."

"I-Ignei?" Her jaw dropped, before muttering to herself. "I knew it."

I smiled at her. "Don't wear it out."

"And this, Lila, this is why I find it better to just not trust people at all."

My head whirled around to see Jackiel peeking through the door, before pushing it all the way open. He had a monstrous grin on his face. You know what? Even if I didn't make that deal with Lila, I probably would've found a way to 'accidentally' kill this guy. He looks insane. *Why bother waiting for the team to show up? Technically I could just kill them both here*. Jackiel's clothes and hair were normal, as they usually were each time I'd seen him. But his face, his face was possibly one of the most unsettling things I'd seen. The moment I'd seen his smile, the way his eyes curled upwards, I knew something was up. It was almost like he'd lost his humanity. But for what? And how? I could practically feel Lila shaking behind me. He looked completely different to how he was when I'd grabbed Lila. There was no mistaking it. He wasn't the same person, at least not anymore. *What an impressive front he put up. But what exactly happened to him?*

"If I was still pretending, I would've said you haven't got that much sleep to be nice. Now, I feel it's okay to say that you look like the kind of guy who would actually kill a room full of people." I snapped, my voice cold. "You're a pretty bad role model for your little sister, you know. And coming from an opposing kingdom, well you're not exactly representing White Castle that well either, are you?"

Jackiel ignored me, his focus reigning on Lila. "Did I hear that right before? You were going to give her, an outsider, a *Sorvian*, the keys to our glorious kingdom?" I could practically hear Lila's teeth chattering behind me.

"Jackiel! Come on! Snap out of it, I don't know what's come over you but quit it. You're threatening over a hundred people right now. You're scaring me."

My flames rose higher as they retreated up the length of my arm so I could reach down. *If Jackiel decides to kill Lila, then that means I don't get any information, huh?* I looked over at Lila, still practically shaking in her high heels. I bent down and tapped the buttons on my heels, watching them fold into each other and turn into a more suitable footwear for combat. Plain old boots. Far better than heels. Lila was smart to make me that offer. Now she's suddenly made herself the most valuable pawn on the battlefield. I just have to get her to the Council, alive.

"Fancy trick, Sorvian."

I groaned, rolling my eyes at him. I was never really keen on being cocky before battle, but this guy was just starting to get on my nerves. "So, you're all talk but no fight then? Come on, show me what you got." Provoking him isn't a smart move, but if I manage to keep him near that doorway, he'll soon realise that he can't blow up that room without it damaging himself in the process, possibly killing him. He'll have to postpone the explosion. *It doesn't matter how weird he looks, he's still human.* "But please, call me Ignei." I raised my fists up, readying myself in a fighting stance.

He seemed surprised at my words. "So, it is true then. Well, I hate to break it to you Lexi, but I have no intention of fighting someone from your family line. I'm not stupid, I know I'll lose. Horrendously. But," he held out his wrist in front of him, his grin widening. He revealed a watch hiding underneath his sleeve. *Isn't that the same watch he was wearing in that carriage? Here I thought Royals wore things a day before throwing them out.* "There is about two minutes left, now. Till that bomb explodes, that is."

"Uh, I just got a question for you, Prince. What time is it?" If it's almost ten, then there's a higher chance I'll be able to win. However, if the elite squad comes in through those windows in the hall, then Jackiel will notice it and try to speed up the detonation quicker, trying to catch the group in the process. I'd better hope they come in through here, help me interrogate this guy and find the bomb.

He blinked, his confident facade lowering. "The time?" He looked almost suspicious, but curiousity overtook him. "Nine-fifty-nine- wait no. Ten o'clock." Now it was my turn to grin. Perfect timing, but that means we only have a few seconds to do everything.

Of course nothing goes the way I want it too. The sound of shattering glass and people screaming came from inside the hall. I swung my head around, horrified.

No! Why'd they come in through there?

Jackiel's confidence returned. "Oh. So that's why you wanted to know the time. Well then, thanks for making this easier for me." I stood there, unable to move. They shouldn't have come in that way. Now, from what I have heard about them, Sorvia's greatest warriors are about to be brutally killed in an explosion. Jackiel looked down at his watch, before clicking a button on it. A small shield made up of crackling dark matter enveloped him, making it impossible to view him from the outside.

"What in the name of-?" I shouted, lost for words. No wonder this guy had seemed like he wasn't sane. I don't even think he's human if he's able to make something like that.

His voice echoed throughout the hall. "It was a good attempt, really. But I don't mind speeding things along, good luck. Oh! And by the way Lila? You made your choice."

Moments before the blast came, I exploded my fire outwards, covering both Lila and me in a fiery haze.

This better be enough, it's the only defensive move I know of. The explosion almost shattered my eardrums, to the point where I only knew Lila was screaming because I saw her mouth wide open. The ground shook, and cracks appeared beneath our feet. I still needed Lila alive, even if those people died, she could still be of use to us. I would've protected the ground we were standing on as well, but it would've been impossible without Lila's feet burning off. An unknown heat radiated from the direction of the blast. It's heat even made me flinch. The blinding white light outside of my fire barrier almost shattered it, and I let out a guttural roar as I tried to hold it together. *I should've taken more defensive classes!*

Sir Lewis should've let me take them as well as offensive! Now we're all doomed. Just as the light seemed to almost obliterate my shield, it stopped. The shaking in the ground halted, and I waited until I was sure there were no aftershocks or any more rubble before lowering the shield. I could hear Lila's sobs as she turned to where the wall that was separating us from the hall used to be.
It was impossible to see anything in the haze. The explosion had been massive, and we were lucky we weren't taken out by it. The bomb must have been planted under one of the stones in the middle to cover such a large area. I turned back to where Jackiel was in that shield of his. He was gone. I wasn't sure whether he survived the blast or not, but he was gone. The smoke began to clear, and multiple multi-coloured domes began to pop up all over the room, with seven in total. The elite team must've been made up of elementals. That's the only solution.

But, wait a minute? The smoke cleared fully, to reveal that the domes weren't made up of anything to do with elementals. I couldn't even recognise what type of magic they were using, or if it was some sort of advanced shield gadget. One by one, the shields dissipated to reveal one extremely tall individual underneath with a handful of people surrounding them. This was the same for each of them. Each of these tall people had on a blue and purple cloak that bore the symbol of Sorvia and one I could not recognise. I stared in disbelief. Who are these people? And-
"Augh!" I fell to my knees as my adrenaline faded. A blistering pain went up my arms. There were no burn marks, it was impossible for me to get burnt. Just the weight of the damage that shield had taken reflected on me, even in the slightest portion I felt significant pain.
Sobs filled the air, with people calling out uncertainly to the others. I saw a tall figure quite

literally walk on air towards me, wearing the blue and purple cloak. They tore it away to reveal a young face looking back at me. She had pale skin with faint freckles on her face and blue eyes. It was matched with blonde hair that was pulled into a tight bun. She grinned at me.

"So, she is an Ignei then, huh?" She bellowed in a deep voice that didn't quite match her appearance.

Does she not realise what just happened? What kind of maniac laughs off a situation like this? I looked around. There wasn't a wall or ceiling to be found within this room and the next few. The explosion had gone as far as putting a massive hole in the castle, cold air breezing through the ten-metre hole that led to outside. "I mean, for a young Flammous to pull off a shield like that against that severe of a bomb, well, it's meant to be impossible. But you Ignei's really do impress the world, don't you?" She grinned, before holding out her hand to me. "I'm Ophelia. It means 'Useful' and 'Wise', at least that's what my parents used to tell me. I am from the Resistance. A group of supernatural beings who joined forces with Krinia and Sorvia to help the world from corruption! I'm pretty high up in rankings too by the way. You, on the other hand, need no introduction! I'm surprised you're still alive considering everything that's happening outside! I'm actually impressed we got here on time before that explosion went off."

I heard the King of Arcarlia speak then. "Outside? What's happening outside? As the King of Arcarlia I demand you tell me what you are! And where are- "

"The King and Queen of White Castle are dead. We did not protect them from the blast in time." Announced one of the other tall people.

A gasp came from the crowd. Some started crying and sobbing.

"Why did this happen to us?"

"Who did this?"

"My friends…"

Ophelia raised her hands up, trying to calm everyone down. "Now, now everybody. Less questions. You should be grateful you're alive anyway. We would've let you all die if it weren't for the fact that some of you are technically innocent in this situation. Members of the Resistance like us don't just kill those who aren't targets. You should be grateful actually."

"Innocent? Grateful?" Shouted King Stafran. "Didn't you just announce that you are allied with Sorvia and Krinia? That makes you the enemy, doesn't it?"

I was surprised to see the King alive, and his two children. Both of them hid behind him, using their Father as a shield.

"Oh! I'm sorry. I guess I can just kill you now and take back our thoughtfulness." She said with the plainest smile on her face. The crowd gasped at her words. Most tried to shuffle away from her, only to trip of pieces of rubble. "Anyways, is that really how you want to be talking to a room full of wizards?"

"Wizards?"

"This is the end of humanity's reign, isn't it?"

"They've come to rewrite our sins!"

"Wizards? So Urugas was right then. You guys really do exist." I breathed, staring at them in wonder. *But they could still be lying. But how else do I explain that magic they pulled off earlier?* "How are you so tall?"

"Ah!" Ophelia clasped her hands together, clearly about to go into a long-winded story before one of the other wizards stopped her.

"Ophelia." Hissed one of them to her. "Don't go spilling our secrets to untrustworthy ears."

"Right! Of course, Dran!" Ophelia beamed. She then leant down and whispered in my ear; "We're so tall because we stop growing at around seventy-five years of age! Then after that, we live till we're about five hundred years old. Ah." She sighed blissfully. "I've seen humanity change so much! And I'm only ninety-seven!" She giggled. "That's why I look so young compared to the others!"

They live till they're five hundred? Since they seem to stop growing at around seventy-five, that means that they barely grow every year. But almost a hundred years being young?

One of the members in the crowd raised their hand. I recognised them to be that speaker from before who was introducing us to the ball. I remember that distinctively because that's when Lila signed to me about the bomb. "I have two questions, for you, um wizards." He stuttered. "How many people couldn't you save before the bomb went off? And adding to that, why are you here? You better answer truthfully, otherwise I'll, uh." He looked frantically around for guards. *Idiot, why would they keep them alive of all people*? "I'll find some guards!"

Dran stepped in for that question while the others remained silent, completely ignoring his baseless threat. "We only had seconds before that bomb went off, but excluding the King and Queen of this kingdom, about an estimated amount of twenty-five. And for the reason we are here, well- "He looked at me when he said this. "I suppose our mission is already finished. So, we saw no point in letting too many others die as well. At least, not the ones who didn't clash with future missions." He said emotionlessly. He looks the oldest. Probably went through the most war out of all of them. The crowd went silent at that, glancing around the room to see who was missing. It was only then that I remembered Lila was still alive. And that was when she grabbed my arm and whispered quietly.

"Mother and Father didn't make it." Quiet tears slid down her cheeks. "Now everything is up to me. I don't want it to be." Her eyes welled up more, tears streaming down faster and faster. "I don't see

Christian anywhere, either. Or your companion, Adrian."

I blinked; she was right. Adrian was out of my line of sight. *Her parents are gone. Brother is definitely not sane anymore. She's the last one.* I sighed. We'd planned to eliminate her family at the same time to reduce the amount of guilt we'd be feeling ourselves. It would be inhumane to do it one at a time. But no. No one chooses how they die. I put my fist against my chest, commemorating the fallen soldier. I hadn't expected Adrian to die, I wasn't entirely sure if he had anyway. He could just be hiding with those two groups at the back of the room, not daring to leave the other members. I saluted him anyway. *I'll find out if he actually made it later.* For now, I never answered Lila.

The speaker from before spoke again. "Okay. But what did that girl there, uh, Ophelia, mean when she talked about what's happening outside?"

A new wizard spoke up this time, he looked somewhere between the ages of both Ophelia and Dran. *Or older. It feels impossible to tell.* "Take a good look out there for yourself. You have no kingdom anymore, let's face it. Before that explosion, there was over a thousand creatures attack your kingdom." He said, his tone cold. "They killed two of our group. Ferocious creatures, they are. Mutant Nats."

Everyone then suddenly turned around to face a surprisingly large hole that was blocked with smoke beforehand, and screams erupted from the crowd. I dragged Lila over there too, curious to see what was going on. I noticed each person was stepping on air instead of the fiery hot ground before us. *No doubt the work of the wizards.* Even my face went pale at the sight. White Castle's Capital, in all its glory.

All up in flames.

CHAPTER 17: LILA

My whole body was shaking. Mother and Father are dead, and now everything's up in flames. Time felt like nothing now. Not moving slow, or fast. Just, an empty void of nothingness. The wizard girl Ophelia's voice was loud, and when I opened my eyes, she was right in front of Lexi and me. "If you girls want to get out of here, I can take you with us back to the Resistance HQ, or Sorvia. Depending on new orders." She turned her attention to Lexi. "I think they'll be glad to see you back in one piece along with Adrian. The other members of your team left the moment you left for this ball. So they're safe. But we're not if we don't' get out of here quick." She then beckoned for a boy to come over, Adrian. He must've gotten in a dome before the explosion. Another Sorvian. Someone I'm meant to hate. But in this situation? I can't hate anyone but myself for my own problems. I'm not sure how Jackiel managed to do all of this, and I'm not sure how to prove it either, but I know he was behind most of this. I just know it. Whether he's a wizard or not is none of my business right now. I clenched my hold around Lexi's arm, giving it one last squeeze

before I let go. I can't keep relying on someone big and strong to help me. But now that I think about it, Ophelia is glowing even brighter than Lexi is. I shook my head. *Come on Lila! Mother and Father would want you to keep going and try to see if there's a way to escape this madness. I mean, wouldn't they?*
Adrian then shook his head at the wizard, before wandering off to join a different wizard. *Dran, I think his name was. Or was it Duran?*
I looked around one last time. People were frantically running away from the castle, or further into it. *They all want to go home.* The grand ballroom where I had spent so much time in, gone. In an instant. It was difficult to comprehend how powerful Jackiel's arsenal is. I was finding it hard to believe that a singular bomb did this. No, he must've had more. The blast radius is far too wide.
"Well? Are you just going to be standing there? We have no idea how long it will take for those creatures to get here, or Overgrown Nats as I like to call them." She added with a wink.
"How can you smile all the time? Isn't this a little bit sad for you?" I asked finally, wiping away my tears with my dusty arm. "And what's a Nat?"
"Well," she said, still smiling. "If I'm all doomy and gloomy like everyone else, how are you guys meant to feel anything other than sadness, anger, and fear? I just try to get a more positive perspective on everything, you know?" She sighed, looking around the area. "It's always so unfortunate when this happens, though. Especially when someone comes across a way for Nats to mutate. Nats are short for Natyss Omega, by the way. The technical term for them. They used to be little balls of fluff that, while it looks cute, would probably tear your face off."
"Slowly." Lexi added, still staring through to the crumbling kingdom. My kingdom. The kingdom I

was meant to rule. All gone, somehow. *Lexi doesn't even look mad.*
Jackiel must have wedged those bombs everywhere across the kingdom. It was the only explanation for how we couldn't have known about this before. They probably went off a minute or two ago, not long before ours did. I looked around at the ruins before us. The ground was steep and jagged, with pieces of what once a beautiful hall now gone. Another rumble echoed in the distance. *More explosions.*
"So, before we go, I do have something to ask you both." Ophelia said as she watched the other wizards taking small groups of influential nobles with them and leaving. I noticed they took some by force. And that they were mainly grabbing Arcarlians. *However, it looks like Princess Jassai already escaped with her family.* I guess information about White Castle isn't needed anymore. I gulped. *Does that mean my significance has dropped? Does Lexi not see a point in me staying alive anymore?* Some people stayed. A death wish. "Do you happen to know if anyone was behind this? It would be good to get a name, so we can track them down. The one in charge, I mean. There would've been hundreds of individuals involved to pull off a stunt this big." She looked right at Lexi when she said this. She thinks I'm just some bystander. Maybe it's best to keep it that way, so she doesn't try and target me. She said she was in an alliance with Sorvia, so it isn't safe for me. *Someone has to keep the Camhok family line alive.*
Lexi nodded, both of us knowing the answer. "The one who set off the bombs was their Prince, Jackiel. I witnessed it, as did she." Lexi nodded in my direction. "From what I can understand, he's lost his humanity. He wanted to kill two birds with one stone as well, eliminate the threats and his parents to earn a solid place on the throne." She then frowned, before

adding. "But I don't understand why he would annihilate his own kingdom. It's the one piece that doesn't add up."

Ophelia nodded. "The motive makes sense, but you're right. Why would he do that? Unless the person he was working with set them off without him realising." Ophelia looked around again. "I'm guessing he escaped?"

"Yes. I'm not sure when, but... prior to the explosion Jackiel had pressed some sort of button on his watch, and he, well-" Lexi was left stuttering her words. "I had not detected anything wrong about him before, but he had managed to summon an opal-shaped shield that appeared to be made of- something."

"Something?" Ophelia arched her brow.

"I'm not entirely sure, it looked like dark matter."

"Hm." Ophelia sighed. "Well, I haven't heard anything even closely related to that description before. But if you hadn't picked anything up about him beforehand, then that watch must've been gifted to him by someone. Someone with powers close to a wizard, maybe an Architect? They are the only ones who can make magical objects."

It felt like my brain fizzled out at her words.

Architect? As in... not a building one? *Scratch that, how are they both so calm in this situation? Who knows when another bomb might go off.* I froze up at the thought.

"Makes sense. But-"

A low growl echoed throughout the space. I felt the hairs on the back of my neck shoot upward at the sound. "What was that?" I squeaked, head swivelling around. But it's not like whatever that was can sneak up on us. The walls and ceiling have been blown to pieces, so we'll see whatever this is coming, right?

"Okay, and that's the sound of a mutant Nat. Sure it sounds a bit different to the others, but, uh," Ophelia fumbled over her words. "We should probably get going. Come on guys!" Ophelia grabbed us both by the hair and pushed us forward. "I really don't want to fight one of those again." She muttered under her breath, a slight tone of panic creeping into her words.

It was only then that I noticed her cloak was covering one of her arms. And it was a dark shade of red. I gulped. How could something even get through to her? She could just throw up the dome immediately, can't she? I silently decided I didn't want to find out what could've possibly done that.

She clutched our hair tighter and tighter as she dragged us along. Everyone else had already run off, not wanting to stay here any longer. *Probably ran off on their own, I doubt they'll get far.* Ophelia then began to pick up speed all of a sudden. Soon she was sprinting. Lexi was able to keep up with her, but I wasn't. I let out a sharp scream when my feet began to leave the ground. *How is she so fast*?! I kicked the air, begging for her to slow down. She didn't. The pain I felt was extreme, as if someone was ripping all my hair out.

"Hey!" I screamed at her. "Calm down! You're going to rip my hair out!"

"I don't think your hair is worth more than your life, kid!" She shouted back. What does she mean by that? A split second after she said that she leapt upwards. I looked at her face to see her eyes glowing a vibrant blue. I looked back to realise we were outside of the castle already. The smoke was thick out here, so much so I could barely breathe. I closed my eyes immediately. *I'm going to die; I'm going to die. I'm going to break my bones when I fall and die.* I braced for impact, feeling the wind howl through my ears as we began to plummet.

Then we stopped. My feet landed gently on a sticky surface. *What the-*

I opened my eyes and looked down at what just saved my life. A glowing blue aroma surrounded a platform that looked like blue glass. It looks like glass, but it's sticky. *What is this?* Ophelia's hold on my hair loosened, and the pain subsided. Slightly. Still staring below at the glass, I lifted my foot up. A sticky blue substance was stuck to my heel, and I pulled further back, and the heel rebounded into the glass, leaving my foot bare. I almost called out in surprise, but a hand was placed firmly on my mouth. I looked up to see Ophelia glaring at me, her joyful facade gone. Lexi also sent me a menacing look. Both held their fingers up to their mouths to tell me to be quiet, before pointing below them. Curious, I looked down again.

There was a large figure underneath the glass, barely visible. We must be pretty high up then, but why? Was it that howl? I frowned. The thing beneath looks human enough to me. From a bird's eye view, I could see a hairy head on top of a rather muscular build. I couldn't make out what they were wearing though. Something grey, tinged with... Is that blood? I started to worry. Someone's bleeding! Right under us, and Ophelia doesn't want us to help them? They could be looking for help themselves, maybe it's even someone I know? A voice called out in the distance. "Hello? Is anyone there? Oh my god- Is that the ballroom?"

My head snapped to where the voice came from. I saw a guard, pretty far away from where we were. He looked like he was in bad shape. Maybe we could get Ophelia to heal two people, she can do that, can't she? He must've been attacked by one of those creatures Ophelia was talking about. What were they called again? Nits? No, Nats. Mutant ones, or whatever that meant. The guard's tone changed drastically when he turned his head to where the person was beneath us. Ophelia clasped her hand tighter around my mouth. Why?

"Oh? Hello-"
The person beneath us leapt forward almost suddenly, and the guard and them disappeared back into the castle. The person beneath us was a grey flash with purple streaks in it. A horrifying sound of bones cracking followed by screams echoed.
I felt my body go stiff. What in the name of Tien was that? Are they... okay?
My hands shook with realisation.
I guess we are going to need that railway system after all.

CHAPTER 18:
LEXI

I could see the fear and horror in Lila's eyes. She has no idea what's happening, or why it's happening. I can understand it. But still, I'm glad Ophelia managed to stop her from talking before that Nat found out we were right above it. At least now she realises how she almost killed us all. We'd landed since that incident, and Lila was still huddled in a corner. Nats already have a natural ability for speed and jumping high. A mutant one like that? Double the speed and jump power. Bigger, faster, far more dangerous. Probably more bloodthirsty too. You can come across the occasional Nat back home, but they are never that strong. These ones are on a whole new level, no wonder they managed to scare a group of wizards that much. This kingdom is done for, well unless the sun rises. Nats hate the sun. Not that it will for a while, it's barely past midnight now. I looked at Ophelia, who had grabbed a map of the kingdom out from one of her pockets and had started mapping out the safest way out of this hellscape. If someone else had been screaming as Lila was, I would've left them. But considering the information

she has to share, that makes her a valuable source. I narrowed my eyes on her. *She better have that information, it's either that or she's done for.*
I slid my hand into one of my arm pockets where I kept one of my special swords. A retractable one that could withstand my flames and heat up the blade enough that it burns through anything it touches. Hopefully it's a last defence move, but as long as we have the wizard, we should be safe. I'd pointed out a two-storey house when we were still up in the air, one that wasn't completely filled with mutant Nats in the streets. From what we could gather, the kingdom was losing population fast. The explosions had only gone off not that long ago, yet people were scarce. Because of this we'd purposely left the doors that were closed alone. *Who knows what's behind them.*
I took a step back to examine our group. First, we have me. The Flammous assassin. The one who'd saved the Princess's life far more than I should have. Then the wizard, Ophelia. The group's lifeline. Her talents could prove far more than useful. Oh, and she's almost a hundred years old. Finally, we have the Princess, who's worth completely relies on the fact that she can provide us information that won't help us in this situation. Plus, she hallucinates. I groaned. Personally, I wish it was Lila who went crazy and not her brother. At least with him I wouldn't feel the need to put my life on the line nearly as much as I do with her. I glanced back at her. She's still rocking back and forth in that corner. I guess she's never experienced death before in her fancy little castle.
"Alright, I've crossed out all the places that the Nats look like they've overrun, or at least the ones in flames. Does this look right to you, Lexi?" Ophelia finally said after close to an hour of waiting. She beckoned me over to take a look.

I leant over to examine the map, surprised by how much she had done. I mean, she could've been done thirty minutes ago, but there's no rushing when your life is on the line. She'd crossed out at least seventy-seven different paths, leaving only two clear paths out of the kingdom. Or at least, out of the capital. "Looks good, but since there's only two paths, don't you think all the survivors would be rushing to get there? It would be hunting season. Why not just fly overhead?"
She shook her head. "I can't, I wasted too much energy on sudden spells. Normally it doesn't take this much out of me, but since I rushed for the spells to be perfect it hasn't exactly worked in my favour." She shrugged, before turning her attention to Lila in the corner. "Well? What do you think, Princess? You've lived here your whole life, so please. Give us your input on this."
Lila finally looked up at that, blinking multiple times. It looked like she wanted to cry but didn't have the energy. Nor do I have the time for her to cry, she can do it later. "Well?" I inquired.
She stood up, then wandered over to us. The map was then snatched out of Ophelia's hands, much to her amusement and mine. So, she does still have some fire left in her. She'll need it. Lila then pointed to a spot that was crossed out as a fatal area. One that had both extreme fire risks and mutant Nats. "There. That's what will be getting us out here quicker." She was pointing to one of their sacred grounds. I sighed. She can't rely on the Celestials to help us now.
I snorted at her choice. "I'm sorry, but that place is possibly the most dangerous spot on this map. I hate to break it to you, but I'm not that eager to die tonight." I pointed at the spot she was looking at. "See the purple circle and red cross? That means Nats and fire. Double trouble. Double risk. We'd be going there with a death wish, especially with

Ophelia's lack of magic energy. We'd have no shield, you realise that? And before you say it, no, we are not using my fire shield. I don't have enough firepower left to fit Ophelia's tall figure." Ophelia probably has some fighting capabilities, and so do I. Plus, I'm currently the only one who can put up the best offence against the Nats. Considering I'm the only one with abilities at the moment. Lila, however, lacks both.

"Yes, I'm aware of that. I'm also aware you have the highest survival chance out of all of us. But something *I* know is that there is a secret entrance there that leads to a railway system powered by magic. It was made ages ago when White Castle was first created, by wizards." She cast a sidelong glance at Ophelia. "Only the heirs to the throne ever know about it. So that means my Father knows, but my Mother never did. She wasn't of Camhok blood, nor was she an heir. I got informed about this ages ago, but Jackiel has no idea about it. We'll be safe once we get there."

Ophelia and I exchanged glances. Ophelia spoke first. "How exactly do you know if this even works anymore? If it was made when White Castle was first created, then that would mean it's," she paused, thinking. "Over two thousand, five hundred years old. I have yet to hear of any spell that could last that long. Plus, how would they even be able to make that back then anyway? No one discovered any other way of transport other than walking until about two thousand years ago. Let alone a railway system."

Lila shook her head at that. "I think you're forgetting who even introduced that system, Ophelia. It was White Castle who chose to share that information with the world. How would you know any better?"

Ophelia went quiet at that. I looked Lila in the eyes. She's serious about this, I can tell. She really thinks that we can stand a chance.

"Additionally, it's been an hour since we last saw anything. For all we know, those paths you'd selected could be blocked now and the Nats could have left the secret entrance already." She added, further strengthening her point.

I found myself nodding along. So, she is finding a way to make herself useful. I was questioning it before, but maybe it's actually really good she's here. I grinned. She's an amazing tactician, how could I not have noticed this before? Her thinking is so logical compared to before. Well, not quite at Granette's level, but she has the potential.

"She's right, you know." I found myself agreeing with her, much to Ophelia's surprise.

"Wait, you're not actually serious? You're trusting the Princess on this?" Asked Ophelia, clearly questioning why she brought me along. "Her entire plan is based on chance, Lexi. Chance."

"So is yours." Lila countered.

Ophelia narrowed her eyes, before leaning against the wall. She glanced at both Lila and I, before sighing. "We're really doing this, huh?" We both nodded. Out of all of our plans, Lila's could get us out faster. It's a risk we're going to have to take. "I hope you know if we die, I'm going to be haunting you both in the afterlife."

I rolled my eyes at her. "Come on. For all we know, we could be missing an essential opening. Let's make sure we have everything we need, then go. Now."

Everyone set to work after that. Lila raided the kitchen, finding food for the trip. She was careful not to pack too much, or any meat. For all we knew, it could bring the Nats to us. Ophelia got us all the weapons we needed, using her craftsmanship skills to make sure they were all sharp. She also gave Lila a quick run-through on how to use a sword. I, on the other hand focused on getting back-up. Luckily, I had kept my CrysTalk with me in one of my pockets. If I hadn't, it would still be in my room, and we'd have no means of getting more assistance from Sorvia. That is, if they'll even help us. I stared at the red screen, silently hoping Granette would be up at this time of night. She better, considering that they haven't had an update on the mission in two hours. I prayed silently to whatever Celestial might be listening.

"Coller, Granette."

It took a few moments to connect. A few, painfully slow moments. Eventually, G's face appeared on the other side.

"Lexi! For the love of Tien! I haven't gotten a single update from anyone. It's been two whole hours! What are you doing?!" She practically shouted into the CrysTalk.

"Keep your voice down, idiot." I snarled into the device. She's going to kill me just by asking how the mission went. "I don't have a death wish."

"Death wish? And hold up. Is that blood on your face? You've got so many cuts…" Her voice trailed off, listing everything supposedly wrong with me. I think it was finally dawning on her that something was wrong. "Okay, what happened? Seriously, spill it."

I groaned, straightening my back as I took a seat on a half-broken chair. "Alright, I don't have long, but I'm gonna need you to send back-up immediately. This is a Tier 5 emergency, Granette." She was stunned into silence by my words. Tier 5 was quite literally the worst thing you could hear. "There was an incident, actually multiple incidents. Prince Jackiel lost his mind and set off a bomb, almost killing an entire room full of people if it weren't for those wizards you guys sent in. King Moralle and Queen Benice of White Castle are confirmed dead, too." I took a deep breath. "Jackiel seems to have obtained some sort of powerful relic, one we believe was made by some rogue Architect. He had possession of mutant Nats and sent them on a rampage all over the capital. Plus, he seems to have planted bombs all over the capital as well. Can't confirm if they've all gone off yet. I am currently accompanied by one of our wizards, Ophelia as well as Princess Lila. Lila has promised us classified information about the alliance in return for her safety." I tensed slightly. "Not that it really matters anymore. Regardless, she has come up with a way for us to escape. Yet we are unsure of the whereabouts and safety of the other wizards. Ophelia is currently out of energy and won't be able to cast anything for a while yet. We require any available personnel to get over here as fast as they can. Ensuring the safety of these wizards should be top priority."

Granette stared at the CrysTalk, probably wondering how everything could escalate so quickly. I was too, to be perfectly honest. Eventually, Granette nodded. "Okay, I got this." Granette said, almost trying to hype herself up. "Okay. Give a sec." She put herself at mute, and even with no sound I could tell she was shouting at the top of her lungs at the guards around her. I could practically see their faces drop with horror behind their masks. They all rushed out, hopefully to get some assistance with the situation. Thank goodness, I can always count on G. Granette then unmuted herself and nodded at me. "Alright, since it's a Tier 5, you should have back-up within the hour. More wizards will use this Quick-Travel ability they have, honestly I don't even understand it myself. But please, promise me Lexi." Her eyes pleaded with me, growing big and slightly watery. "Please promise me you'll survive. If you don't, I am going to make sure I pee on your grave every time I see it."

I laughed softly. "Promise. And please don't."

We both shared a quiet laugh together, knowing it could be our last.

"You have such a bright future, Lexi. Don't waste it." G stood, then saluted me. "Good luck, Soldier Ignei."

I saluted her back, a weak smile on my face. "Same to you, Coller. Ignei out."
The screen went blank, and I stared at it for a little while. I could feel their eyes on me.
"Well then." I looked up at our group of misfits, more determined to make it out alive now than ever before. "Let's get moving."

-Anasia Edwards-

CHAPTER 19:
LILA

I'd kept the map with me to make sure we were going the right way. Even though I knew these streets from the back of my mind, it was impossible to decipher what building was what in all of the rubble. So far, we hadn't encountered a single Nat. And I was glad. I had no interest in dying today, nor did I any day. The cold feeling of metal against skin had eventually become comforting. The sword Ophelia had given me was tied to my arm with a bit of rope she found. I'd only been given a quick lesson, so they weren't going to depend on me to be slaying anything. In fact, I was still depending on them if I wanted to survive. My beautiful dress was ripped, and I had cuts on my legs and arms from climbing over rubble. My heels had been tossed aside, and now I wore someone's boots. I had no idea who had worn them before, but I didn't exactly want to meet them. Most importantly, I myself had changed entirely. I'd thrown the scared teenage girl away and replaced with someone else. Someone who wanted to see the sun rise and fall just one last time. While Ophelia was a wizard and had almost a hundred years worth of battle experience, I felt safest with Lexi. She had supported me when she didn't need to. Even if we were both enemies. It turns out the stories I'd read about were right. Life or death situations do bring people together. Even an assassin and her target.

I think we just passed Christian's house just now. I wasn't sure how to feel about that if I was being completely honest. Sure, I had cared about him. But during the ball, he had been so... I can't even bring myself to describe a word about him. Nothing else but 'past', and 'dead'. *At least, I'm pretty sure he is.* I shook my head. That shouldn't matter. What matters is that I'll get out of here and make sure these people get remembered. That's all I need on my mind right now. That's all I need. *Because I'm a changed girl, no, I'm a changed woman!* With that, I almost tripped over a piece of stone in front of me. *I take most of it back.*

A soft growl came from his house. That sound was all we needed to leap behind a particularly large piece of rubble. Lexi had her hands out, ready to burn it to a crisp if it came anywhere close to us. I'd never actually seen what it really looked like yet. Not that I wanted to, but I couldn't help but feel curious. I knew Ophelia knew, but I wasn't about to ask her. She barely trusts me as it is. In my eyes, she'd put on that happy mask to everyone who was at the ball to make them feel safer. Now, she couldn't care less how I feel. I know how she feels about me though. A liability. Heavy footsteps came from behind us, and the sound of a creature sniffing the air. I wasn't worried about it picking up our scent, though. We'd gone through so much rubble and dust that I'll be surprised if we even smell human anymore. I remember that the mutant Nat has the physique of a human, but that was only from a bird's eye view. Who knows how they really look? A yelp came from a good distance away, whether it was a human or animal I couldn't tell.

Regardless, I heard the Nat race away in the sound's direction. It will probably be a while till it gets back. That'll give us some time to get away.

After a few seconds, Lexi shot upwards. She signalled to us that the coast was clear, and we continued on our journey.

Hopefully we won't encounter anymore of those things.

Around halfway through our journey, we found ourselves blocked by a massive mound of rubble. Two buildings had collapsed, one on each side resulting in a big barricade made out of their remains. I turned to see Ophelia glaring at the rubble intensely, as if she could move it with her mind. *She might be able to, but she's ran out of energy.* I turned back to the mound and began devising a way around it. *It's either we go through it and cause enough noise for the Nats to hear us, or we find a way around.* I rubbed my temples. *Both could end badly.*

It was Lexi who looked like she might have some idea on what to do. She was standing there, deep in thought. I had a feeling she had come to the same conclusion as me. *Either way, something is going to hear us.*

Lexi then turned her attention to me, a sly grin lighting up her face. Oh? Has she come up with a plan already? I shook my head. Of course she has. She's basically our small groups leader. Lexi then began to approach me, much to my surprise. *Her plan involves me?* She then proceeded to give me a tight hug, one so tight it felt like the air had evaporated inside me. *This isn't normal, she has to be sacrificing me* I thought, panicked. Since when did Lexi give out hugs randomly? That's when the ground around us began to heat up drastically. For a moment, I thought that another bomb was about to go off and take us out with it. Then I felt a sharp feeling of heat curl around my legs, my feet to be more specific. I looked down to see flames gathering around Lexi's ankles, and it was only then when I realised what her plan was.

Oh no.

Before I had a chance to scream, we were propelled into the air in a split second. The feeling of my feet leaving the ground for what felt like the fifth time today overwhelmed me, and I thought I was about to faint. Smoke filled up my lungs as we shot higher and higher, passing through the cloud of smoke and reaching a staggering height before we gradually began to come down again. I frantically looked around, worried a Nat might appear out of nowhere because of the trail of flames we left in our path. Instead, there were none to be seen when we landed. My feet eventually touched the ground on the opposite side of the rubble pile, and I immediately sunk to my knees, writhing out of her grip. I stared at Lexi with a pleading look. *Please, never do that again.*

Lexi shrugged, then propelled herself back over to go collect Ophelia. It was then that realisation dawned on me. *She did me first because I was lighter.* I frowned. *I was basically her test subject. I could've died*! I rose unsteadily to my feet, surveying my surroundings. Lexi would be coming back with Ophelia at any moment, and it's now my duty to make sure there aren't any Nats to greet them. I sagged. Not that I'd be much help anyways. Instead, I stood there awkwardly. Who am I kidding? I'm not that selfless. If I saw something that wanted to kill us, I'd probably run away as fast as I could and leave the others as bait. The familiar feeling of Lexi's flames rushed over me again, and I looked up to see a bright light emerging from the smoke. With me, Lexi was able to keep her flames steady for the whole time.

But now her flames are spluttering as she gradually makes her way down. Because of Ophelia's larger figure, she must be having a more difficult time. *I guess I really was a test to see if she could even do it.* As they came more into view, I could make out their figures more clearly. By the looks of it, Ophelia was wrapping her arms and legs around Lexi as a toddler would do after being given a piggyback. I did my best to hold my laughter in. Lexi's expression was blank, focusing on landing cleanly. Ophelia's face however was bright red, and she'd turned her face away from me so I couldn't see her properly. I moved backwards a little, giving them space to land. However, before they could, Ophelia's grip on Lexi loosened.

Without any warning, Ophelia fell backwards and landed flat on the ground. I could see her face twist in pain. She didn't make the largest sound as she fell, but it was loud enough to make me cringe. Lexi whipped her head around to give her from what I can guess was a nasty glare, before hovering in the air a little longer to see if a Nat might be coming. *At least, I think that's what she's doing.* The sound of a soft growl came again, except it was further away. We all stayed dead still for at least two minutes. Sweat trickled down my forehead. I didn't even bother to wipe it away. Until Lexi seemed sure it was safe, none of us moved a muscle.

Lexi's shoulder then relaxed, and she landed firmly on the ground. She then held her hand out to Ophelia, who took it reluctantly. I exhaled a breath of relief. *I'd trust Lexi's judgement over anyone else's. Assassin or not.* We then continued on our journey, except this time more cautiously. All in complete silence. Yet a question was lingering on my mind. *Where is everyone?*

We came across three more Nats until we reached the sacred grounds. The first two had given up searching for us and ran off searching for more prey. The final Nat hadn't been as easily fooled and attacked us almost immediately. This was when I finally saw what they looked like. The Nats have the physique of a man, but it was completely covered in dark grey fur with purple streaks along their backs. They had razor sharp claws instead of fingernails, ones that had managed to scratch at Lexi's arm before she thrust out a fireball that had incinerated it at once. It also had a long tail, thin and barely visible like a mouse. Its face was pretty horrific, however. It had piercing red eyes that looked like a fly's eye, and fangs that hung outside of its mouth. To finish it off, it had little buds dotted along its back. What they did, we never got to find out. And I hope we never will.

Lexi had managed to patch her injury up fairly quickly, much to my relief. Now, we stood in the centre of the sacred grounds. It was the only place that hadn't been blown up. At least Jackiel had some decency not to blow up the place of Celestial Tien. It was in mint condition, a shrine dedicated to the Celestial of the Land and Sea. The brazier inside was still lit, flames flickering unfazed as it always is. I sunk onto one knee in front of the flame and motioned for the others to do the same. If we want any luck on our escape, we better show some respect for the owner of this entire world.

We stayed there, bowing for a few more moments.

Please, Celestial Tien. Help us. Let us make it out of here and warn the rest of the world of Jackiel I thought silently.

The flame flickered brighter and higher then, reaching the top of the shrine before shrinking back down. It was as if it heard me. I could see Lexi marvelling at it. Even Ophelia had her mouth gaped open a little. The flame started to drift in Lexi's direction, leaving her looking puzzled.

"At least your brother has some form of respect." She said calmly. They were the first words we'd uttered since we left the house.

I nodded. "He knows better than to annoy the Celestials."

Lexi cleared her throat then. "Our back-up should be arriving in the next five minutes. It would be best if we could get a move on now, since they'll be attracting the most attention from the Nats." Her eyes lowered slightly, as if she were worried. "I just hope a few of them will be able to return home."

Both Ophelia and I nodded, finally agreeing on something. "Alright then Princess. Show us the way out of this hell." Ophelia said matter of factly.

I nodded, before entering the shrine. The others followed. "Below here, there should be a lever somewhere." I grunted, my hand reaching under the brazier and fiddling around for it. "It should be about... aha! Here."

A soft click sound was made as I pushed the small lever up. Everyone was quiet as the seconds ticked by, waiting for something to happen. I stood up after the minute mark came and looked at the others. "It-it should be working now."

Even Lexi, who had originally trusted me, clearly started to have doubts. "Well? Did you flick the wrong lever maybe?"

Ophelia shook her head, now glaring at me. "No, Lexi. There's probably only one lever there. Why would they make an extra one?" Ophelia groaned, before kicking a small pebble in front of her. "I knew we never should have trusted you! Now look where we are." Her eyes returned to Lexi. "Come on. The information she promised you is probably fake too. She just sent us on this wild goose chase for nothing."

"I didn't! You just have to give it time-"

"We don't have time, Princess." Ophelia snarled at me. "We probably could've been out of here by now,

but no. Now we are going to have to wait for that back up team to get here and save us. And they probably won't think to come this far into the capital for their own safety!" She massaged her temples, before looking back at Lexi again, who had been quiet. "Let's leave her. She hasn't got a thing that she can help us with, don't you get it?"
Lexi stayed quiet, listening. Her eyes then narrowed. "I don't think this was a waste of time."
Ophelia's eyes widened. "What? She basically lied to our faces! If we stay here any longer, we are going to be the next ones dead."
Lexi sighed, rubbing her temples before pointing at the brazier. "Let me show you both something. Since none of you have the intellect to work this out." She spat, glaring at both of us. "The brazier lit up when we entered here and bowed to it, correct?" We nodded. "By traditional means, that normally translates to a message from the Celestials themselves. But think about it." She held her hand out to the flames, to which they responded by wrapping around her wrist like a snake enveloping its prey. I gasped. "Normal flames at a sacred site don't do this on their own. I was wondering why it kept drifting to me, but now I'm almost certain. So, here's what I've concluded. Considering that I'm a Flammous, or an Ignei to be more specific, certain flames call to me. Those flames are ones that have been ignited by someone of Ignei blood. Are you catching on?"
"Uh, no…" Ophelia said, still confused.
Lexi groaned. "Just watch me." She then raised her hand up and the flames from the brazier followed pursuit. It was a beautiful sight. "I'd recommend ducking, by the way." Both Ophelia and I both ducked, but with her on her knees with her head touching the ground because of her height. Lexi then waved her arms around in a circle, and the flames began circling the room, lighting it up even more

than before. The circle of flames began spinning with Lexi's command, getting so close to me it singed some of the hairs on top of my head. So, this was an Ignei at work. I gazed at her wonderful display, almost forgetting that we were having our own mini apocalypse. Stunning. Then, Lexi twisted her arm slightly and flames stopped. She then whispered one word quietly to herself.
"Show."
The flames sunk into the ground around the brazier immediately, and the shrine's floor tiles began to move, descending and falling into itself to form a staircase leading below the ground level. It continued descending into the darkness, and at the end Lexi's expression showed she was rather amused with herself. Meanwhile, I was starstruck. I felt jealous at that moment, even though I shouldn't. She'd just technically saved us. All while showing off at the same time. I pinned my jealousy down deep in my mind. She deserves to show off after that, that was magical. But Ophelia had more questions than praise.
"Okay, so that was cool. That I understand. What I don't understand is what you mean by an 'Ignei must've lit the fire' in order for you to control it. Didn't your family line originate from Sorvia?" Ophelia questioned.
Lexi looked surprised at that, then shrugged. "As far as I'm concerned, you're correct. My family originated in Sorvia at least a thousand years ago. Past that? No idea. I'll see what I can find in the records when we get back. For now," Lexi grinned at us, before holding her arms out. "Let's ignore all that for a little while. Welcome to our escape."

CHAPTER 20: LEXI

I held out my hand for the whole way down the stairs, illuminating the path so we wouldn't trip. It was clear to us all that both Lila and Ophelia hated each other's guts, at least I was confident Ophelia did. But if what Lila said is down here is down here, we're all going to have to put our differences aside. I honestly never thought I'd be the kind of person to say that. I looked back at Lila, who was in close pursuit behind me. She'd never seemed like the type to put her life on the line for anything. Yet now I respect her as she was a Sorvian herself. She didn't seem to care that we were a unique duo, an assassin and her target. She still knew we all had to get out of here somehow. I turned back around and grinned to myself. *She'd make a fine soldier one day, hopefully she'll join our ranks.* I'll definitely recommend her for her bravery and cleverness. In the past two hours, she'd gone from a scared, slightly annoying teenage heir to the throne to someone I could actually trust. A rare thing for me to come across, trust. Especially in such a small amount of time. I frowned as I thought back to that brazier entrance. I don't recall there being any Ignei's who'd fled from Sorvia. Back then there wouldn't have been a need to. However, right now I need to focus on getting out of this hellscape. Confusing family-related problems can come later. We'd been descending these stairs for a while now, at least it felt like a long time. All in complete silence. So, I decided to ask something that's been on my mind lately. "Hey Lila." I called out to her, ignoring Ophelia's immediate grumble at the name.

"Remember when I asked you about how you knew about my powers? I don't see how Jackiel would be able to tell you that, now that I think about it. Sure, he knew about my abilities. But by the sounds of our conversation I don't think he mentioned that. So, how did you know? Even after inhaling a whole bag's worth of Snooze Memory?" Ophelia's eyes widened at that.

"What did you just say? A whole bag of Snooze Memory?" She looked surprised. "Holy cow!" She turned to me. "When was this?"

I paused, thinking. It felt so long ago now, even if it wasn't. "About two days ago now, actually three. It's technically morning now, isn't it?"

Ophelia looked dumbfounded. Her attention turned to Lila. "How are you not in a coma right now? You should at least be dead!" She asked. I could practically see the clogs in her brain failing to work. "That makes little to no sense, I hope you realise that." Her eyes narrowed at Lila suspiciously. "Are you really human?"

Lila looked surprised. "Coma? No, in fact I just felt a bit drowsy the day after." Lila looked back at me again. "I mean, I don't see why you bothered wasting that bag on me anyway. The 'Snooze Memory' or whatever you call it is only temporary. Plus, that's a horrible name." She pinched her nose, as if for added effect.

I stared at her. "What do you mean, 'temporary'?"

"I mean it stopped working about an hour after I woke up. I remembered everything, even that outrageous lie you told me that night." She started to laugh. "Can't believe I fell for that; I'd wanted to talk to you about it for ages afterwards."
I stopped walking all together. My brain felt like it was malfunctioning. I did give her the Snooze Memory that night, didn't I? It wasn't something else? *No.* I shook my head. It was the Snooze Memory I gave her. I remember checking the bag the next morning, there was nothing left. But… that doesn't make sense. How does she remember everything, still? I've never heard of someone being resistant to Snooze Memory before. "Huh. So, Snooze Memory doesn't affect you then. That's interesting." I said quietly, as if I was still not sure whether it was myself. "I've never heard of that before."
Ophelia shook her head. "Neither have I, the stuff can sometimes knock you out for hours depending on your resilience. And that's just a small amount." She looked Lila up and down, as if searching for clues. "You really are a unique person, Princess Lila. That is, if you are."
"I am, Ophelia. What do you think I am?" Lila groaned. "Just because you think I'm a dumb little Princess doesn't mean that I have nothing unique about me."
"Aw. You took my line." Ophelia pouted. "I wanted to call you dumb little Princess."
I continued down the stairs in a faster pace to avoid them and their pointless argument.
"You know, from the report I got about you it's like the only thing 'unique' about you was your materialistic mindset. It's not my fault I find it a little suspicious that someone like you has that advanced of a mind for Snooze Memory to not work on them."
"You guys have a report on me?" Lila's attention turned to me. "Is anything about me private?"

I paused for a moment, then turned to face her with a little grin. "I know you wet your bed five years ago on the 15th of-"

"Okay! I get it. Ugh, that's so weird how that's in a report. How do you guys even know that?"

"An Assassin never spills her secrets." I responded calmly. *G told me. I actually don't know how she found out about that either. It wasn't even related to the mission.*

Ophelia cut back into the conversation. "I'll have you know I'll be running tests on you when we take you back to Sorvia. You're not normal, Princess."

Lila froze. "What?"

The debate about the Snooze Memory ended as soon as we reached the bottom of the staircase. I sighed. "Well, we're here." I closed my eyes, focusing on the flames in my hand and imagined them spreading to every corner of the room. When I opened my eyes, the room was well lit, perfectly illuminating something of a waiting area. A small cube with a singular door was placed on a railroad at the end of the room, clearly the transport Lila was talking about. My heart did a small jump at the thought. *I can finally go home*! I turned my head around to Lila, about to ask her where the system went when a loud, thundering step came from the top of the stairs. More steps coming down, slowly but surely. It felt like my heart stopped. Huge, heavy steps. And they were getting quicker with each one. Those aren't the steps of a human. *No.* They're far too loud and aggressive. Any normal person would be cautious if they were going down a random passageway leading into darkness. *Nats.* Maybe even more than one. And they're coming down to us. Frantically, I looked at Ophelia, who was just as shook as me. She looked at me with wide eyes, then shook her head. She still doesn't have enough energy. *Damn it! I forgot to close the entrance before we went down!*

I could tell Lila was trying her best to hold back a scream. She knew better now that she had seen what they could do. A low, monstrous growl came from the steps. *Definitely a Nat.* We all backed up, and I returned the flames to my one hand, quietly stepping towards the cube. The lights around the room went out in a second, with the only source being from my hand.

"But I didn't see any Nats around here, where did they come from?" Ophelia whispered into my ear; her eyes fixated on the staircase.

"I don't know, is there a chance they were attracted to my flames?" I replied, my hand shaking with uncertainty. *Are they perhaps coming here because of me?*

"Keep your voices down!" Lila hissed at the both of us. We fell silent.

Eventually we were completely backed up against the cube. Lila fiddled for the handle, but I stopped her once I heard more growls coming from the steps.

There *are* more of them. If they hear us open a door, we're done for. I whirled my head around, thinking of a hiding spot before I spotted one. I tapped them both on the shoulder, before pointing above the cube. If we could get above that, we'd be hidden in the shadows and hopefully with all the dirt and grime on us they won't detect us. No questions were asked. Ophelia helped Lila climb up first, with her raising Lila up to stand on her shoulders and quietly crawl on top. I was next, quickly extinguishing my flame before Ophelia grabbed me and hoisted me up onto her shoulders. I tried my best not to grunt at the sudden movement. It wasn't long before I was up there with Lila, which left just Ophelia to get up here. We both held our hands out, trying our best to pull her up without making a sound. It wasn't easy, but eventually my raw strength managed to pull her massive body up and on the roof of the cube. But not without her foot banging on the side. Since the cube was hollow, the sound echoed throughout the system. The growls became louder almost instantly, proving how fast they were. Ophelia barely had the time to swing her leg over before the first Nat appeared at the bottom of the stairs. We all held our breath, not daring to make a sound.

Four more Nats came up behind it in seconds, each one hissing and scraping at the other to get through. The last Nat to arrive however, was different from the others. It was even bigger, and instead of red eyes its eyes were completely black with no soul. Once the Nat's had gone further into the room, the only thing that was visible were their red eyes, darting around and glowing in the dark. The bigger one was completely invisible in the shadows. Since I had extinguished my flame, the room was pitch black except for the light coming from the staircase. The way the light made the Nats flicker in the darkness had the atmosphere take a whole new level of eerie. Now it was a matter of if they would give up hunting for us or force us to fight back. *I prefer the first option* I thought silently.

It was dead silent in the room besides the sound of the Nats sniffing for their prey, for us. I quickly regretted ever coming on this mission. If I didn't, then maybe I wouldn't be in this situation. If I didn't agree to this, then maybe I would be at home, thinking about what our next battle should look like.

No Lexi! I scolded myself. I can't die with regrets. That means I never really lived up to everything I wanted. *Come on. Survive. Just a little longer.* I could hear Lila gasp beside me, and the sound of a small metal object dropped onto the floor, clinking on the cold stone. Then, everything went quiet. For a moment, I had thought that the Nats were going to leave. They'd stopped sniffing around. But I knew deep down that they weren't. I could see their eyes in

the dark, their red menacing eyes looking in our direction. I gripped the hands of Lila and Ophelia tight, bracing for death. That's when one of those hands left my own. When a yelp came out of the darkness. When Lila got snatched in a second.
The red eyes immediately turned to a new spot in a darkness, to where Lila must be. I didn't waste a second. I could hear her screams already, but I wasn't going to let her die. *Why not? Why? Why Lexi? If she dies, they'll be satisfied and move on.* Said the tiny voice in my head. Yet the larger voice, the one I listened to said otherwise. *Save her. Save her and you won't die with regrets. Save her and you'll die a hero.* I chose the bigger voice. *She is technically under my protection after all.*
A split second after Lila was taken, I had sprung into action, lighting up the room with my flames in seconds. I could see Lila now, already a little bit bloody and having two Nats try and take her away from the other. *They're gonna rip her apart* I realised, horrified. I jumped in immediately, weaving and dodging one of the Nat's attacks and replacing it with one of my own. Before a single blow could reach me, at least one of their limbs got obliterated by my blasts. *I'm not letting anyone else die today.* I repeated in my head, drowning out my own battle cries as both their arms exploded into flames. Another Nat tried to swipe at me, and instead of attacking back I went on the defensive, engulfing my body with flames so it wouldn't be able to go anywhere near me. The remaining Nats backed off, screeching in terror. To them, I probably looked like some sort of demon stealing their food. Which I suppose, I am. A retreating Nat tried to run up the staircase, to which I responded by blasting it with a massive fireball. One down, five to go. *These things are easier to bring down than I first anticipated.*

It was at that moment that an additional Nat came from my blind spot, swinging its claws in an attempt to swipe at my face. The attack took me by surprise, and my hands exploded as I propelled myself backwards. The Nat's attack still hit me, however. Its claws had grazed against my skin ever so slightly, yet it cut deep. I winced from the contact. While I was still in the air, I swung my leg around to collide with its face after it launched after me. I didn't have enough time to fully immerse my foot with flames, so the Nat was only hit with a few sparks. Still, the impact managed to blind it temporarily, resulting in the Nat hurling itself backwards to scratch at its eyes in agony. I took the pause in battle to launch a fully-fledged fireball at it, which exploded on impact and left the Nat up against the wall, its charred body falling in a heap onto the ground. *So they might be a bit of an inconvenience* I thought.

More Nats began to advance towards me. I swerved and dodged their attacks again, hitting as many as I could in places that I had been taught were instant kill zones. The two who were fighting over Lila were eliminated quickly with that tactic. Four down, one to go. The final normal-looking Nat knew better than to leap at me. Instead, it went on all fours and the buds along its back began to burst open. Sharp spikes shot up from where the buds were, and the Nat then formed a ball-like shape. I quickly realised what it was doing and yelled at Lila. "Get to the cube! Let Ophelia help you up!" She obeyed my orders immediately, sprinting for the cube and leaping at it. I didn't get the chance to see if she made it on, I was too focused snatching my sword. The flames hadn't done any damage to my clothes, I made sure they were above my clothes and not directly on them so they wouldn't burn off. I pressed a button on the sword's hilt, to which the sharp blade emerged from the hilt itself. I focused my flames onto the sword and watched it glow bright red, searing with heat. Just one swipe with this, and I can eliminate this Nat immediately.

The Nat had sped up enough for it to charge at me, rolling at high speeds toward me. I treated the situation as I would with a red flag and a bull. It charged me, and at the last second, I leapt out of the way and brought my sword down hard and fast, cutting through its surprisingly rough exterior with just one singular strike. When it came out of its ball form, it was cut clean in half. I took some deep breaths, leaning on my sword, exhausted. That fight had taken nearly all of the energy left out of me, even though it was so short-lived. To think I was so scared of these things before, I suppose I didn't know their full potential then anyway. A blow suddenly came from behind, hitting me harder than anything I'd ever felt and sent me flying, knocking me right against the stone wall on the other side of the wall. I felt one of my ribs crack from the impact. Probably some internal bleeding as well. I grimaced, writhing in pain on the floor. *Where did that come from?!*

A scream came from where I originally was before. I struggled to open my eyes, but when I did, I saw the massive Nat from before with black eyes holding up Ophelia by the throat. How did it get her? She was so high up. Realisation shot through me. That Nat must've been the one to grab Lila! Fear clouded my mind. *No, no, no. We need back-up, and we need it now. I can't win this with my injuries, and Lila can't stand a chance against that thing.* I punched the floor with frustration. *How could I have forgotten about it before? It's clearly more intelligent than the others, it was just watching the whole situation unfold.* My eyes widened in horror as I realised what I just thought. *It's intelligent.* Fumbling in another one of my pockets, I pulled out my CrysTalk, wincing from the energy it took for me to do so. I coughed up blood and spat it out. I think I was missing a tooth, I'm not sure. I held it up in front of me, checking to see if it was broken. It had many cracks, but hopefully it still works.

"Coller, Granette." I croaked. I didn't know who else to call. I didn't know who she assembled for the rescue team, so she was my only hope.

She picked up almost immediately. I tried to speak, but she wouldn't let me. "What's your location?" She said, not even flinching at my injuries.

"T-the shrine for Celestial Tien. Further inward of the capital. D-down the stairs at the bottom." At least I can get some help, since Ophelia and I can't do anything.

Granette nodded. "Sending them to you right now, they've already got the wizards, so we were already waiting for you to call and tell us where you were. Lexi, you cannot die. Hold on until they get there." Granette then looked at another screen, nodding at it. "Turns out you're close to them, so expect a whole team of trained professionals to help you guys." Her eyes started watering up as I felt mine closing. "Hold on, Lexi. You did your best."

Then everything went black.

Five Years Earlier

"Try again!"

Sire Lewis's voice bellowed, clearly annoyed. I winced from his tone. My body felt exhausted. I looked over at Sire Cleo, a clear face of disappointment on her face. Even her?! I thought in horror. No! Sire Cleo likes me! She's nice. She can't think I'm weak. I strained my body to recreate the shape I'd been tasked to make with more determination. The aftermath would be painful, but I can't let Sire Cleo down! Fire curled all around my arms, eating away at the poor fabric that remained. I spread the fire out into the space in front of me and closed my eyes. In my mind, I imagined my hands moulding a piece of clay into a small puppy. I gave it cute little ears with tiny points at the end, carefully adding the fur to go along with it like I was creating a painting. I then moved onto its' face, forming the dog's snout and button-like nose. I gave the puppy a toothy grin, with a little bit of drool falling from its' mouth. Its' eyes were sad looking, despite the puppy's big smile. I frowned. No, it's supposed to be happy! I tried again with its' eyes, but it turned out the same. I continued remoulding its' eyes to perfection, yet always having the same result.

Exasperated, I decided to leave it and worked on the rest of the body. I gave it a big body so that the puppy could grow up to be big and strong. Some sweat slowly started falling from my forehead, dropping onto my arms and dissolving in the arms. I can hear the crackling of it. Why must my fire be so loud? I pouted. It's so exhausting too. Suddenly the puppy's body disappeared. I gasped. That hasn't happened before. I felt someone tap my head.

"Stop it Lexi! Snap out of it!"

Who's that voice belong to? It sounds familiar. Actually, what am I doing here again? I pondered quietly to myself. Why am I making this puppy? Why is everything so dark? I can't feel my arms-

I snapped out of my daze as a hand collided with my head, which sent me flying. I landed face-first on the ground in shock. "Wait- What?" I mumbled, my head feeling woozy. What was that? I felt someone grab the collar of my shirt and yank me off the air. I yelped in surprise. "Ignei! You could've killed us all!" Sire Lewis shouted into my ear, making me flinch. He's so loud. Wait, what does he mean? "I thought you already knew how to control your abilities, yet here you are letting it consume you! What did I do to have such a useless student?" He snapped. "Take a look at the room!"

I anxiously raised my head to see the sandy walls stained with black marks. The room also felt unnaturally hot, as if something had just exploded in here. I gulped. Did I do that? I heard Sire Lewis groan, then he dropped my collar. I collapsed onto my knees and screeched as my knees grazed on the hot, hard ground. Tears slid down my face, blurring my vision. "I- I'm sorry." I sniffed, rubbing my eyes as the tears fell. I'm here to control my abilities! I wouldn't be here if I already could. Why is he so cruel?

"It's okay, Lexi." I heard Sire Cleo say, walking over to embrace me in a hug. "Oh my! Your arms are still quite warm-"

I yanked out of her hold and ran out of the room, tears streaming down my face. I heard Sire Lewis shout something after me, but I couldn't hear it. I ran through the hallway at an uneven pace. My knees hurt! Sire Lewis is so scary! I eventually stopped running after a while, standing in the empty hallway. There wasn't many people in the Main Building today. Which I was happy about. I froze. Wait a minute. Sire Lewis is going to be so mad that I ran away! Same with Sire Cleo! I gulped. I can't go back now; I'll go back to my dorm. I decided, hoping they wouldn't follow me there. I wandered around the corner, lifting my head at the right time to see a young, tall boy with a sour look on his face. However, he didn't see me. I yelped in surprise when he walked right into me, almost knocking me over. I steadied myself at the last second to avoid falling, sidestepping away from the oblivious boy as fast as I could. His eyes blinked as he searched the area around him before his eyes finally set down on me. He looked angry. Wait, why is he mad? He bumped into me! I thought defensively. I should be mad! "Watch where you're going!" He snapped. I almost laughed at his high-pitch voice; it didn't match his appearance at all. "Hey! What do you think you're smiling at?" He shouted, his face going a dark shade of red. "What are you even doing out of your dorm?

As your superior, I demand that you go back to your dorm!"

I blinked at him, confused. "Superior? You're not an adult. You're definitely not a Sire either." I crossed my arms in defiance. What a filthy liar. Wait a minute, what is he doing in the girl's section anyway? My jaw dropped in realisation. He's one of those weirdos! "You, tall guy! What do you think you're doing in the girl's training area? Go back to your side of the building!" I watched his face go an even deeper shade of red.

"Huh?! What are you talking about? This is the boy's side! What are you doing over here?" He said, looking more irritated than before. "Where do you even think you are, little girl?"

"Little girl?!" I shouted at him. "I'm not that short! I'm average height!"

"Yeah right, it's a miracle you haven't been mistaken for a long-lost Dwarf." He snorted in amusement, the redness fading from his cheeks. "Little girls like you shouldn't be preparing for TOUC. You've still got ages to go, meanwhile we only have four years."

I gasped at him. "Hey! I'm also participating in TOUC in four years! I'm ten! I'm not a little girl, I already have two Sires." I said smugly, crossing my arms against my chest. Take that, weirdo boy.

The boy burst into laughter. "Oh really? Do you even know what a 'Sire' is? You look six at best. Just because it sounds like you got a good education doesn't mean you're older!"

"Oh yeah? You wanna know who I am? My name's Lexi-"

"I don't care about your name, kid." He bent over to pat me on the head. "Go back to Mummy and Daddy like a good girl, okay?" My face went red-hot with rage.

"My name is Lexi Ignei!" I shouted at the top of my lungs. "I will be participating in TOUC in four years, with all the other eleven-year-olds like you!" I held

out my hand to ignite a large flame, having it twirl through my arm into the shape of a bunny hopping along. "And I'm not that short!"
He took a step back in surprise. "What the hell?!" He shouted, realisation suddenly flickering across his face. "You're Lexi Ignei? I'd thought she'd be taller."
"Stop making fun of my height!"
"Fine!" He shouted. "I mean, sorry." He mumbled, running his hand through his hair. I took a moment to look at him. He had silky hair that bobbed up and down without any wind to aid it, all in a dark brown hue. His eyes were a piercing light blue that were intimidating enough without his angry looking face. I tilted my head at him. That's weird. He has blonde eyebrows. How strange.
"Hey, why are your eyebrows like that?" I asked with a blank face, diminishing the fire bunny.
"My eyebrows?" He said, suddenly getting defensive. "T-they're natural, okay? It's not that big of a deal." He took in a deep breath. "And I, uh, I apologise for what I said earlier. I hope you forgive me, Miss Ignei."
I cringed at his words. "Never call me that again." Why does everyone always do that? I guess I kind of wanted him to stop calling me a little kid, but do I always have to rely solely on my name alone to prove my worth? A vibration came from one of my pockets. Oh, it's my CrysTalk. I grabbed it out of my pocket, before regretting looking at the screen.
"Lexi Ignei is in the Restricted Area for Female Participants. Please leave before you are forced to."
"Eh?!" I shouted, lost for words. He wasn't lying? But that would mean... I'm in the boys area?! Sire Lewis is going to kill me, how did it even know I was here? I sprinted back the way I came, far away from the boy. I heard a voice come from behind me. "My name's Kri! Kri Renur. It was nice to meet you!"
I collapsed onto my bed back at the dorm. I grabbed the blankets and pulled them all the way over me,

hoping I could hide my face from the world. Sire Lewis gave me an earful when I got back to the girl's area. He'd stopped me just before I made it to the hallway where my dorm was, as if he'd been waiting for me. He told me about how I almost ruined the Ignei family's reputation and informed me that I shouldn't look forward to our next session. I froze up just thinking about it. Why is Sire Lewis so scary? I sniffled, burying my face in my pillow.
"Was it Mr Lewis again?" I heard Granette ask, sitting on the foot of my bed. We'd become roommates the start of this year, and she eventually became my first friend. She's also apparently really talented and smart for her age. Sire Lewis probably made sure we shared a dorm.
"It's Sire Lewis. He'll beat you up too if he hears you say anything less." I grumbled. "You would think life as an Ignei, would be easy, with the fame and power. But it's not!" I grabbed my pillow and threw it across the room. G tapped me on the shoulder gently. "It'll be okay. When we graduate, we'll find a place far, far away from the war. Then we'll be okay, right?"
I turned to her in surprise. "Wait, really? Would we be allowed to?"
She burst into laughter. "Of course not silly! That's why we'll sneak out, and we can start a farm!"
"Oh, right." I smiled. "That sounds like a lot of fun. I can't wait!"

CHAPTER 21: LILA

Present

I stared in horror as Lexi dropped her CrysTalk, finally unconscious. Her flame continued to flicker in the darkness, continuing to illuminate the room. She was our only chance, and I couldn't quite hear what she was saying. *You can only hope she was getting help* I thought. Ophelia then started choking more aggressively. The hold that the overpowered Nat has on her is tightening. It takes longer for a wizard to die, from what I've heard. They require less than humans. Less oxygen, less food, less water. It's a miracle they live longer than us. That Nat had already thrown me off the cube, so here I was lying on my stomach. Defeated. The Nat only seems to care about Ophelia, the wizard. But Ophelia won't live any longer if I don't try to help her now. I gritted my teeth, slowly crawling back up to stand. I unsheathed the sword from my holder, and locked eyes with Ophelia. Without another hesitation and ignoring the pain running through my entire body, I launched myself at the Nat, sword in hand. Lexi had made it look so easy when she annihilated the other Nats, but this one threw her around like a paper doll. I knew I stood no chance, but if I can get its attention on me then maybe Ophelia can get her magic back in time. I swung my sword at it, coming on its arm with all the strength I could muster. It barely even went into its arm. I panicked. *I'm not strong enough.* Tears pricked down my cheeks as I continuously swung at it, chipping away at its arm.

The creature didn't even bat an eye at me, nor try to stop me. It doesn't even see me as a threat. It's instead focusing its energy on getting rid of the stronger ones first, then dealing with me. Almost all of my hope dwindled away. *Come on*! I kept bringing my sword down, harder and faster each time. I didn't care if I got tired. I couldn't think of another way to get its attention! *Wait a minute.* If its main skin around the body is this tough, surely it has a weak spot. I took a step back to analyse it, much to the creature's amusement. *It finds me entertaining. Why does everyone feel that way about me*? Well, I'll just have to use it to my advantage then. I have to take a guess at the weak spot now. I don't have the skills to find out its exact location like the others. Ophelia's face had gone a deep shade of purple by now, and she was struggling even less in its frightening grip. I had to do whatever I needed to do now.

Much to my own surprise, I ran up to the wall to use it as a support beam and leapt onto the creature's back, careful to avoid the spores decorated all over its backside. I then wrapped my arms and its neck and pulled tight, grabbing my sword and attempting to slit its throat. The overgrown Nat quickly realised my intentions and tried to throw me off, prioritising its life over Ophelia's, throwing her away with breath still in her body. It shook me around, running in circles to try and wrench me off of it. The Nat gave a deafening growl as it did this, terrifying me even more. *Augh! What have I done?* I quickly realised the only way off of it was to kill it right then and there or be launched off its back. I attempted to slit its throat again, my sword shaking in my hand. *Come on Lila! It almost killed Ophelia! And Lexi! Lexi, the assassin who saved your life! Come on! Do them a favour and kill it now*! I thought, desperately trying to convince myself to just do it already.

All of a sudden, I was flung off its back and thrown right up against the wall next to Lexi. I hit my head on the wall, hard. I began to zone in and out, the world a blur around me. All while the Nat approached, eager to finish me off. I tried to move away, but I had no strength left in my arms or legs. I stared at it, barely with reality as I accepted my fate. Maybe this was just meant to be. We were never meant to get out of here, were we? I closed my eyes, waiting for the impact.

But it never came. Instead, the smell of water and earth materials was inhaled by my nostrils. The sound of wind howling echoed through my ears. And the heat of fire made me wince. I opened my eyes to see a bombard of people sprinting into the room, all wearing different colours but with the same symbol. The symbol of Sorvia. Lexi managed to send reinforcements. A spark of hope flickered in my chest, burning brighter than before. A young boy wearing a dark green cloak emerged from a flower growing out of the ground. Another two emerged from the ground as well, except from weeds. A boy with water surrounding him sent a massive torpedo of water that turned into ice when it hit the Nat, freezing it on the spot. In the span of twenty seconds, around twenty different people arrived. A mix of elementals, wizards, and normal soldiers. All had the same target in mind. Kill the Nat. Once it was frozen, the group all yelled at each other on who would get to kill it and such. Eventually, it became a race on who could kill the Nat first. It was dead within the minute. All my effort to do it myself, and these people had finished it off so quickly. The Nat didn't even get a chance to fight back, not that I could imagine it doing so. Its body thumped onto the ground, finally unmoving. I felt like I could finally breathe again. *These guys are strong.*

I stared at the group that now took up a majority of the room. Some of the wizards and elementals rushed over to Ophelia, helping her up and offering her some healing herbs. While a majority of the group rushed over to where me and Lexi were, all with the same thought on their minds. *Is she okay?* Not that they cared about me, or anything. They only noticed me after a medic crew came in and took the hospitality of Lexi, was my presence known. The boy who had frozen the Nat came up to me, bending down on one knee in front of me. His dark brown hair bobbed up and down almost unnaturally, with piercing blue eyes staring me down. A unique thing about him would be that his eyebrows were a light blonde. *Did he dye his hair? I wasn't aware Sorvia had access to* that. He smirked at me. "So, you're the Princess of White Castle, huh? How does it feel to-" The boy who had emerged from the flower cut him off before he could finish. "Hey! Kri! Leave her alone. From what our reports say, she was the one who helped Ignei. If anything, she's done a good deed for Sorvia."

The boy named Kri shrugged. "So? She's still technically the enemy, Dan."

Dan rolled his eyes at him, yanking him away from me. He then looked at me with much kinder eyes and held out his hand. "I'm Dan, Dan Grotheel. I'm a proud Terranine. And I'm guessing you're Princess Lila Camhok, right?"

I nodded slowly, not sure whether I could trust him or not. *Terranine, Earth Elemental.* I looked over at Kri again. *Liquarn, Water Elemental.*
Dan helped me up, slinging an arm around my shoulder so I could stand easier. "How did you know we were here?" I asked, genuinely curious.
"That would be with the help of Lexi. She'd managed to contact one of our Tacticians, G, your location. Since we were all in the area after we'd rescued Arthuriel over there after he got cornered by a bunch of Nats," he pointed to where a Wizard stood, quite clearly avoiding everyone. "We had managed to get here quickly, and lucky we did otherwise you guys probably would've been dead." He shrugged at the words, as if he couldn't care less. "Well, obviously if Lexi had passed then that would put us at a serious disadvantage, considering she is the last Ignei and all."
"I've heard that phrase before. Aren't her parents still alive?"
"Who knows? Just disappeared one day. Not that it matters if I really knew or not, you're not exactly in a position to be earning valuable information like that. Regardless, you'll be coming with us."
I looked at him, surprised. "I'm sorry, what?"
"We have direct orders from the Council to return you to Sorvia in one piece." He grinned. "Looks like the Council are really interested in you, Princess. You'd better get ready though, Sorvia is the last place you want to get recognised as a Crown Princess of White Castle."
I stared. "Do you know what this 'Council' even wants from me?"
He grinned even wider at that. "A trial. One to decide whether you live, or you die."
"And it's all up to you."

EPILOGUE

"You failed."
Mused the Stranger, leaning against one of the buildings. Jackiel grimaced at his words. He'd anticipated every single one of their little group's movements. Ignei, Lila, and that wizard's group to be more specific. They'd abandoned the castle to stay in a building until they could formulate a plan. They'd then decided to use that old railway system to get out, thinking he wouldn't have known about it. Then Lexi opened it, giving him further indication that his plan was working, and their location. He'd sent the mutants down there to kill the wizard then take both Lila and Ignei unconscious, but alive. It wouldn't have mattered if they'd managed to get into that cube beforehand, that thing won't start. It's over two and a half thousand years old, and Jackiel knew that they needed a wizard's magic to activate it. Which their wizard was incapable of doing. What he hadn't anticipated was for an entire small army of supernatural individuals to appear out of nowhere, suddenly knowing where they are. *That overgrown Nat must not have hit Ignei hard enough* He pondered. It should've, then her CrysTalk would've been broken, and she wouldn't have any last moments of

consciousness to call for help. Jackiel frowned. Now Sorvia has both of them.

"I didn't fail." Jackiel finally replied, watching with the black-hooded Stranger as the Sorvians escorted the group out of the railway system. "Just had an unanticipated move be played against me. That's all."

The Stranger snorted at that. "You're so childish, Jackiel." He sighed. "But do not fret. This is but the first step in our plan. Once they take those two to Sorvia, it gives us even more reason to get Arcarlia on our backs to regain the 'stolen' Princess. They'd have no idea about the truth. They did just survive a nightmare after all. If they think Sorvia is the cause of it, then they will almost definitely join forces with us."

Jackiel nodded, surprised. He hadn't thought of that. And that upset him. "True. But you should see to it that our experiments with Nats are finished. That stronger one we added didn't stand a chance against that other group from Sorvia. Next time, we should bring in the-"

"Don't be too hasty now." Snapped the Stranger. "Things like this take time. We'll only resort to that if all our plans go to hell."

Jackiel nodded, embarrassed. "Of course."

The Stranger looked back at the group again. "I understand you want your sister to join you but remember. Our main focus is getting Ignei, do you understand? She doesn't even realise it yet, but she is our key to winning this world. All we need to do is win her over."

Jackiel said nothing to that. He still wanted to prioritise his sister. He couldn't care less about Ignei. The Stranger knew that too. But he also knew when the time came, Jackiel would do the right thing.

The Stranger continued. "Disrupting the sacred land of Tien was a risky move to play, however. If we do that again, I fear she may come down here herself and kill us both."

"Why not come down now?"

"Simple. She knows she can't kill me on her own, but if we repeat this move a second time, the other Celestial's will join her."

"Why can't she kill you, exactly?"

The Stranger laughed at that. "You sure do ask a lot of questions, boy. But I'll answer this one. It's simple, really. You can't exactly kill the Celestial of Death himself on a one-on-one battle, can you? Even if it is one of the strongest Celestials in all of history."

Jackiel smiled. "No, no you can't."

The Celestial grinned, taking off his hood. "We will take this world, one kingdom at a time. With only one singular kingdom having supernatural beings as half its population, it puts us at quite the advantage. But as I like to say, 'The brightest flame always burns out the quickest'." He looked out to the still-burning capital. "Only the strongest may survive the flames of death, young Apprentice."

-Anasia Edwards-

ACKNOWLEDGEMENT

Writing this book took lots of patience and support from a number of people. Inspiration wise, so many of my favourite books and authors took part in giving me a reason to write. Without them, none of this would be possible. Reading your books and marvelling at how much effort and time you put into them has given me a spark to write and share it with others. However, I would like to thank some of the people who helped along the way.

I want to thank some of my proofreaders for all the work they have done to help make my book better. They have given me constructive feedback on how to make my writing better and are overall superheroes in my eyes. I want to thank Taryn and Ryan. Your help was greatly appreciated!

To family and friends whose support and positivity took a massive part in making it all possible. Without your help, I wouldn't have had nearly as much motivation as I did to finish it. (I hope your proud!)

To my teachers who encouraged me to follow my passion and see where I went with it. Your

~ ~

encouragement was heavily appreciated, and I would like to thank you all for helping me to pursue this magical journey!

To the authors who gave me inspiration for my ideas, and whose books I still love to read.

Thank you all for being my favourite comrades in this journey!

THE BEGINNING:

Before writing this book, it had begun as an assignment in one of my classes. While the original storyline is very different to how it is today, the characters and their feelings and motivations never changed. After I had submitted it, I had felt that the story wasn't quite over yet. (After all, I had left it on a cliffhanger myself!) A month or so later, I decided to continue writing on it on a separate document. A year and a half later, the 'story' had reached 50,000 words with at least three different storyline changes until I finally settled on the one. Nine months later, I had finished writing it with 80,000 words and a mindset brimming with excitement. With the encouragement I had received from friends, family, teachers, and peers, I managed to complete it almost two and a half years after I had begun! I hope to turn this into a series, with my writing style advancing through each book!

Now, for a snippet into one of the Council's points of view, and a hint for the next book. Introducing, Bravo!

~~

-Anasia Edwards-

THE COUNCIL

The Council sat in their assigned seats in the Chamber, discussing amongst themselves quietly while they waited for Brain to arrive so they could start their meeting. It was only an hour after the Assassin and her group were rescued, and they'd be arriving back at Sorvia late afternoon. Bravo's smile twitched. *Why in the name of Tien are we doing this early in the morning? We all heard the update, what more information could they have to offer?* She thought quietly to herself, her fingertips clicking on her chair's armrest in thought. *I suppose this is a unique case, but couldn't it wait till dawn? Unless Ignei has been killed, I don't see any point in this meeting.* She almost frowned at the thought. Almost. *No, I doubt Ignei could be killed by a mere Mutant Nat. She has far too much potential to be wasted on such a feeble thing.*
Bravo looked over to where Brain's chair sat, still empty. He was nowhere to be seen, which was unique considering he was the one who organised this meeting in the first place. Bravo suspected

~~

something must be amiss. Her eyes scanned the space around them, not that there was much to look at. It was all a black abyss, the normal pathway leading up to the Council members was gone. The Council merely floated in the dark space, still missing a member. *It isn't like Brain to be late. Something important must have come up, it's the only explanation.*
She could hear Mortal groaning, as if sick of his conversation with Fox already. Bravo turned to meet him. His bushy eyebrows were furrowed in annoyance, and his eyes kept darting between Fox and Bravo as if he were unsure about something. It was Fox who started up a conversation with Bravo. "Hey, Bravo." He nodded at her, his fiery red hair burning brighter with each word. "You're closest to Brain. Where's he at? Hm?" He questioned, clearly bored with himself.
Bravo shrugged in response. "I wish I could tell you, but I honestly have no idea. Something must have come up."
"Correct as always, Bravo."
She jumped at the sudden voice, and whirled her head around to her left, revealing Brain sitting comfortably in his chair. Bravo straightened her back, attempting to look more professional before nodding in his direction. Everyone had gone silent, waiting for Brain to address the crowd. *No one questions how he pops into existence randomly. It's a secret he keeps under lock and key.* Brain cleared his throat. "Now, our meeting. I have some unexpected news to share with you all this morning." His cold eyes narrowed. "Fox." He said with no emotion in his voice. Bravo could feel the hairs on the back of Fox's neck raise. The Chamber was left in an uncomfortable silence. Internally, Bravo was panicking. *What did Fox do? Now he's being picked off?*

~~

-Anasia Edwards-

This wasn't the first time something like this had happened. There used to be eight members in total. Now there's five. Two of them were picked out in unscheduled meetings like this, meanwhile the last one just disappeared one day. No one knows where she went. Brain continued, his attention facing forward into nothingness.
"It has come to my attention that the information shared in our meetings have not stayed in our meetings. Can you confirm this?"
"W-what? Brain, you know I'm faithful to you all, this is crazy talk-" Fox stuttered.
Bravo could imagine Brain rolling his eyes at his words. *The only way Brain could say an accusation like that out loud means he has heavy evidence. I wonder what else Fox did.* Bravo sunk into her chair. *Here's to thinking I was starting to like the guy. How disappointing.* Mortal and Dagger both stayed quiet, knowing what was about to happen. Brain would lay all the evidence out and give him a few final words. Then Fox would drop into the pit of nothing. Bravo paused her thinking for a moment. *Then again, Fox is good with words. Maybe he can wriggle out of this predicament?*
Brain yawned before continuing, clearly bored with the conversation. "I have many different witnesses stating that you were giving away information at a public bar while in a drunken state." Brain then grabbed a scroll out from his chair. "Let us see, eighteen witnesses in total. Six females, twelve males. All range from the ages of twenty to fifty. Stories all fit in perfectly together. Plus, it looks like you gave away your own personal information as well." Brain sighed, before setting his scroll down. "Really Fox, I thought you were better than that." Brain then held his hand up, signalling for him to have his final words as a member of the Council. She

~ ~

could hear Fox struggling to form words, but eventually he finally did. "B-Brain, this is all a big misunderstanding! You have to understand! J-just give me a second chance! I'll never drink again. Does that sound good-"
Fox didn't even finish his sentence before the sound of his chair plummeting into the darkness was heard. I slowly turned my head to see both Mortal and Dagger staring at the now empty spot where Fox used to be. *Then there were four. Half of the Council is gone now.* Bravo sighed. *I was hoping Fox could actually come up with a reason for Brain to not do that. Sad.*
Brain cleared his throat. "Now that he's gone, I can explain the reason for your being here without it being leaked to the public." He sighed blissfully. *Brain is something else* Bravo thought, not sure whether to be afraid or not. "As you all know, Ignei's team and the other wizards were rescued from White Castle along with the Whienan Princess. In return for her safety, she has promised us important documents." He paused, as if making sure we all knew what he was talking about. "Perfect." He said, satisfied. "It has also come to our attention that the source of the Capital's downfall was none other than the Prince himself. From some of our reports, he seems to have obtained a relic that grants him abilities that none of us can even comprehend at this date and time."
Bravo leaned in, suddenly intrigued. "Oh? A wild Architect then? Is that what you're hinting at?"
Even Mortal seemed to be more interested in the conversation. "Interesting. There's only six documented Architects living right now, and they're all under the Wizard's jurisdiction. Convenient?"
"Hm." Dagger said in agreement.
"Yes, it does seem that way." Brain agreed. "But we can't rush to conclusions yet. We've done a background check on the Architects already, and

~~

none of them have shown any signs of fraying away. Nor have they even left the hideout." Brain paused. "Yet that isn't the main part of the information I called you all here for. Something unexpected has come to light, something we can't ignore."
"Oh?" Bravo inquired.
"We've received a message from Krinia, a few of their Scouts had decided to explore the Capital for clues on why the Prince may have blown up his kingdom. Something interesting they found is that there were no bodies discovered, nor was there any sign of life besides the rescue team. Animals are excluded in this, however. It seems the Mutant's main focus was humans." Brain took a deep breath before continuing. "The most disturbing thing the Krinian Scouts found was a nest. Upon closer inspection they realised it wasn't any normal Nat nest, but in fact a power hoarding nest. This is just a guess, but," Brain hesitated. Bravo was surprised. He never stutters on his words. "They believe that the Nats dragged the bodies there and let this core that they found absorb the body's energy and turn it into power. An estimated maximum amount of power it could hold?" Brain gripped the sides of his chair tighter. "Enough to kill a Celestial."
The pieces clicked together in Bravo's head as the room erupted with Mortal's outbursts. "Kill a Celestial? You're joking. Nothing of this world can do that except for the Celestials themselves-"
"That's what the Prince wants then." Bravo said, interrupting Mortal. The Council members stared at her with interest. "It also tells us he's working with someone powerful. The Prince must have decided ruling one kingdom isn't enough, and he wants to rule the world. However, in order to get the power you're talking about, there's no way a mere, powerless human could've done it on his own. You said he had a powerful relic?" Brain nodded. "That

~~

settles it. The Prince is known for being a child genius, and whoever they're working with must have an intellect of something higher in life. And the power to mimic an Architect's handicraft."
Dagger and Mortal stared at Brain and Bravo. Eventually Mortal said something. "But, that means nowhere in the world is safe, Bravo."
Brain nodded. "He's right. If this Prince and his superior continue with this, they may not pose just a threat to us but the very foundation of our world." He gritted his teeth. "However, that means this war needs to end if we are to succeed. Which may be the most difficult task of all." His eyes then filled with hope. "This partnership between Ignei and the Princess may very well save Sorvia. Better yet, the entirety of Mistlon."
"They need to stay together; our world may very well depend on it."

~~

-Anasia Edwards-

ABOUT THE AUTHOR:

Anasia Edwards lives comfortably in South Australia and is the author of *A Tale Etched In Fire*. She currently attends High School. Some of her hobbies include art, writing, reading, and hanging out with friends and family!

She loved participating in all sorts of creative projects from a young age such as art and writing.

This novel is the result of her passions, and one of her greatest accomplishments.

~~

Sorvia

~~